USA TODAY BEST SELLING AUTHOR

KRISTEN PAINTER

BOOK
FOUR

MOODY
AND THE
BEAST

Moody and the Beast
Shadowvale, Book Four

Copyright © 2020 Kristen Painter

Shadowvale isn't your typical small town America. The sun never shines, the gates decide who enters, magic abounds, and every resident bears some kind of curse.

Exiled king of the goblins, Robin Gallow, has no choice but to live in Shadowvale. That was the deal he made with his ex-wife and current queen of the goblins in exchange for the antidote to the poison she gave him. Now, the town has become his prison and his world is closing in on him. It's enough to drive a man insane.

Theodora "Moody" Middlebright wants nothing to do with Shadowvale or the royal beast she's about to spend the next year of her life with. But her father owes the man a debt and he's too unwell to pay it himself. So Theo has come in his stead. Doesn't mean she's one bit happy about it. But then Theo hasn't been happy about anything since her mother died.

Turns out, Theo's sharp wit and brash attitude are the breath of fresh air Robin didn't know he needed, and the two somehow hit it off. But when his trust issues and her secrets collide, their budding feelings for each other are threatened with extinction.

Can Robin learn to trust a woman who's kept her true identity hidden her whole life? Will it even matter if Theo thinks he's the beast everyone believes him to be? Or will love give them both a brand new start?

CHAPTER ONE

Theodora Middlebright glared at the enormous rusty gate blocking her path. She tucked the braid at her left temple behind her pointed ear. She was knee-deep in weeds on an overgrown dirt road that clearly hadn't been used for as long as this gate hadn't been opened. She let out a long sigh that did nothing to make her feel better.

Stupid gate. Stupid town. Stupid exiled king. "Anytime you want to open up, go right ahead."

Nothing happened. Of course it didn't, because this wasn't Limbo, and you couldn't give commands to certain inanimate objects and expect them to obey like you could at home.

But then, if she were home, she'd be getting up right about now to go work at the bakery. Then in a few hours, she'd leave that job, rush home with whatever day-old goods she'd bought for breakfast, make sure her father was all right, then dash off to her second job of cleaning.

It was a hard life. Made harder by living under the rule of Queen Vesta. As monarchs went, she was probably pretty typical. She was as capricious as she was beautiful. She was occasionally kind, and she was occasionally cruel. Perhaps more than occasionally.

Theo believed that was the way rulers were, because that random cruelty kept their subjects from getting too comfortable. Her father always said there were two kinds of rulers. Those who wanted their subjects to love and respect them. And those who wanted their subjects to fear them.

Queen Vesta seemed torn between those choices, although in Theo's estimation, Her Royal Highness leaned more toward fear with each passing year.

But everyone gave Her Grace some leeway because they knew Queen Vesta had been tormented by the exiled king. How the incredible anguish he'd put her through had left her scarred and fragile. How she'd risked everything to save the citizens of Limbo and Livion, their sister kingdom, from being enslaved to the orcs. For that, Queen Vesta's cruelty was grudgingly tolerated.

It wasn't like the citizens of Limbo had a choice.

Regardless, Theo would still rather have been home. Well, mostly. At least then she would have been with her father instead of standing in the middle of nowhere trying to get a worthless gate to open and let her in.

"Open, gate." Nothing. She growled. Maybe she could pick the lock with her dagger, but with her luck she'd end up damaging the blade.

Her hands clenched. She knew this was a chance for a year away from her problematic life, but she still did *not* want to be here. She shouldn't be here. But here she was. Dang it. All because of her father's bad choices, her unrelenting sense of duty, and her stubborn unwillingness to see her foolish father die in prison.

Why did she have to be such a good daughter? Why did she have to be single? If she were married, this wouldn't be happening. But to be married, she'd have to find a man willing to put up with her and everything that came with her. And she generally found that being around most people only added to her crankiness. She didn't care if she had a reputation for being moody. Who wouldn't be with her life?

And, of course, if she were married, her father would probably be the one standing at this gate.

That couldn't happen. There was no way he'd survive what she was about to take on.

This was all because she loved him. That much was obvious. Perhaps she loved him too much. She might even love him more than he loved his wagering. Because that was something he loved dearly. Did he love betting more than he loved her? His inability to stop gambling away all their money and family possessions certainly made her wonder.

Her hand went to the little emerald-and-starstone pendant around her neck, one of the few things she had left of her mother's. Certainly the most precious. Theo had managed to keep it from her father's clutches by never taking it off.

She also locked her bedroom door at night.

She wasn't sure he would have actually snuck into her room and tried to take it, but a locked door seemed like the best possible solution. Just in case.

Enough of this. She put her hands on her hips and glowered at the offending hunk of vine-covered metal. "Seriously. Just standing here. Waiting."

The gate didn't seem impressed. Not enough to move, anyway.

She sighed again, this time the kind of long-suffering, out-of-the-diaphragm, heaving sigh that seemed to clear out every last bit of air from her lungs.

With her next inhale, she thought that if her mother were still alive, she would have whipped Welten Middlebright into shape. His gambling had always been a problem, but it had escalated after her death. Which was when his illness had set in as well.

Caralynne Middlebright had been a sharp, loving, no-nonsense kind of woman. A little on the plump side, which had made for the best hugs, and a hard worker who'd always had a kind word and warm embrace for her only child. She'd smelled of sugar and vanilla and sometimes cinnamon. That's how Theo remembered her mother.

She'd been the guiding light that had kept Theo's father on the straight and narrow. She'd also kept a tight hand on the purse strings. She'd worked long, early hours in the royal kitchens as a pastry cook. That money had kept them in good stead and sent Theo to one of the best lapidary schools in the kingdom. Theo had been happy then. They all had.

And then Caralynne had gotten sick.

Theo sucked in a ragged breath as the memory of her mother's passing came crashing down on her, along with the anger and bitterness that always followed.

If her mother had still been alive, Theo wouldn't be standing here.

But her mother wasn't. And Theo most definitely *was* standing here. She swatted at a bug that tickled her neck.

Theo glared at the gate a little harder. "Oh, for crying out loud, are you going to open or not? I know I'm not the one who's supposed to be here, but I'm here to take his place. It's all the same. You might as well let me in. I thought you were supposed to be magic, but I guess you're just a dumb hunk of metal."

The gate didn't budge. Not even a creak from one of the rusted hinges.

That really didn't leave Theo much choice. She'd walked here from the closest bus stop, which had to be six or seven miles away. She wasn't about to spend the next couple of hours walking back. Besides, she didn't have enough money for a ticket to the nearest portal to Limbo anyway.

And what good would going home do her? Or her father?

This big debt would still be unpaid. As would all his little ones, of which there were plenty. And all of that would only serve to darken her attitude further.

No, she was here for the duration. The good news

was she had youth and persistence on her side. Plus, she was strong. And had a talent no one knew about. A talent she'd kept to herself since she was a child, when her mother had told her it would be useful to her one day if she kept it secret.

She glanced around to make sure she was alone and that her secret would remain that way. Seemed so.

With a frustrated groan, she grabbed the tattered bag she'd dropped at her feet earlier and gave it a heave up and over the gate.

It landed with a soft *thunk* on the other side. Then she shifted into her most favorite of forms and launched herself into the air.

She flew up and over the gate easily, making only the slightest sounds, and landed on the other side a handful of seconds later. The gate had looked even rustier up close. She ruffled her feathers once before turning back to her human form.

There was a road on this side. A well-maintained, paved road. Good. That would make traveling a little easier.

She hoisted the bag's strap onto her shoulder and set off walking. She took a few steps before stopping to look back at the gate. "Not so tough now, are you?"

The gate did the same thing as earlier. Nothing. Then a breeze sailed past, and she heard creaking. Just a tiny noise that lasted a brief second. But she'd heard it.

Stupid gate.

With a frown, she started walking again. Her father had given her the map on the back of his indenture agreement, where it had magically shown up. But the paperwork was tucked in her jacket pocket. She'd had plenty of time on the bus to memorize the directions. As long as nothing had changed since the map had appeared, all would be well. She had decent recall, better than most goblins, maybe. Nothing extraordinary. But she was observant, and that helped.

In all aspects of life, really. You learned more by letting other people talk than you did by filling the air with your own words.

That was another of her mother's lessons. *Listen to learn. Not to reply.* Those words suited Theo just fine. She wasn't much of a talker. Never had been.

Talking could get you into trouble. Being quiet rarely did.

The road wound through a forest that was darker than the sky above because the trees were too close to let the light of the moon and stars through.

Didn't matter. Her eyes were sharp. She could see as well in the dark as she could in bright sun. Better, possibly. That was one of the gifts of being a changeling, the rare offspring of a goblin and fairy union. Typically, the children of a goblin-fairy marriage favored one kind over the other. But once in a purple moon, a changeling was born.

Her mother had known right away what her daughter was and instructed Theo all her life to hide her truth. Caralynne knew all about hiding truths.

Out of necessity, she'd hidden the fact that she was a fairy. Limbo was the goblin kingdom, and Livion was the kingdom of the fairies, the fae major. Not to be confused with the insect-sized fae minor who lived in most forests.

The two kingdoms had been at odds for ages. So when Caralynne had married Welten, she'd kept her heritage a secret. A family secret, she'd liked to say.

The truth would have meant the end of her job as a royal pastry chef. And a much harder life for all of them. At least until Queen Vesta, a fairy herself, had united the two kingdoms by marrying the King of Limbo. Traitor that he was.

But old habits died hard, and even after the merge, Theo continued to hide her fairy blood as a way of keeping her connection with her mother alive. Besides, if people knew her truth, they'd like her even less. The fae, major and minor, could sometimes be sly and conniving. Of course, goblins had their faults, too.

Theo wouldn't have changed who she was for the world, though. Being a changeling meant she had the benefits of many of her forms, even when she wasn't in them. Ordinary goblins, like her father, had better-than-human senses. But hers were even better than that.

She thanked her fairy mother daily for those gifts. Theo thought about how her parents had met in the woods surrounding the kingdoms. He'd been fishing. She'd been hunting berries. Her mother had always said she'd fallen for Welten because he'd made her laugh.

Theo could believe that. Everyone liked Welten. He was a charmer. That's how he'd gotten away with being in debt to nearly everyone he knew for so long.

But even the congeniality of friendship thinned when an imbalance existed. His illness had bought him a little more leniency, but as the illness became more serious, her father's friends were starting to realize their hopes of being repaid would die with him.

She swallowed at the knot in her throat. She didn't want to lose her father, but every day brought the inevitable closer. She was terrified to lose him. Not just because she would be alone in the world then, but because she was afraid of what that would do to her.

How much angrier would it make her? How much more would people avoid her? She had a reputation, after all. Of being moody and sour and therefore unpleasant to be around. Could it get worse?

She didn't want to learn the answers to those questions. Not now that she was going to be away from him for a year. And there was nothing she could do about it. Nothing she could do but serve that year and get back to him.

So yes, she'd do the allotted time. But she wasn't going to be happy about it.

If His Former Royal Highness thought he was

getting a little ray of sunshine to do his bidding, he had another think coming.

*

Robin Gallow stood on the balcony of his quarters, watching the lightning bugs zip through the dark and dangerous forest surrounding his home. The red streaks of light they left behind were as beautiful as they were deadly.

Those lightning bugs were his only real subjects now. Not that he wanted any.

Despite the way he'd lost the throne, he didn't miss being king that much. He certainly didn't miss the complexities of royal life. Or the need to act a certain way around certain people, all in the name of diplomacy.

And he absolutely didn't miss his treacherous ex-wife. May that deceitful fairy sink into the bog of despair, never to be seen again.

He tugged absentmindedly on the braid by his right temple. Off in the distance, a low, feral howl broke the silence. A hellhound, no doubt. One of the rarer denizens of the dark acres. Still not as deadly as his ex-wife.

He should be sleeping. But sleep had eluded him for years. Since he'd come to Shadowvale, really. Some nights, he managed it. But on most, like tonight, he woke after a few fitful hours and knew that was all he'd be getting.

So he came out here to take in the air and think.

Too much thinking at times. Enough that his thoughts were overwhelming. His head was stuffed with them. Thoughts of regret, revenge, and loss. Scenes he replayed over and over, wishing he could do them differently. On those nights, darkness pulled at him, and anger stirred in his soul.

He fought it, but his life, such as it was, had become a rather melancholy exercise in maintaining his sanity.

Still, he had a lot to be grateful for, and he tried to remind himself of those things. He had his health. Barely. His home was beautiful. Even if it was as much a prison as it was his residence. He had his job as foreman of the mines, which actually required far less work than he put in. But what goblin didn't find joy in the presence of beautiful jewels?

He also had the company of his staff, especially Elswood, his valet turned butler. The one member of his royal household staff who'd stayed loyal. That was something, wasn't it?

It absolutely was. And yet Robin often pondered how terrible a ruler he must have been that only a single member of his staff had sided with him. The rest had gone with Vesta. He knew she'd bribed them with money and jewels and promises of the fine life they'd have under her rule.

How much of that was true now? Vesta wasn't exactly a keeper of promises. No doubt there were those who regretted siding with her. He hoped there were, anyway. Even so, he wished most of them no ill will.

Everyone did what they had to in order to survive.

But he had very little communication with anyone in Limbo now. In the beginning, a few acquaintances had responded to his letters, but shortly after that, his letters had been returned, unanswered. Very clearly opened and read, but then resealed and sent back.

He got the message. He was persona non grata, as the saying went. At least in Limbo.

He yawned as he leaned against the railing. Maybe there was sleep yet to be had. Might as well try.

He trudged back inside—to his enormous empty bed—and did his best to sleep, praying only that if he did, it would be deep and dreamless and free of fairies.

He'd had nightmares enough already.

Chapter Two

Theo walked for hours. In part because her destination was deep in the heart of Shadowvale, but also because as she went through town, she slowed to take it all in. Shadowvale was nothing like the Kingdom of Limbo, and having never been outside of the kingdom, she wanted to see as much of this new place as she could.

Some of the shops were open, and as tempted as she was to go in, what would be the point? She had no money, and her person was required elsewhere. And soon.

So she walked on, content to look. She stopped outside a few of the food shops, mostly to inhale the delicious scents. Her stomach growled, but again, her purse wouldn't let her indulge. She clung to the thought that there would be food soon. There had to be. Wouldn't room and board be a requirement?

She lingered at the window of the chocolate shop. She wasn't sure how often she'd be allowed out once she entered service. It was very likely she'd have no days off. She'd be a servant, after all. And the lowest of all the servants, being the newest addition and only temporary.

There was no reason to think any liberties would be extended to her. Not when she was here to fulfill a debt. She was expecting a tough year with few comforts, so whatever happened, she'd deal with it, just like she'd dealt with every other hardship that had come her way. That was one thing her life had prepared her for.

After what seemed to be the heart of town, the streets became residential. The homes were so different from the thatched cottages and treehouses and stone bungalows of Limbo. The homes here all looked so pretty and perfect. Some had lights on inside, even at the late hour, but she knew that Shadowvale's citizens were from all walks and creeds.

What must it be like to live in a town like this?

Supernaturals abounded here. So did humans. Although they weren't as interesting to her now as they'd been before she'd spent nine hours with them on the bus. That had been plenty of time to study that species. Amazing how much some of them snored. And with their mouths open.

An owl hooted far off, and not long after that, a wolf's plaintive howl split the night. She liked those sounds. They made her feel at home. As much at home as she could feel in a strange place like this.

The homes got bigger. And bigger. And scarcer. And then they went away altogether.

Not long after that, she passed a school. Home of

the Tigers, the sign proudly announced. Real tigers? That couldn't be, could it?

She picked up the pace a little anyway.

She was in the country now, surrounded by nothing but trees and fields. Mountains rose up in the distance all around her. The sky above was bright with stars. It was lovely, really. A lot like Limbo. She kept going.

Next up was a cemetery. Last Rest, it was named. A cluster of winged cats mewed at her from their perches on the headstones and from the top of a mausoleum. She wiggled her fingers at them. They were cute. They'd probably try to kill her if she attempted to pet one, but cute was cute. Even when it was deadly.

The cemetery faded behind her, then the fields disappeared, too, and there was nothing but woods.

An enchanted forest, to be exact. That's what the sign had said at the beginning of the road that led into the amazing forest. The trees were incredibly tall and thick, and the air smelled like magic. Green and woodsy with an underlying hint of darkness. Very much like goblin magic. And fae, she supposed.

She could understand why the exiled king made his home here. So far, this part of Shadowvale felt the most like Limbo. She shifted her bag to her other shoulder and trudged on. She was close now, according to the map in her head.

The trees covered the road like a canopy, hiding the stars. It was dark, but clumps of sprite moss provided some light. Enough that every so often, she could just pick out a face in the bark of a tree, the sign a wood nymph lived there.

She kept going, a little bothered that the walk was taking longer than she'd anticipated. She knew she'd slowed through town, but she was used to walking, and she'd picked up speed once she'd gotten past the houses. She'd run, but it wouldn't do to arrive sweaty.

Was that a hint of lavender in the sky? The sun must be on its way up. Or was it?

She'd heard the sun didn't shine here. That the skies were permanently gray, because the witch who'd created the town had done so to keep her vampire lover safe.

If that was really the case, Theo was fine with that. Like most goblins, she preferred the cool shadows of the forest to the blazing sun. Limbo had bright days, but also long shadows. Its thick forests provided steady breezes, and the surrounding mountains meant daylight was short because the peaks blocked all but the highest sun.

She turned down another street, wider than the one before. Blackthorn Drive. At the post, she stopped and stared back the way she'd come. The sky had to be lightening, because she could see the green of the leaves. Just like the forests of Limbo. No wonder the exiled king had come here.

Although she wasn't sure he'd had much of a choice.

She faced forward again and noticed that the forest started to change at this point. The trees grew more twisted, the bark and leaves darker. Almost sooty. Like they'd been burned. She inhaled. There was no acrid smell of ash.

She walked toward an iron arch across the road ahead. In the curve of the arch, *Dark Acres* was spelled out, but there was no gate, thankfully. A raven sat on one side of the arch, watching her as she passed beneath it.

Signs of other houses appeared as she continued on. A chimney here, a weather vane there, the peak of a roof, a curl of smoke. But if she tried to see the house itself, or see more of it, all traces disappeared. The fog around her seemed to thicken. She stopped looking around and concentrated on following the map in her head.

Eventually, she came to a street sign. Candlewick Court. She peered through the trees where the road bent. Mist rose off the pavement, making it hard to see the place that would be her home for the next year.

Then a breeze caused a break in the fog, and she got a better look. The house that lay beyond was every inch goblin royalty. The deep-purple roof, curved gray stone walls, and embedded gems were all reminiscent of Fangmore. The palace he'd left behind.

Right down to the skulls worked into the accents.

It was a good reminder that while she was here to fulfill a debt, she needed to keep her wits about her. The king was exiled, not powerless. He was still a ferocious warrior. He hadn't become king of the goblins because it was his birthright. He'd earned it in battle, just as every other goblin king had. In his case, by single-handedly capturing the orc king.

She'd do well to remember that. She started walking up the long, curving drive. He'd do well to remember she was also a goblin. Half, yes, but that half was just as fierce as could be, and as far as he would know, she was a hundred percent goblin. She would not be mistreated while she was here. Nor would she sacrifice her personal security.

If the exiled king thought she'd be his new plaything and warm his bed during her tenure, he'd soon discover just how wrong he was.

She took a deep breath as she climbed the stairs to the wide front doors. The stair risers were skulls, all facing out. The door handles were metal cast to look like bones. A mosaic of amethysts, iolites, and a mix of other gems decorated the sides of the doors, letting in some light, but allowing no one to see in.

The entrance was beautiful and creepy. The true goblin aesthetic. She raised her hand to knock, but the door opened before she made contact.

The goblin who answered was not the king, but based on his livery, she had a pretty good idea of who he was. Elswood Hardencourt. The only member of the royal staff who'd left with the king. That much she remembered from her history.

His appraising glance raked over her. "Who are you?"

He had to know she was a citizen of the realm. Her pointed ears and the iridescent sheen of her black hair gave that away. They matched his own. Although her hair was lacking the abundant streaks of silver threaded through his. And his hair, perhaps as a concession to living in the human world, was too short for the traditional braids.

She made herself answer as pleasantly as possible. "I am Theodora Middlebright. I've come to fulfill the debt owed by my father to His Royal Highness Robin Gallow."

She dug into her jacket and took out the hard leather tube that housed the official indenture document. She handed it to him. "It's all there."

He removed the scroll, unfurling it. He scanned the binding document. The map on the back had disappeared. Perhaps because she'd arrived?

She knew each word of the indenture by heart, but the gist was her father had lost a game of slip one night in the palace kitchens. Out of money, he'd foolishly wagered a year of his life in service to the cunning card player across from him, a young man all had thought to be the butcher's well-to-do cousin.

A young man who'd turned out to be the newly crowned king.

Elswood looked up at her. "This debt is owed by Welten Middlebright."

"Yes, that's my father. The arrangement allows for a substitution so long as it's for the better." When Elswood still hesitated, she frowned, struggling not to snap at the man for failing to recognize the former king was getting a superior deal with her serving in her father's place. "Are we going to stand here all day, or are we going to let the former king know I'm here?"

Elswood's gaze narrowed to seemingly focus on the little magical clock embedded in the heart of the document. She could see the numbers ticking down through the parchment, although they were backward to her. They'd turned from green to red three days ago, a warning that the time to make good on the debt was running out.

His gaze lifted again, but he seemed to be looking beyond her and not at her. "You chose an unusual time to arrive."

Did he mean the early hour? "I came as quickly as my feet were able."

"I meant that there are only a few days left to begin the year owed on this note. Any later, and the note could have been called due."

"I'm sure you can understand my reluctance." Not to mention her father had only recently told her about the indenture. And then only because she'd caught him packing and forced it out of him. As if he could have done this.

Elswood backed away from the door. "You might as well come in and get to work, then."

"Thank you." She exhaled softly, relieved that her year in service, for all that she was dreading it, had begun. She stepped inside.

"Door, close." The door did as Elswood commanded. Then he looked at her. "Follow me."

Interesting that standard goblin magic worked in

this house. But she didn't have long to ponder it. Or much of anything, really. He walked fast, barely giving her a chance to gape at the home's interior. The exiled king had spared no expense in decorating. Rock crystal chandeliers, velvet drapes and brocade upholstery in vibrant jewel tones, vast displays of antique goblin weaponry, battle-scarred helmets, even a full suit of antique battle leathers on display by the entrance to some grand hall. Several large, open geodes displayed their gem interiors under spotlights that caused them to glitter.

The home looked exactly as she'd imagined an exiled king's home might look.

It also looked very unlived in. But she didn't guess His Lordship had much in the way of company after being cast out of his kingdom. There were consequences for the sins he'd committed.

Elswood led her through a simple swinging door and down a set of steps. The décor changed as they passed through. It became much simpler. More utilitarian.

She was in the servants' part of the house now. The part she'd become the most familiar with, she supposed.

"I'll take you to your room first, then introduce you to Mrs. Baton. She's the housekeeper. She can introduce you to the rest of the staff. I don't have time for such things, as I'm His Lordship's butler and very busy."

"I'm sure," Theo said. She quickly added, "Thank you for your time."

He glanced back at her like he wasn't sure whether that had been a sarcastic remark.

It almost had been, but she'd modified her tone at the last moment. She smiled all the same to reassure him. As soon as he looked away, she stopped smiling. Curbing her natural inclination to bite back was going to be a chore.

They went farther into the bowels of the house. All the windows were narrow transoms near the ceiling because this floor was technically underground. A sort of daylight basement. They passed an enormous kitchen with two women in it, another workroom that contained a long table, a couple of closed doors, a room that might have been an office, then they turned down a hall.

He took her to the room at the very end.

She doubted that with all these sleeping quarters, this was the only one available, but whatever. The location was perfectly acceptable to her. She didn't want or need to be near anyone. In fact, this was better. The farther she was from other people, the less likely they'd annoy her. And she them.

Going by doors, there were enough rooms for a staff of twenty. She'd seen two women in the kitchen, one much younger and clearly a helper. So a cook, a scullery maid, a housekeeper, Elswood, and who else? Maybe a footman? Perhaps a gardener? And her?

It didn't seem this house employed many more than that.

She hoped that meant there wasn't all that much work to be done instead of there being an overwhelming amount she'd have to handle on her own. Her shoulders were strong, but there was a limit to what anyone could do in a day. Taking on more than her fair share would definitely make her grouchy.

Grouchier.

He unlocked the door with a key on a chain attached to his waistcoat, then detached the key and handed it to her. "Get settled, then come to the kitchen. Five minutes. No more."

She took the key. "Yes, Mr...." She couldn't very well call him Elswood. But he hadn't introduced himself either, and she didn't want him to know she already knew who he was.

"Mr. Hardencourt."

"I'll be right there, Mr. Hardencourt."

He gave her a little nod and left.

She tucked the key into her pocket and pushed the door open. The room was simple. A narrow bed with a stand next to it barely big enough to hold the bedside lamp. A small dresser and a chair. A slim mirror on one wall. Utilitarian to the extreme. She'd managed with about the same at home. What mattered was that there was a window and that it opened. Did it?

She closed the door, dropped her bag on the bed, and stood on the chair to inspect the window. It opened easily, and the screen was simple to remove.

A sense of relief went through her. She'd have a chance for fresh air. An escape, if needed. Which she imagined she would. Often.

The window looked out onto a simple stone path, then the dark, twisted woods beyond. Interesting. Hopefully, the path wasn't much traveled. She glanced down both sides of it as far as she could see. Did it go around the entire house? Might be worth checking out.

She left her bag on the bed. She could put her few things away later.

The kitchen was a big, bright space with an enormous marble island in the center. A round woman with an easy smile wiped her hands on her apron. She had a little smudge of flour on her forehead near the edge of her white cap. "Hello there. Mr. Hardencourt had to take care of something. He said we have a new staff member. How nice. We haven't had one of those in…well, since Lolly replaced the last scullery maid five years ago. Welcome."

Theo nodded. The woman reminded her ever so slightly of her mother, making Theo like the woman instantly. It never hurt to be friends with the kitchen staff. "Thank you. I'm Theodora Middlebright. I'm here for a year's service."

"Nice to meet you, Theodora, always glad to have more help. Many hands make light work. I'm Mrs. Applestock. I'm the cook."

The younger woman Theo had seen earlier came in with a flat of eggs.

Mrs. Applestock pointed to her. "That's Lolly. She's the scullery maid, although she pitches in with housekeeping sometimes, too."

Lolly grinned and waved. "Hi."

"Hi, Lolly." The girl was a little too cheerful, but Theo chalked that up to not having anyone new around in a long while. "You can call me Theo."

Both women were in simple lavender dresses with white aprons. Neither of the women had the pointed ears or shiny hair of a goblin. Theo wasn't sure what they were. Human? Was that possible? Working for a goblin? Shadowvale was an interesting place.

A stern woman entered, and Lolly's smile vanished. The young woman bent her head and went to work wiping down what looked like already clean countertops.

Theo took Lolly's change in demeanor as a warning.

"Theodora?" The woman had shimmering steel-gray hair that gave off subtle purple hints. Goblin, definitely. A thin braid flowed back from each temple to be twisted into an elaborate knot with the rest of her hair. Her ears tapered toward the sky, and she wore the same deep-purple livery as Elswood. The clothing had steely trim with tiny skull buttons. This had to be the housekeeper. The woman in charge of everything Elswood wasn't.

"Yes, I'm Theodora. You must be Mrs. Baton."

"I am. Come this way, Theodora, and we'll see that you're properly attired."

Theo glanced back at Mrs. Applestock and Lolly. Mrs. Applestock gave her a sympathetic smile. Huh. A smile in her direction. That was new.

She kind of liked it.

Theo followed Mrs. Baton. She had no other choice. But the very idea of wearing the livery of the king who'd tried to sell his own citizens into slavery...her skin already crawled.

But this was what she'd agreed to. All to keep her father from the damp, dirty cells beneath Fangmore Castle should the queen have called in the debt.

She wondered what this home was called, but she supposed she'd learn that eventually. She had three-hundred sixty-four and a half days to find out.

CHAPTER THREE

After a few restless hours of staring at the ceiling, Robin gave up on sleep and got dressed for the day. That was one task he was grateful he no longer needed Elswood for. He'd never needed Elswood for it, but a king was expected to maintain certain standards and abide by certain rules of etiquette. Having a valet assist him with his clothing and weaponry was one of those rules.

Fortunately, Elswood had gone from valet to butler with ease.

It was also fortunate that exiled kings could generally make their own rules about the help they needed. The fact that he still kept a staff was mainly because of the size of his house. It was ridiculously large. But then, he'd built this house never imagining he'd live in it without a big family.

There was no way he'd be able to maintain a house this size by himself. And keeping staff helped in another way because the fact was that living in such a monstrously large place alone would have been the pinnacle of loneliness.

At times, it still was.

He'd built this house thinking it would be a sort of summer palace. A place to retreat to when he and his queen needed to get away from life in Limbo. As such, it would be filled with staff when he and Vesta were here. When it had become plain that wasn't going to happen, he'd still expected more of his staff to follow him when he'd been removed. Not just the household staff, but some of his ministers and secretaries. Those who knew he was innocent of the charges she'd leveled against him.

As it happened, Vesta had not only encouraged him to build this house for them, she'd turned the staff against him. All of them. Save Elswood.

He wondered what the citizens of Limbo thought of him now. If any of them remembered him fondly, or if he was the villain in all of their tales of days gone by. So many years had passed.

It didn't matter. Not much. He'd never leave the confines of his restricted life. Which meant he'd never leave Shadowvale. It was a fate he was more or less resigned to.

He zipped up the waxed twill jumpsuit he wore to inspect the mines, tugged on his steel-toed boots, and grabbed his hard hat. He tucked a small steel knife into his boot, then strapped a longer, malachite-handled dagger into a specially made loop on his jumpsuit. No self-respecting goblin went anywhere without a blade of some kind.

Fully dressed, hard hat under his arm, he made his way toward the stairs. The lack of sleep had left him with little appetite, but he liked to stop by the kitchen anyway.

Mrs. Applestock was one of his favorite people. And her biscuits, which she made every morning, were always a hit with the miners. She made a double batch just for them on the days he visited the mines.

He jogged down the stairs and through the house, barely seeing the surrounding luxury. It was all just window dressing. His hours were spent in the more personal areas of the house.

The opulent sitting rooms, ballroom, and dining hall were meant for company. Something he never had.

He went down the back stairs and strode into the kitchen. "Good morning, Mrs. Applestock."

She smiled at him as she pulled a large tray of biscuits from the oven. She put the pan on the marble island, then gave him a little bow. "Your timing is impeccable as always, Your Lordship."

"I try." The smell of warm biscuits made him rethink his lack of appetite. He settled onto one of the stools at the island.

"Sire." Lolly put a mug of coffee and a little pitcher of cream in front of him, then went back to sweeping the floor.

"Thank you, Lolly." He inhaled, taking in the clove and cardamom that were the necessary ingredients to all good goblin coffee. There was nothing like it as far as he was concerned.

He slid over the sugar bowl and added a couple spoonfuls to his mug, then a quick pour of cream.

Mrs. Applestock gave him a rather disapproving but motherly look. He smiled. He'd come to enjoy those looks more than he could say. "Your Lordship, you know I can have Lolly take all of this up to the small dining room."

Lolly nodded. "Right away."

He shook his head. "I know you can. And you both know I don't like to eat up there. I much prefer the company of beautiful women anyway."

Mrs. Applestock chuckled. "Shall I pack a basket for you to take, then?"

She always asked, and he always said yes. It was their ritual. "Please."

Lolly's frown wasn't missed. He knew she wasn't a fan of accompanying him to the mines. The girl had dated one of the miners, a holler troll by the name of Billy, but had broken things off a while back. Now she balked every time there were biscuits to carry.

He felt for her. He understood all about having an ex you didn't want to see. He gave her a short reprieve. "I'll have a biscuit now with my coffee before I leave. What kind of jam is there?"

"Blackberry jam and peach preserves. But is that all you want? I could make hot cakes. With cod sausages and baked sugar beans and some of those buttered mushrooms you like."

"As tempting as that sounds, I'm fine with just a biscuit and coffee. Blackberry jam, please." Finding the appetite for a biscuit was one thing. Finding it for a full goblin breakfast was another. Although he gave Mrs. Applestock credit for learning to cook such a spread. She'd adapted her skills marvelously to his tastes.

She brought him a plate with two piping-hot biscuits, along with a crock of butter, a crock of blackberry jam, and a knife.

There was no point in telling her he'd wanted only one biscuit. He already knew he'd eat both. Her biscuits were that good, especially when they were hot from the oven. Warm and buttery with the kind of soft, crumbling texture that made them melt in his mouth.

Their deliciousness was exactly why he took them to the mine with him whenever he went. They made the miners happy to see him, and he much preferred to keep people happy.

He split the biscuits, spread them with butter, then added a thick layer of jam. This would hold him until he got back, that was for sure.

"Mrs. Applestock, have you seen Mrs. Baton? She's not in her—oh. Excuse me."

Robin glanced up to see who the voice belonged to and looked into the most interesting green-gold eyes he'd ever seen. "Hello."

She stared at him. "Hello."

She was wearing Gallow House livery, but he'd never seen her before. And there was no way he would have forgotten that beguiling face or those eyes. Or another goblin in the house. She had to be with that hair and those ears and those braids. "Did Elswood hire you?"

"No, I'm—"

Mrs. Applestock stepped closer. "This is Theodora, Your Lordship. Just arrived. She's here to—"

"Your Grace," Elswood interrupted as he strode into the room. "My apologies. I was just coming to find you to let you know about the new girl." He glanced at her. "Mrs. Baton is waiting for you in her office."

Theodora shook her head. "I was just in there, and she wasn't—"

"She's there now," Elswood snapped.

"Yes, sir." She did a quick, clumsy curtsy and left.

Far too soon for Robin's liking. "I didn't know we were hiring a new girl. I approve. Although I'm not so sure of that term. She looks more like a woman to me."

"Yes, Your Lordship." Elswood smiled indulgently. "She's come to serve a year's indenture."

Robin shook his head. "I don't recall anyone owing me a year's service."

"It's quite an old indenture, my lord. It was produced nearly twenty years ago."

"Twenty? But I'd only just become..." His long-gone title didn't need to be spoken to be understood.

Elswood knew. He nodded. "Yes, Sire, you had."

"Sounds like rubbish. There's no way I would have indentured a child. She couldn't have been more than six or seven, then."

"Nine, I believe. And you didn't indenture her. It's her father's order. She's fulfilling it for him. He is unwell, apparently, and unable to do it. And the terms of fulfillment were nearly up. Another few days, and he would have been in default. Such a thing would have sent him straight to the dungeons."

"Not likely. I'm no longer king. I can't very well claim any rights to payment or send the man to jail."

"No, Sire. But the queen can."

"I see." But he didn't. Not fully. Didn't matter at the moment. What mattered was the incredible loyalty this woman had to her father to give up a year of her life for him. Loyalty like that, a rare commodity in his world, intrigued him. And although he had no interest in an indenture, the idea of someone new in the house was welcome. "She'll be here for a year, you said?"

"Yes, Sire. I've put the document on your desk."

He nodded. "I'll look at it later. When I return."

Elswood hesitated.

"What is it?"

"If I may, Your Lordship...there are only a few days left on the indenture. If you don't sign off on it soon, the clock will run out."

"I promise. As soon as I return."

"Very good, Sire. Is there anything I can do for you today?"

"No." The things Robin needed, no one could provide. The key to this prison of a life didn't exist.

Elswood bowed. "Enjoy your day, Sire."

"Thank you." Robin turned back to his biscuits. "Wait. What did you say her name is?"

"The girl? I mean, the woman?"

"Yes."

"Theodora Muddlebranch or something."

"Very good." He gave Elswood a quick nod. "You're dismissed." The name meant nothing to him.

Elswood left, and Robin's mind wandered, the woman's name tumbling through his memories as he hoped to latch on to something. He felt like he should remember the name, but twenty years ago?

He'd practically been a boy then. Just crowned, having won the battle of First Moon against the orcs and, in doing so, earning himself the throne. It hadn't been planned. But battles were funny things that sometimes took unexpected turns, and he'd known the Threadbare Forest in and out from his time hunting starstones there.

He'd had a hunch where the orcs' king would be. And he'd been right. Robin had followed that hunch, found the orc king alone, and captured the old man single-handedly. He'd earned a few scars from the fight, but he'd prevailed.

And just like that, the throne of Limbo had become his. A gift from the aged and heirless sitting king.

But the name Muddlebranch eluded him. Like one of those lightning bugs in the woods surrounding his home. Not that he'd want to catch one of those.

He sighed and took a bite of biscuit. It was still warm, the jam sticky-sweet, and he made short work of the rest of it. Why couldn't he place that name, though?

Mrs. Applestock set the big wicker basket of biscuits in front of him. They were covered with kitchen towels, as always. "I put a few crocks of jam and butter in there, as well, plus some spoons. Lolly'll be ready to go when you are."

"Thank you. The miners will be thrilled." He picked up the second biscuit. "Say, I know Lolly doesn't like making the trip since the incident with Billy."

Mrs. Applestock rolled her eyes. "Aye, the perils of young love. But she'll be fine."

Robin shook his head. "No point in torturing her. She can have a break. I'll have Theodora carry the biscuits."

CHAPTER FOUR

Theo stood in Mrs. Baton's office, listening to her explain the policies and procedures of working at Gallow House, which was how they all referred to the place. But as Mrs. Baton droned on, Theo's mind wandered.

Mostly to His Lordship. And how he was nothing like what she'd imagined. How was he not a craggy old man? Stooped with age and graying?

He looked very much like a warrior capable of capturing the orc king. Tall and strong and lithe with that feral goblin grace. His braids could use redoing, but otherwise a perfect example of the male of their species.

In fact, he looked more like the king's son than the king. The king's *hot* son. So not like the monarch himself. True, goblins didn't really show their age until their seventh or eighth decade, but how young was he?

She tried to remember her history, but there hadn't been much about King Robin. After all, he was a traitor to his kingdom. What more did anyone need to know than that? The libraries and schools contained only officially sanctioned books, so trying to uncover more than what was taught would have meant searching out other sources. She worked far too much to spend her time researching the history of a bygone ruler.

Not even her father liked to talk about King Robin's time on the throne. She knew because she'd pressed him before she'd left. She'd wanted to know as much as possible about the man she was about to serve for a year.

But her father had mostly just smiled and shaken his head and repeated the things she'd already learned in school.

Things like Robin Gallow was a traitor to the goblin nation. He'd won the throne, but only because he'd been in league with the orcs and had had a plan to turn the citizens of Limbo over to them as slaves. Very soon after marrying him, Queen Vesta had uncovered the plot just in time and banished him, saving her homeland of Livion and the goblin kingdom, Limbo.

Making her the savior of both.

That was the gist of everything contained in the history books. And those books were approved by Queen Vesta's cultural minister.

So all her life, Theo had imagined King Robin to be this beady-eyed tyrant with a cruel smile and an unnatural need for power.

Not the exceedingly handsome man who'd been eating jam-and-butter biscuits with the enthusiasm of a child on All Saints' morning. Certainly not the man who'd been kind and cordial with his staff. Was it possible his time in exile had changed him?

She doubted it.

"Are you listening to me?"

Theo straightened. "Yes, ma'am. Sheets must be ironed. Towels must be folded in threes, and pillows are to be fluffed at turndown."

Mrs. Baton frowned. "Correct."

A knock on the door was followed by the appearance of Mrs. Applestock's cheery face. "Sorry to interrupt, but the biscuits need carrying down to the mine."

Mrs. Baton's frown went nowhere. "That's Lolly's job."

Mrs. Applestock wasn't deterred. "His Lordship has requested that Theodora do the carrying today."

Mrs. Baton's lips pursed like an invisible drawstring had suddenly been pulled. She narrowed her eyes. "I'll send her along."

"Thank you. Trout potpie for dinner tonight," Mrs. Applestock added before she disappeared.

Mrs. Baton's sharp gaze turned to Theo. "You'd better be on your best behavior, girl. I can't imagine why he'd ask for you, except that he must already suspect you're not up to this job."

"I'll do my best." Because biscuit carrying required a high level of skill. But she kept that comment to herself.

Mrs. Baton pointed toward the door. "Well, go. Don't keep His Lordship waiting."

"No, ma'am." She took her time walking back to the kitchen. She wasn't going to hustle just because Baton said jump. Do that once, and it would always be expected. She didn't want Baton thinking she had any great pull over her either.

Besides, only the exiled king could declare her service void, and Theo wasn't about to let that happen. Such a tragedy would immediately call her father's account due and result in him doing time in the dungeons. That would be the end of him in a few short days.

As much as she despised the exiled king, she felt rather certain she could get into and stay in his good graces.

She hoped. At least he was easy to look at.

She walked into the kitchen and found him putting his plate in the sink. What kind of royalty cleaned up after themselves? Lolly was at the other end of the long sink, scrubbing a pan, and Mrs. Applestock was sitting at the far end of the island, poring over a cookbook and making notes on a pad of paper.

Theo cleared her throat softly. "You asked for me, Sire?"

He turned. And smiled. At her. It seemed like a benevolent smile, but that was probably part of his act. Didn't matter. She knew what he was all about. He leaned against the sink like he relaxed in the kitchen all the time. "Yes. I'd like you to accompany me to the mines today."

"You want me to carry the biscuits." It wasn't a

question. More of an impertinent statement, but he didn't seem to take it that way.

He nodded. "Yes, please."

Please? She didn't mean to frown at his use of that word, but apparently she had.

"It's not far, and I like to walk. I hope you don't mind. It's good exercise."

"Whatever you wish." It wasn't up to her how they traveled, but walking suited her fine.

"Good. Go get changed. You have something more appropriate for the mines? The household uniform is a little much for where we're going. If you need one, I could probably dig up another jumpsuit for you. It would be a little big on you, though."

His fit him very well. She'd noticed. She blinked as the rest of his words registered. "I have jeans and short boots and a jacket."

Lolly looked over her shoulder, still up to her elbows in suds. "That should do it. Gets a little cold down there."

Theo nodded. "I'll be right back." She ran to her room, shucked the wretched uniform she'd just put on, and got into her street clothes. It was a welcome change. She wasn't much for the uniform, but she knew she'd have to get used to the blasted thing, seeing as how she'd be spending most of her time in it.

That would save wear and tear on her own things, she supposed. That was a plus, seeing as how she hadn't brought much with her. Not that she had much to bring.

She returned to the kitchen. "Ready, Your Lordship."

He was chatting with Mrs. Applestock. He turned and looked Theo over. The briefest hint of something sparkled in his eyes. "All right, let's go."

He picked up the big basket off the counter and handed it to Theo.

Their fingers touched when she took it from him, sending sparks through her. Sparks? She almost recoiled. She wanted none of that. She was *not* attracted to him. At all. Nor would she be. In fact, those sparks revolted her.

Except…they didn't.

He was a traitor, she reminded herself. He excelled at making people believe one thing when another was happening. Nothing else about him mattered.

She clutched the basket handle tightly and kept silent as she followed him out.

He didn't go through the front doors. He didn't even go back upstairs to the main part of the house. Instead, he went past Mrs. Baton's office, past the hall that went to the staff quarters and straight ahead down the main passage. It ended with stairs on both sides. He went left and up, then out through a much more utilitarian set of doors.

They opened onto a large stone courtyard. A long, paved drive led out from it. She'd walked part of that drive when she'd first arrived. She hadn't realized it went past the front doors and then around the side of the house to where they were now. She inhaled the fresh air, taking in the earthy scents of the encompassing woods.

The courtyard was a large rectangle, although the edges had been rounded to maintain the curve of the driveway that fed into it. The surrounding forest came as close as possible to the buildings that flanked the three sides. First was the main house, the back structure had a four-door garage, and across from the main house was a small cottage.

But the garage was what caught her eye. One of the doors was up, and a car had been pulled out.

She knew nothing about cars, but this one was beautiful. Sleek and curvy and the color of fresh butter. The car had no top, and the inside was all white leather. A man in Gallow House livery was wiping the outside with a cloth.

Robin waved at him, and he waved back, smiling.

"You have cars?" She regretted the question as soon as she spoke it. The very sentence violated part of what Mrs. Baton had told her this morning. A servant was never to address their lord. They were only to speak when spoken to and then with as brief an answer as possible.

His eyes narrowed, and he looked at her in amusement. "Yes. Does that surprise you? I even know how to drive. Not that I go far."

The last comment didn't seem to be directed at her. She nodded anyway. She couldn't be more brief than that.

He was still looking at her. "Why do you ask?"

Well, that wasn't a question she could answer

without speaking. "I don't know. You're walking to the mines. I guess I thought there was a reason for that. Like you had to."

"No. I just like the air. I drive sometimes when I go out. Which isn't often. And like I said, not very far. And not for long." He sighed as they crossed the courtyard, and it seemed to her that there was a lot he wasn't telling her. Not that he owed her an explanation for anything he did. "People tend to stare a lot when you're royalty. Even in a town like this."

That sounded more like an excuse or a justification than a genuine reason. Who wouldn't stare at a car like that? But she just nodded, keeping her thoughts and words to herself.

He pointed to the little cottage as they went by. "That's where Henry lives. The man I waved to who was wiping down the Packard. He's my chauffeur, but his services aren't required all that much. Once in a while. Mostly, he takes care of the cars."

"Why don't you—" She closed her mouth abruptly. Once again, she'd forgotten herself. She was only to speak when spoken to. A hard thing for anyone to remember, she imagined. Eventually, it would become habit.

He smiled. "Why don't I what?"

They started down a path through the woods. It was worn enough that the dirt showed through and a few weeds had popped up. The weeds were as black and twisted as the trees.

She shifted the basket to the other hand. It wasn't heavy, but it wasn't light either.

He glanced back like it mattered if someone was watching, then reached over and took the basket. His hard hat was tucked under his arm. "Here. Let me."

"I can manage." Panic sluiced through her. Did he think her so weak that she couldn't carry biscuits? She'd never survive this job if he believed that. "Really, it hardly weighs a thing."

"It weighs enough, especially when Mrs. Applestock adds a few crocks of her blackberry jam. Besides, I always carry the basket."

She looked at him, no longer caring what the proper protocol was. "You do?"

He screwed up his face in amusement. "Do you really think I need a maid to help me?"

"Then why…" Maybe she should stop asking questions. But she couldn't figure this man out.

"Because…it's expected of me. Exiled or not, my life is governed by a few restrictions I seem powerless to circumvent. And I've learned over the years that things are easier if I abide by those constraints."

She had so many more questions. As long as he wasn't objecting, she decided to ask a few more while she took in the forest around them. "Why are you powerless? Your life is your own now, isn't it?"

He snorted. "Not hardly. I am still very much controlled by the woman who put me here."

"Who's that?"

He looked at her like she was a blooming idiot. "Queen Vesta. But you must know that, or did you not come from Limbo?"

"No, I did. I just didn't realize…never mind." She knew Queen Vesta had banished him, but she'd never really considered that the queen had chosen for him to reside in this location. The queen must have wanted him somewhere she thought he'd stay contained. Which meant she still considered him dangerous after all these years. But if that was true, why make him continue to live in the style of a king? Theo didn't get it. But then, she'd never had a reason to understand the ways of royalty. Or to care, frankly.

"You ask a lot of questions. And don't seem afraid to talk to me."

"My apologies." She hated apologizing when she wasn't really sorry, but she was well aware of her faults. And her need to keep him happy. "I'll learn."

"Don't." He laughed softly. "I like it."

She studied him, wondering what he was up to. "I can't afford to be dismissed. My father wouldn't survive the dungeons."

"I would never send him there."

She had no assurance of that. Not with this man's reputation. "Perhaps not, but you know how an indenture works. It's in the magic of the thing. If the clock runs out, or if the indentured fails in some way, the debt comes due. In my father's case, he can't pay it, so he'd be sent to the dungeons. And he won't survive there. Not long. Which means I'd lose him."

Her next breath sounded ragged even to her own ears. "I think it would be the end of me as well."

CHAPTER FIVE

The emotion that had slipped into her voice wasn't lost on Robin. "Your father is ill? That's why you're serving his time?"

The woman intrigued him to no end. And not just because she was beautiful. She was the most interesting person he'd talked to in a long time. Not that he met that many people. Or had a chance to. Almost none outside of his staff and the miners. And they all pandered to him in the way people did with royalty. Some intentionally, some without realizing it, but it left him with almost no genuine interaction. It wasn't much of a way to live.

He supposed that was exactly what Vesta had intended when she'd dreamed up this prison.

But that didn't mean he was about to spill all his secrets to Theodora, as enticing as she might be. He'd slowly learned the extent of his imprisonment over the years. Such secrets were his to share or not, but he thought not was probably the smarter choice. Sometimes, he thought the things he'd learned were all that kept him alive.

She nodded. "Yes, that's why I'm here in his place."

"Your loyalty is commendable. I mean that. It's a rare quality. At least it's rare in my world."

She shrugged. "I didn't even know about the debt until a week ago."

"The indenture is nearly twenty years old. What suddenly brought it to light?"

"I found my father packing. He wouldn't tell me why at first, then I found the indenture scroll sticking out of his bag. He told me not to bother with it, but I'm not one to listen. Not with him. When I read what was on that document..." She exhaled like there was pressure on her chest. "I had no idea such a thing even existed. All those years, he'd kept it a secret. Or maybe he'd forgotten about it, I don't know. But I knew immediately what I had to do."

Robin still needed to know more. "Despite the magic connected to the indenture, it still came from my rule. And I'm not king anymore. So why not ignore it?"

Her eyes narrowed. "And run the risk that the Overwatch shows up at our door when the timer runs out and then stand helplessly by while they put my father in shackles and drag him off? No, thank you."

The Overwatch was what the people called the Royal Guard. In his day, they'd been a rather benign force that served mostly to handle crowd control at official events. But he knew other rulers had used them very differently. Vesta was definitely the kind to do exactly that. No doubt by now she'd turned them into a fearsome unit.

Robin frowned. "But again, the indenture is mine. Not Vesta's. I doubt she'd care about any debt owed to me."

"Maybe not. But I couldn't take the chance. Do you even know what happens when the timer ticks down and the indenture comes due? Who gets notified? You're no longer in the kingdom. Should I have risked the chance that the queen wouldn't be alerted?"

"I suppose not." She was right. Magic was funny that way. When the bespelled timer went off, who would have heard the alarm? He couldn't fault Theodora for her actions.

She shook her head. "I would never speak ill of my queen, but I believe she would have called the debt due, had it landed on her desk. I couldn't take that chance. As I've said, my father is not a well man. I'd very much like to make his last days easier."

"And yet, you're here. For three hundred and sixty-five of those days."

She scowled. "Again, I had no choice. And better me than him."

"Such a sacrifice for both of you. Your mother must miss you terribly as well."

Her gaze darkened ever so slightly. "My mother passed. Quite a while ago. I'm surprised you don't remember that."

"Why would I remember that?"

"Caralynne Middlebright. The name means nothing to you?"

He squinted, trying to remember. Then his mouth opened as a sudden memory flooded him, and he stopped walking. "Middlebright? I remember *that* name. Caralynne was the head pastry chef in the royal kitchens. She was your mother?"

Theodora nodded. "Yes."

"Of course. I am so sorry. May she rest in the bright light."

"Thank you." She touched the pendant at her throat.

Robin put a hand to the back of his neck. "I know exactly who your father is now. We played slip, along with a few others, until the wee hours of the morning. No one knew who I was. I wore a hat and told them all I was the butcher's cousin. It was one of the last times I was able to enjoy an evening like that. Soon after, I was too well known. I had so much fun. But he lost terribly. To me."

"He always loses."

"And that's where his indenture came from."

"Yes. My mother claimed he offered up a year of his life in service when he ran out of funds, but he told me that when he admitted he didn't have the funds to pay what he'd lost, and it was revealed who you really were, the indenture was created automatically. I suspect my mother's version is the right one, but it doesn't matter now." She sighed. "I will say you were very kind to give him as many years as you did to pay it off."

"I'm sorry it happened at all. If I remember correctly, I tried to forgive it, but your father refused. Said he'd have the funds shortly and it was nothing to worry about."

"He says that about every debt he incurs. It will never be true, but he's too proud to admit that, and so his debt increases steadily."

They started walking again, following the path in silence for a few moments.

Robin was lost for a moment in happier times. "Your mother made the best spice cake I've ever eaten. Her oatmeal cookies were equally as good. I was so sorry to hear of her passing."

"Thank you."

"She made my coronation cake, you know."

"I didn't know that."

He nodded. "She wasn't the only one, but she was in charge of it."

"Thank you for telling me that. My father says you sent beautiful flowers when she passed. I'm sure it was your secretary or one of your ministers."

He stopped walking again, causing her to stop as well. "It had to have been my secretary. I was barely nineteen. I'd been king for all of six months. It was still a novelty to me. Still something I had to pinch myself every morning to believe. I was finding my way. Honestly, I had no clue then what I was doing."

"You knew enough to arrange a marriage for yourself with Queen Vesta."

He shook his head. "I had nothing to do with that. Believe me. I would have chosen very differently than that spoiled fairy princess. A fairy. What was I thinking? But the ministers and diplomats and ambassadors all promised me a marriage with the fairy king's daughter would unite Limbo with its sister kingdom of Livion once again and make us a force to be reckoned with."

"So you did it."

He stared into her pretty green-gold eyes. "We do things sometimes because we believe they're what's right and best. And turning it down would have meant the possibility of more war. I was ready for an end to the fighting, not looking to start it afresh."

She made a skeptical face.

"You don't believe me."

"Goblins aren't a people who shy from battle."

"Yes, I know. We have a reputation for being fierce and bloodthirsty. And for loving gems beyond all reason." He grunted softly. "I am much more the latter than the former."

"And yet, you won the throne."

More accidental than purposeful, but he wasn't about to confess that. He started walking again. "I had no idea Vesta would be my downfall. Although, again, I should have known better than to wed a fairy. Such duplicitous creatures."

Theodora snorted.

He looked at her. "You find that funny?"

"You and your plans to enslave us all were your own downfall. Queen Vesta saved us."

His feet froze in place. "What are you talking about? Vesta dethroned me. Destroyed my name.

More than that, she poisoned me and exiled me here." Not that Shadowvale was such a bad town or his house such a terrible location. He was just so alone. And so trapped.

Theodora's eyes narrowed. "I don't know how she did what she did, but without her, we'd all be orc slaves right now."

He set the basket and the hard hat down to put his hands on his hips. "Is that what you think? Is that what everyone thinks? I know Vesta told lies about me, but…" His fury made him unable to continue.

She scowled at him. "It's not what the Queen says. It's our history. It's why you were exiled. Everyone knows you betrayed your kingdom and your kind."

He could do nothing but stare at her. "None of that is remotely true."

She frowned. "I don't want to argue with you. I need to fulfill my father's indenture. Whatever you need to believe is fine with me."

The woman was utterly mental. He leaned in. "Your precious Queen Vesta poisoned me so she could have the throne. This place? This town? That big home you've come to work in? It's my jail. And if you think the citizens of Limbo aren't already slaves, you're dead wrong, because I'm sure Vesta's got you all doing exactly what she wants."

Theodora stared at him with such willfulness he nearly laughed. "Again, I don't believe you."

She might be beautiful, but she was as lost as they all were.

He took a deep breath, then exhaled, his shoulders slumping as the air left him. "No one does. And no one did. That was the problem. She had too many on her side. Too much already in place."

He picked up the basket and the hat. Why should this new woman be any different? The only one who knew the truth was Elswood, but then, he was the only one who'd been there with him. At his side.

He started walking again. After a brief moment, Theodora fell into step alongside him.

Baton, Applestock, and Lolly had all been hired after he'd arrived here. By him. Granted, Baton was a cold fish, but she'd come highly recommended through a contact of Elswood's.

Robin had employed Mrs. Applestock and then Lolly through recommendations from Amelia Marchand, the witch who'd founded this town and the closest thing Shadowvale had had to royalty until he'd moved in. He considered her a friend, although she wasn't someone he wanted to bother with his problems.

Amelia, for all her power, had her own issues to deal with. Perhaps that was why he felt a kinship with her. Although since her niece, Emeranth, had moved to Shadowvale, Amelia was notably happier and had definitely become more social.

He wanted some of that happiness for himself. But he knew that was unlikely to happen. He had no family. No true, deep friends. And an ex-wife who would undoubtedly do him in should word get back to her that he'd lifted a finger toward freedom.

Some days, he was half convinced the wretched lightning bugs were her spies. But then, Vesta didn't need spies with the constructs she'd put into place. Blasted fairies and their curses. Witches had nothing on fairy magic.

He glanced over at Theodora. He knew nothing about her. She could very well be working for Vesta. A plant sent to watch him and report back on how he was handling things. That would be a shame if true. Despite Theodora's wrongheaded beliefs about him, he was already starting to like her. At least she engaged him in conversation.

But would those conversations go straight back to Vesta? He'd have to test Theodora somehow. Slip her some misinformation and see if it traveled beyond her. But how? It would have to be something really big for Vesta to respond.

That response could be deadly. If he was going to test Theodora, he had to be very sure he wasn't opening up a crock of eels.

Until he managed to suss out Theodora better, he'd have to keep the lovely woman with the bewitching eyes at arm's length and watch his words.

Vesta didn't need any more reasons, real or imagined, to torment him.

Theodora suddenly sucked in a breath. He realized he'd been watching her so long he'd lost sight of where they were. He looked forward to see what had made her gasp.

The mine entrance was just ahead. He supposed it

was rather something if you were seeing it for the first time.

"That's the mine?" she asked.

He nodded. "One of them. The biggest one."

"It's so pretty."

He gave it a fresh appraisal. The entrance had been cut into the mountainside and then fortified with steel beams, a steel support structure, and wide gates that opened in the middle. All very necessary and very serviceable. But there was nothing utilitarian about the arabesque curves, green and purple metal, and the multipaned glass inserts in and above the gates that let light through.

Amelia had told him she'd designed it after a long-lost art deco Metro stop in Paris, one of her favorite cities. She'd said there was no reason something couldn't be functional and beautiful. He didn't disagree. Although he'd never been to Paris or seen pictures of the Metro stop, so he couldn't say how true the homage was.

"Looks like the lair of an enormous dragonfly, doesn't it?" Theodora asked.

"It does." Seemed befitting that a place that produced such a spectacular array of amazing gems would have an entrance that was something more than just a hole in the mountain. He nodded. "That's what they call this mine. Dragonfly."

"Really?"

"Yes." He smiled. "Amelia, the woman who designed it, likes beautiful things. She built this whole town."

"Is she a goblin, too? Wait, she also built the town? For her vampire lover, right? Then she's a witch."

He was impressed Theo knew that much. "That's right, she's a witch." A witch who as probably as powerful as Vesta. Maybe more so.

Then again...he wasn't really sure.

CHAPTER SIX

Theo just stood there, marveling at how gorgeous the entrance was. And all for a *mine*. Amazing. The gates were swung open, and she could see inside. The light that came through the glass panels only reached a few yards into the mine. After that, it dimmed, of course, but strings of clear bulbs glowed brightly, helping to pick out the path that led deeper into the mountain.

"Have you ever been in a mine?"

She shook her head, glancing at His Royal Highness. "But I did a little training towards becoming a lapidary."

His brows lifted. "You're a lapidary? How wonderful."

"No. I only began the training. I never finished it."

"Not your thing?"

"I loved it. But when my mother died, the tuition money for the Royal Stonecutters Academy went with her. Even at the primary level, the cost was more than we could afford." After that, Theo had gotten the rest of her education at the regular school. Just the basics.

His face fell. Almost like he actually cared. "I'm sorry to hear that. What did you do instead?"

She'd taught herself as best she could, but outside of the Royal Stonecutters Academy, that was considered an inferior way to learn. "I went back to the common classes, got my papers, then did whatever I could. Mostly baking, like my mother, in a shop in town. Did a little cleaning at night to make what extra I could, to try to keep the collectors from our door. That's what I do now. I work at a bakery in the morning, then go to a cleaning job."

He didn't say anything for a moment. "Losing your mother changed everything, didn't it?"

A moment of anger welled up in her, but Caralynne's death had been no one's fault. Her illness could have happened to anyone. Theo exhaled the bad feelings as best she could. "It did."

She was ready for a new subject. She looked at the basket he carried and thought about the fresh biscuits and jam inside. Her stomach grumbled softly, but she swallowed down her hunger. "Those biscuits won't stay warm much longer, even with those towels covering them."

He smiled, which made him terribly handsome. "Mrs. Applestock puts a warming pad in the bottom. They'll be plenty hot. But you're right, we should get in there."

She didn't blame him for not offering her one. It wasn't his job to feed the servants. No doubt he assumed that had already been taken care of. If he thought of it at all.

He tipped his head toward the entrance as he put his hard hat on. "Let's go, then."

She followed alongside, astonished to find that, other than feeling like she was starving, she was actually enjoying her time with him. If this was a sample of her coming year, it wasn't going to be bad at all. She liked being outside, liked seeing new things, and, much to her personal disappointment, liked spending time with the exiled king.

For a traitor, he didn't seem like such a bad guy. It was no surprise he claimed Queen Vesta was the villain. She'd made it plain on numerous occasions that she expected and anticipated a smear campaign from King Robin. She'd said he would paint her as the evil fairy queen out to destroy him.

She'd been right, too, although it hadn't happened on the large scale she'd predicted. Just in person. Which wasn't much of a smear campaign, as those things went.

But Theo could wonder about all that later. Right now, they were walking through the mine's entrance, and there were a lot more interesting things to concentrate on.

A short, squat man who looked like he could lift a mountain came toward them. He was covered in blue-gray dust and decked out in the same kind of outfit Robin had on. A jumpsuit, boots, and a hard hat.

He grinned broadly, his teeth gleaming white

against the grime darkening his face. "Your Lordship."

"Grent. Good to see you, old man." The exiled king stuck his hand out like a commoner. But then, that's all he was now.

The man, a holler troll judging by his low brow and square jaw, shook Robin's hand like they were old friends. Or at least well-acquainted ones. Grent looked at the basket. "I smell biscuits and blackberry jam. The workers will be happy about that. Give Mrs. Applestock our thanks."

"I will."

"Spriggs." Grent called another worker over, also a troll. "His Lordship has brought us biscuits."

Spriggs grinned. "Thank you, Sire." He took the basket with a nod and a bow to King Robin.

As he left, the exiled monarch gestured toward Theodora. "Grent, this is Theodora Middlebright. She's come to work at Gallow House for a year."

Grent stuck his hand out. "Pleasure to meet you, Miss Middlebright. I'm Grent Hawthorne. I'm the second-shift manager here at Dragonfly."

How odd that he'd want to shake the hand of a servant. She did it anyway. "Nice to meet you, Mr. Hawthorne."

He laughed. "Call me Grent." He had arms like pillars and hands that could have cracked bones. "Well, shall we start the day's inspection?"

His Lordship nodded. "Lead on."

Was she supposed to follow? She wasn't sure. She wanted to go. Seeing a working mine would be amazing. But she'd been brought only to carry biscuits. And she'd barely done that. She stood there, torn with indecision, as the two men began walking away.

King Robin glanced back and stopped when he saw she wasn't moving. He motioned for her, giving her a quick smile and a wink.

A wink. She nearly fell over. His behavior was patently unkinglike. But she went after them, catching up in a few steps.

They stopped at an entrance checkpoint where Grent signed off on a clipboard, then handed Theo a hard hat. "Regulations."

"I understand." She took it and stared at the inside, not sure which was the front and which was the back.

King Robin took the hat from her, turned it around, and set it gently on her head. It went down over her eyes. He took it off again, adjusted something, then replaced it. This time, it sat right. "There you go."

"Thank you, Your Lordship."

"You're welcome, Theodora." He gazed into her eyes for what seemed longer than necessary.

Her throat felt hot and tight, and her stomach did a weird flip. Probably from lack of food.

He turned to Grent. "Good to go now."

Grent started walking again. They followed the path of lights until the cavernous passage split into four smaller tunnels. Men and women passed them, all dressed in jumpsuits and hard hats, some carrying pickaxes, some pushing carts of stones. Many looked like trolls, but there were other species mixed in. Dwarves in abundance, but maybe even a few humans.

It was louder here with the whine of machinery and the sounds of digging. That was fine with her. It covered the rumbling of her stomach. Whatever. She'd been hungry before. She'd live.

The air smelled of stone and oil and sweat. It wasn't altogether unpleasant. It was one of the many smells of work, something Theo was intimately acquainted with.

Grent headed into the first tunnel on the right. He spoke over his shoulder to Robin. "The hunt for that vein of opal we were getting close to last week has paid off. We've struck a nice seam. Should give us a substantial bit of ore in another day or two."

They didn't go far. After just a few more yards, he stopped them near a cluster of workers chipping away at the rock wall. A visible vein of milky, iridescent opal shone blue and green in the lights. It couldn't have been more than a half-inch wide, but the color was almost neon against the tan rock it was embedded in.

"Wow." Theo reached out to touch it, then caught herself.

Grent smiled. "Go ahead. It's really something, isn't it?"

She slid her fingers along the narrow strip of gem. It was smooth and cool to the touch. "It's beautiful. I've never seen anything like this."

His smile was proud and steady. "Wait until we open this up a little more. I predict it'll widen up considerably another two or three feet in." He went over to one of the worker's carts, dug around a bit, then pulled out a chunk of rock.

He brought it back and turned it so the opal fragment was visible. "Look at the color in this. Some of the best we've come across to date." He handed the rock to Robin.

"Excellent." Robin held it up and nodded his approval. "I can't wait to see what next week brings."

Theodora felt the old itch to work with the stone and turn it into something amazing, but her chance to become a lapidary had come and gone.

They went through all four tunnels the same way, inspecting the new finds and talking about what might be on the horizon. Robin took samples along the way, collecting them in a little bag at his waist. Theo saw more gems than she'd thought possible. Besides the opals, there were emeralds, amethysts, tourmaline, topaz, and in the last tunnel, sapphires of all colors.

But they never ventured into each tunnel more than fifteen feet, maybe less. Twice, Grent went quite a way deeper, gathered samples, then came back to them. It seemed odd that Robin, who was there to inspect the work, didn't actually do that in two of the tunnels.

She kept her mouth shut about it, though. What did it matter to her how he did, or didn't do, his job?

When they were through, they said goodbye to Grent, who made sure Mrs. Applestock's now-empty basket was returned, Theo handed over her hard hat, and they headed back to the house by the same path.

Theo carried the basket with His Lordship's hard hat in it. Something gave her the boldness to ask the question burning in her mind. "How is that possible? All of those gems in one mine? That shouldn't be."

"No," Robin answered. "It shouldn't be. But this is Shadowvale, and magic rules. The mines were all created with magic, which means the natural laws don't exist. It's a good thing, too. Those gems, the sale of them anyway, are what keep this town going. The money pays for all the things we enjoy here. Those mines fund everything the town needs. From the fire department to the schools to keeping the roads nice. Of course, magic helps with some of that, too."

She just stared at him, trying to process that. "So if the natural laws don't exist, then anything is possible? You mean with the mines, right?"

"I mean...anything is possible with anything in this town."

Her mind ran with that in a hundred different directions at speeds she couldn't keep up with. But she wasn't done with her questions about the mine.

He laughed. "Go on, ask. I can see you're practically bursting with something."

She took a breath. "How did you get the job of mine foreman?"

His brows rose as if that wasn't the question he'd been expecting. "Amelia gave it to me."

"Does she know you don't really inspect the work going on?"

His smile went stiff, then faded. "She knows what I do."

Theo shrugged. It wasn't her place to comment on what he did. She knew that. But he was a traitor to her people, and that made her bold. Even so, her words slipped out before she really thought them over. "Must be nice to have a job like that."

Robin stopped abruptly. "What exactly are you implying?"

Her heart began to race. This was exactly why her mother had told her to speak less and listen more. She'd been foolish. She'd been lulled into thinking his kindness meant they were friends. They were not. Nor did she want to be friends with this traitor king. She shook her head and kept her eyes down, unwilling to look at him. "Forgive me. I apologize, Your Lordship. I spoke without thinking. I shall endeavor to remember my station."

She could only see him from the knees down. He wasn't moving.

"No, you won't." His voice was gruff. Then he sighed and shifted slightly. "I don't want you to. You're not a servant. This is not your station. You're a woman who gave up a year of her life to take her father's place."

She still couldn't bring herself to look at him, but she didn't know what to say either.

He sighed. "I can't go down those tunnels."

That got her head up. She didn't understand what he meant, though. "Why not, Sire?"

He made an odd face. Almost like her use of his title made him uncomfortable. "Because I am physically unable. Just like I am unable to stray from this path." He peered at her, as if he was watching her eyes for her reaction.

"I still don't understand."

"Don't you?"

"No." She shook her head, genuinely clueless.

He crossed his arms as though he was attempting to keep from lashing out. "Queen Vesta didn't just take my throne, she took my freedom. My life here is cursed. I can't stray too far from the house or from any of the routes she's determined I am able to travel. When I say this place is my prison, I mean exactly that."

CHAPTER SEVEN

Just like that, Robin had shared the secrets he'd held close all these years. Part of his decision to spill them was he'd grown weary of keeping them, but the thought had also occurred to him that his revelation might be the perfect way to test Theodora. If she told Vesta that he'd figured out her scheme to confine him, Vesta would be sure to react.

Of course, she had to know he knew. He'd lived here long enough to have tested the boundaries. But he'd never said a word about it to anyone except Amelia and another man who'd tried to help him, Deacon, and he'd sworn them to secrecy.

How would Vesta take the news that he wasn't keeping silent any longer? For as much as she liked power, she also craved adoration. Being exposed for the terrible person she was wouldn't win her any popularity contests.

She might erase the restrictions to make him seem like a liar. Or tighten the reins in retaliation.

The latter worried him. If his world grew any smaller, he would go mad.

Theodora peered at him. "You can't leave the path?"

"Not far." As much as he hated to make a fool of himself, a demonstration seemed in order. "Watch."

He stepped off the worn path, bracing himself, hands out. He found what he was looking for in two steps. The wall was as invisible to him as it was to anyone, but only he could feel it. He put his hands flat against the invisible divider that kept him from the rest of Shadowvale. "There. You can't see it, but I promise, the barrier is real, and I can't get past it."

She looked skeptical. He didn't blame her. She put the basket down and stepped off the path to stand beside him. She stuck her arms out, waving them around and reaching past his hands. "I don't feel anything."

"You won't. You're not the one Vesta cursed."

She still didn't look convinced. "Any mime can pretend there's a wall when there isn't one."

"You want more?" He took his hands down, put his shoulder against the barrier, and leaned in against it to the point that it would have been physically impossible to stay upright without help. Then he smirked at her from his slanted position. "Could a mime do this?"

She stepped back, eyes widening ever so slightly. "There really is a wall."

He pushed off the barrier to straighten himself. "I have no reason to lie about this."

"And this exists everywhere you go?"

"Everywhere. In some places, it's as narrow as the

breadth of my outstretched arms. In my house, I can go anywhere I want. Thankfully."

"How did you figure it out?"

"Trial and error. Years' worth." Why not tell her the whole truth? In for a penny and all that. Or maybe he was just happy to share his burden with someone after so long. "Upon imprisoning me here, Vesta told me I wouldn't be able to leave the house. I argued with her until she allowed me a little more freedom than that. Little did I know how confined I was still going to be."

"How awful. Have you sought help from anyone?"

He wasn't sure if she genuinely cared or was just trying to make him feel better, but speaking the truth was so freeing he didn't care. "When Amelia came to welcome me, I confided in her, but she's powerless to do anything against a fairy curse. Same with another man who tried to help me here in town. Not long after Amelia's visit, she offered me the job as foreman."

"Her way of helping?"

"I think so." He thought back to that day. "When I told Vesta about the job, she laughed. She thought my working like a common man was some kind of downfall, so she loosened the restraints enough to make it possible. But I was happy to do it. Happy to have something else to fill my days with."

"I can imagine." Theodora tilted her head as if she was doing just that.

He hoped it wasn't lost on her that Vesta's opinion of the common man was less than favorable.

He went back to the path and picked up the basket. "We should go back."

She just nodded and joined him on the path. "All right."

Then she put her hands out, eyes squeezed shut. "Forgive me."

"Why? For what?" He peered closer. She was very pale. "Theodora? Are you—you don't look so—"

She tilted toward the ground.

She awoke with no sense of the time that had passed and realized very quickly she hadn't hit the ground because *he* had caught her.

She was in his lap. In his arms. Resting against the trunk of a tree where he must have carried her and sat. It was only two steps off the path. The basket was next to them.

He was gazing down at her with concern. "There you are. How are you feeling? You passed out."

"Oh no, this won't do." She tried to get up.

"I don't think you're in any position to move just yet. Now, again, how are you feeling?"

She shook her head. He was so near. Too near. His scent filled her nose, and she was all too aware of his body beneath hers. "I'm fine." She was reluctant to tell him the reason for her fainting spell.

"That's clearly not true. Why did you faint? It's not that warm. People who are fine don't faint for no reason."

She shrugged and refused to make eye contact. If she told him his staff had failed to offer her something to eat, she might get them in trouble. And they, in turn, might take that out on her. "There's nothing wrong with me. Just tired, I'm sure. We should go."

He inhaled like realization had struck him.

She looked at him and saw what might have been horror in his eyes. "Why are you looking at me like that?"

"Are you pregnant? Is that why you took your father's indenture? Are you using this year away to hide the truth from him? Or from the father? Who did this to you?"

"No! You have definitely been left alone with your thoughts for far too long. Not that it would be any of your business if I was." She laughed suddenly at the ridiculousness of it all. Then something occurred to her. "Why did you look so terrified when you thought I might be pregnant?"

He blinked rapidly, like he was trying to sort out his words. "Because you'd have the child while you were here. Which would mean a baby. In the house. I don't know anything about babies."

Her laughter became uncontrollable to the point she could barely speak. "And you think...you'd have to raise it?"

"Well, I... That is..." He frowned. "It's not *that* funny."

Except that it was. She finally caught her breath. "I'm not pregnant, I swear. Just hungry."

His frown deepened. "Didn't you eat?"

"Not since I finished the last of my food on the bus here, no." She had to get off his lap. She shouldn't be on it to begin with, and now she was lingering. She rocked forward onto her knees.

"No one offered you anything at the house?"

"I'm sure they all just assumed I'd eaten." She still felt weak, but she'd had enough rest. And staying here wasn't doing her any good.

"Unacceptable. Someone should have asked you." He immediately stood and held his hand out to her. "Can you make it back? Would you like me to carry you?"

"Yes. And *no*." Reluctantly, she took his hand and let him help her up.

"Good. We'll go at your pace. As soon as we arrive, we'll get you fed. And you're joining me for dinner tonight."

A wave of panic swept through her. "What? I'm sorry, Your Lordship, but I don't think dinner is such a good idea."

"Why not? You're the daughter of a woman I liked very much. Practically a guest."

"Forgive me, but I am not your guest. I am your servant. Indentured or not, that is my position in your household. Treating me any differently will at the very least cause resentment in the rest of your staff. I don't want that. I just want to serve my year without incident and be done."

He let go of her hand. "I see. Of course. How foolish of me to think differently."

Had she hurt his feelings by turning down his offer? Or worse, offended him? Royal egos were so fragile. Or was he that starved for company? Regardless, she felt for him, but she couldn't change the reality of her situation. She leaned against the tree they'd been sitting under. "I'm sorry. It's not that I don't appreciate your kind offer. I do. Perhaps under different circumstances…"

His expression remained unchanged, and he said nothing.

She had to do something to salvage the moment. "Queen Vesta actually poisoned you?"

"Yes. She also laced my soup with sleeping powder. When I woke up, I was here in Shadowvale in the home I'd built for us. I felt like I was about to die. I've never been so sick in my life. That's when she told me that if I wanted the antidote for the poison, I'd have to agree never to return to Limbo."

"So you agreed."

He nodded. "What other choice did I have if I wanted to live to fight another day?"

"None," Theo answered softly. Had she misjudged him? Had Queen Vesta lied about him? About what he'd done? "Why would Queen Vesta do that if you weren't guilty of betraying the kingdom?"

"Because she wanted the throne for herself. It's that simple. She doesn't want an equal union between the sister kingdoms. She believes, like many of the fae, that Limbo should once again belong to Livion and be ruled by the fae. Which it is now."

"Then you didn't plan on turning all of us into orc slaves?"

His gaze narrowed. "I captured the orc king. That's how I won the throne. The last thing I would have done was arrange anything with the people who most wanted to remove my head from my shoulders." He leaned in, obviously angry. "So *no*. I did not plan on turning all my countrymen into orc slaves."

He sounded convincing, but she still didn't know if she believed him. After all, she'd grown up *knowing* he was a traitor. Changing that belief in a split second wasn't the easiest thing to do.

He held his hands up. "I know. You don't believe me. I get it. But if you're going to live in my house for a year, you'd better at least give me the benefit of the doubt."

She thought about that for a moment, then nodded. "You're right. I can at least do that much for you."

"Thank you." He picked up the basket, then offered her his arm. "Let's get you home."

Gallow House wasn't her *home* and never would be, but she kept that to herself as she accepted his offer of help. She didn't want help. Especially from him, but she still felt a little unstable. And turning him down might only anger him further. Better to let him help her and soothe the tension between them. Fortunately, it wasn't long before they walked back into his house. He took her directly to the kitchen, where he made her sit at the island.

Mrs. Applestock greeted them with her cheery smile, taking the basket and giving him back his hard hat. "Biscuits gone, are they?"

"Gone and greatly enjoyed," Robin answered. He put the hat on a hook near the door. "But we have a problem."

"Oh dear." She knotted her hands in her apron. "Was there not enough jam?"

"Plenty of jam," he said. "The problem is Theodora hasn't eaten in days. She fainted on the way back."

Theo shook her head. "It hasn't been—"

"Oh my stars. You poor child. I'll take care of that immediately." Mrs. Applestock rushed to the wide, double-door refrigerator and started pulling things out, piling food in her arms and on the island behind her.

Robin took the seat next to Theodora. "I wouldn't mind a sandwich myself." He looked at Theo. "What do you think? Ham and cheese?"

Mrs. Applestock waved a long, crusty baguette in the air without missing a beat. "I have just the thing for that!"

Theo nodded, amused by all the fuss on her behalf. "I'm not picky. Ham and cheese would be perfect." Her stomach growled in agreement.

"Excellent," Mrs. Applestock said. "I'll make you both a picnic for lunch."

In what felt like mere minutes, Mrs. Applestock spread an array of food in front of them. Ham-and-cheese sandwiches made with the loaf she'd shown them. Red and green grapes. Deviled eggs. Three kinds of pickles—sour, sweet, and hot. Cucumber salad. Potato salad. Macaroni salad. Smoked salmon and cream cheese pinwheels with little sprigs of dill. Pita chips with fish dip. And lastly, a chopped salad of cold shrimp and vegetables with vinaigrette.

And then came the desserts. A platter of chocolate chip walnut cookies. Little cheesecakes each topped with a cherry. Half-sized iced lemon scones. Chocolate pots. White chocolate raspberry truffles. Rhubarb pie with a visibly flaky crust. All accompanied by a bowl of freshly whipped cream.

Theo had never seen so much food in one place. She was frozen by indecision and, despite her incredible hunger, just stared at it all, trying to decide what to eat first.

Robin didn't have that problem. And when he saw that she had yet to put anything on her plate, he started helping her. "Here. Have a sandwich. That's the main thing, right?"

She looked down at the serving he'd put on her plate of crusty baguette with ham and cheese and nodded. She didn't need to be told twice. She picked it up and tucked in.

She ate the sandwich and kept eating. Everything was so delicious. And there for the taking.

Robin did the same, but she was aware of him watching her, too. Was she eating too much? That couldn't be it. Every time she slowed down, he pushed her to try something new. Was he just curious about how much she could eat? He was hard to read.

Mrs. Applestock beamed. "Would you like something else? I could make some tuna salad. Or there might be some cold chicken left. Or some salmon mousse, maybe? Oh! Cheese and crackers?"

Theo's mouth was full, so she just shook her head until she could swallow. "This is more than enough. I am overwhelmed with food. And it's all so good. Thank you." She glanced at Robin. "And thank you, Your Lordship."

"Where is that girl?" Mrs. Baton's voice rang out from the hall. "She should have been back by now. If she thinks she can—" Mrs. Baton walked in. As soon as she saw Robin, she smiled. Tight-lipped. But a smile all the same.

She glanced at Theo. "There you are, Theodora." Her gaze flicked to the spread of food on the island, then to His Lordship, then back to Theo. Her smile left her face. "Miss Middlebright. Staff does not eat with His Lordship."

Theo's mouth was too full for her to respond, and Mrs. Baton kept on going so that Robin couldn't even answer.

"I am so sorry, Your Highness." Mrs. Baton bowed her head. "I promise this impropriety will *not* happen again."

Robin seemed amused. "The only impropriety was that no one bothered to offer Miss Middlebright anything to eat upon her arrival at Gallow House. And as it happened, she hadn't eaten in quite some time. Because of that, she fainted on our return from the mine."

Mrs. Baton stiffened.

All traces of his amusement disappeared, and his countenance became stern. "I find that lack of care and hospitality alarming. Don't you, Mrs. Baton?"

She paled. Then nodded rapidly. "Yes, Your Lordship. It won't happen again."

"I don't suppose it will, seeing as how I don't foresee any new staff coming to work here. Unless you're leaving us, Mrs. Baton, and we need to replace you?"

Remarkably, she paled even further. "No, Your Lordship."

His smile returned in a flash. "Excellent news, Mrs. Baton. I would hate to lose someone as competent as you. Ham-and-cheese baguette? We have plenty."

"No, Sire, thank you." She bowed again, then caught Theo's eyes. "When you're done, Miss Middlebright, if you could come to my office?"

Theo nodded. "I will."

Mrs. Baton left. Quickly.

As entertaining as that had been, Theo had to wonder how much trouble Robin had just gotten her into. Whatever it was, she would manage. And be grateful that he cared enough to see that she'd been fed. She'd had enough food to last until tomorrow, if need be.

His kindness had her second-guessing everything she'd thought about him. With each passing minute, he was even less like she'd imagined. But more time in this house, and more time with him if possible, would help her decide.

Until then, she'd do what her mother had told her. *Listen to learn.*

Fortunately, listening was easy. Especially when those you were listening to didn't know you were there.

CHAPTER EIGHT

Robin reclined on the wide, two-person chaise on the balcony outside his bedroom and watched twilight overtake the sky. It was especially beautiful in Shadowvale, because dusk meant the clouds slipped away to let the stars and moon shine through.

Seeing that happen never got old. And sometimes, that glorious reveal of the night sky was the only thing that got him through the long days.

He smiled suddenly, because that didn't feel exactly true anymore. Not with the curious Miss Middlebright in the house. He already wondered what tomorrow would bring with her. Funny that he was actually looking forward to tomorrow. When was the last time that had happened?

Not in many, many days. Years, even.

He'd signed the indenture document as soon as he'd returned to his quarters. The red clock, ticking away on the paper, had vanished. He wondered how the rest of her day had been after he'd left her.

No doubt Mrs. Baton had put her to work dusting rooms that really ought to be shut up altogether from lack of use. Or maybe polishing the ballroom floor that had never actually been danced on. Perhaps ironing tablecloths meant for a dining table that would never see a meal?

He leaned his head in his hand as he dug his elbow into the cushion a little more. He'd been foolish and impetuous to ask Theodora to dine with him. And while he knew what a stir such an evening would cause among the other staff, he still wished it was possible.

Oh, Mrs. Applestock and Lolly wouldn't care. Neither would Henry. Fenwick, the gardener, wouldn't give it a second of thought. But Mrs. Baton and Elswood would definitely think it improper. And they wouldn't be quiet about it either.

In different circumstances, he wouldn't care. But if anyone on his staff was reporting back to Vesta, something that was an absolute possibility, he couldn't risk making Theodora or her father a target of the queen's anger.

Maybe not a big thing if Theodora was already on the queen's payroll. But if she wasn't...that could be very, *very* bad.

Such a shame, because he longed for company. And he *liked* talking to Theodora. Even more so now that she'd agreed to give him the benefit of the doubt about his past. He ground his teeth together in frustration. What other terrible things had Vesta made people believe about him?

She was the one who ought to be imprisoned. That wretched fairy hag. Why couldn't she fall into the moat of Fangmore Castle, where she would be devoured by the eels that lived in it?

Things like that never happened to the right people.

"Good evening, Sire." Elswood walked out from the bedroom, carrying a tray. Somewhere in the forest, a raven cawed. "Your evening repast."

"Thank you. Just set it on the table." He wasn't all that hungry, even for his usual before-bed snack of a hot toddy and cookies. He glanced at the tray as Elswood put it on the small side table. Mrs. Applestock had included more than the standard amount of cookies. And they were iced oatmeal, his favorite. Maybe he'd have one.

A little movement caught his eye, and he realized he was being watched. He smiled at his unexpected visitor. "Hello there, little cat."

The sleek black cat, glossy even in the dim light, sat on the balcony railing. Robin's quarters were on the second story, so the creature had put in some effort to get here.

Where the cat had come from, he had no idea. He knew Shadowvale had a few strays, but this one looked well cared for. Although perhaps a bit thin. But then, what did he know about cats? Not much except that they were good climbers.

He changed positions slightly to see the creature better. No wings, so not a meowl. Just a regular housecat. Except this one was watching him rather closely. Did cats do that? He wasn't sure. He'd never had a pet of any kind.

Elswood hmphed at the sight of the animal. "That won't do." He waved at the cat. "Get lost, you scrawny pest."

The cat hissed at Elswood, who then raised his hand further.

"No," Robin snapped. "Leave it be. It's not a pest. I think it's just hungry."

Elswood lowered his hand. "As you wish, Sire. But those creatures can carry disease."

Robin shot him a look. "The same can be said for any being. And this one isn't hurting anything." He thought for a second longer as he studied the creature's slender frame. "Fetch a dish of salmon from Mrs. Applestock."

Elswood's pinched expression said he clearly didn't care for that request, but he nodded anyway. "Yes, Sire."

As he left, Robin moved to the end of the chaise. Slowly, so as not to startle the cat. "Hi there, puss. Are you hungry? Do you like fish? I do. But then, goblins tend to have an affinity for seafood."

The cat blinked once, then lifted a paw, licked it, and cleaned an ear.

"I'm a goblin, by the way." He snorted. "Used to be king of them, but I suppose that doesn't matter one bit to you."

The cat changed paws and moved on to the other ear.

"You're very handsome. Or pretty. Whatever the case may be." A pet might be nice. He'd never considered it, but he already felt less alone. "How did you get up here, hmm? You must be a very good climber."

The cat stopped cleaning and went back to staring at him. Then it meowed, a squeaky little sound that showed off nice white teeth and a little pink tongue. It jumped down, tail curving into the air, and took a few strides toward Robin before sitting down again.

Robin thought he might not need a pet, but this little animal might need him.

The cat looked around as if inspecting the place.

Robin held back a laugh. "This is my house," he explained. "You could live here if you want. I've never had a cat. Or any pet. But I can learn. I'm a fast study, too. I would take the best care of you, I promise."

He was bargaining with a cat. Had he lost his mind? Maybe. All things considered, he was okay with that. For a while, the cat just sat there, cleaning. Were all cats so fastidious? It was an admirable trait.

Elswood announced his return by clearing his throat. He was carrying a second tray.

Robin glanced up at him. "A whole tray for one dish?"

Elswood frowned. "Mrs. Applestock insisted on sending an array of options in case salmon wasn't the preferred choice."

Robin laughed. "Of course she did."

Elswood set the tray on the end of the chaise. "Besides the little dish of water, there's raw diced salmon, cold salad shrimp, and a can of tuna. Packed in water, not oil. Mrs. Applestock thought it important that I tell you that. Also, I am to tell you she has a tin of sardines at the ready if required, but will not be sending milk or cream. She said that's not good for cats. Upsets their stomachs, despite what you see on television."

"Is that so? Glad she knew that." He checked out the tray. Mrs. Applestock had used the good china and had added a sprig of parsley to each food dish. He almost laughed. She was a treasure, that one. He gave Elswood a nod. "That'll be all for the night, thank you."

"Very good, Sire." Elswood bowed and left.

Robin looked at the cat. Its little nose was sniffing the air, making its whiskers quiver. He smiled. "Something's got your attention. Want to see if you like any of these?"

He moved the tray to the floor, then pushed it toward the cat before sitting back to see what the creature would do.

As the cat approached the tray, Robin kept talking to it. "Do you have a name? I feel like I should call you something, but I don't know if you're a boy or a girl. And I'm not sure I could tell even if I looked."

The cat glanced up at him suddenly.

"Yes, I suppose that would be rude of me as well. All right, then, what shall I call you?"

The cat sniffed all three bowls and settled on the one in the middle. The salad shrimp.

"Shrimp, hmm? I would have guessed the tuna first. Further proof I know nothing about cats." He settled against the chaise and watched with great curiosity. The animal ate with more delicacy and grace than he'd expected. There was no gulping down of the food, but careful, dainty bites.

"How about Pepper?" Robin asked. "You were rather spicy with my valet. Which is fine. He deserved it. For the record, I would have never let him hurt you."

The cat looked up, licking its chops.

"Pepper is black, too."

The cat went back to the bowl, clearly less invested in the conversation than Robin.

He didn't mind. "And Pepper could be a girl name or a boy name."

The cat kept eating.

"All right, Pepper it is. I'm going to assume you're a boy. Unless you decide to tell me otherwise."

Pepper finished the shrimp, had a few bites of the salmon, then a few bites of the tuna, and finally jumped up onto the foot of the chaise, where he went to work washing his face. Again.

Robin realized he'd been smiling the whole time he'd been watching the cat. "You might be just what I needed, little one. You and our new Theodora. But I think if you decide to live here, we're going to have to get you a collar. That way, if you get lost, it's clear where you belong."

Finally clean enough, Pepper yawned, walked up the chaise until he was across from Robin, then flopped down next to him. Not touching. But beside him all the same.

"Do you live in the enchanted forest? I know

there are meowls there, but they're not exactly cats. Is that really a safe place for you to live? There are hellhounds in there. I just heard one last night."

Pepper let out a little sigh.

"I suppose you've done all right protecting yourself." Robin put his hands behind his head. "You look very soft. Can I pet you?"

Pepper's eyes were half shut. He seemed amenable. And maybe a little sleepy. A bird flew past the balcony, and he didn't budge.

Robin took the chance. Slowly, he moved one arm down and traced his fingers over the curve of Pepper's head. "You are soft."

Pepper's eyes closed all the way, and he started to rumble.

Robin inhaled in surprise. "You're purring, aren't you? That means you like this. Or you're happy right now. Either way, I know it's a good thing." He nodded. "I could totally have a cat."

Pepper put his head down, closed his eyes, and gave a big exhale as if the weight of the day had just been lifted off him.

Robin stroked the animal's back, pausing to feel the vibrations of joy filling his little body. The cat was thin, but not to the point of being worrisome. And Robin figured a few days of good eating would help that tremendously. If it didn't, maybe a vet visit would be in order.

He almost laughed. He was making plans for the animal, and he had no idea if the cat would even stick around. One day at a time.

Before long, Pepper seemed sound asleep, and for the first time in a long time, Robin felt the pull of sleep himself. He closed his eyes, one hand resting on Pepper's side, and drifted off.

When he awoke, he was still on the chaise, but Pepper was gone, and someone had covered him with a throw.

None of that surprised him so much as the fact that the sky was pink with dawn. He'd slept the entire night.

That shocked him so much that he sat bolt upright and blinked at the sky in disbelief. Clouds were already rolling in to mute the rising sun. "How is that possible?"

He looked around for any sign of the cat, but Pepper had definitely left. Robin's hot toddy and iced oatmeal cookies were still on the table beside the chaise, cold and untouched. But the dishes of tuna and salmon were now as empty as the dish of shrimp, proof that Pepper had been there.

A few black hairs remained on the chaise cushion, too.

Robin got up, expecting to be a little stiff from his unusual sleeping spot, but he felt fine. He stretched and walked to the balcony. No sign of Pepper in the garden below either.

Robin frowned. Dark Acres was an especially dangerous part of the enchanted forest. Certainly no place for a stray cat. He hoped the little creature was all right. And that he would come back.

Maybe he'd tell Mrs. Applestock to add proper

cat food to the grocery list. Some cans of that fancy stuff. They could put a dish of it outside in the garden. Just in case. And he'd say something to Henry about keeping an eye out. In fact, maybe Henry already knew about the cat.

Or Fenwick. If anyone had seen Pepper before, it was Fenwick. The man spent his days caring for the grounds.

With new urgency, Robin jumped into the shower and got ready for the day. There was no trip to the mine today, so he could look for Pepper all he wanted. Or at least, as much as the confines of his curse allowed.

He threw on track pants and a T-shirt. If he was going to be out hunting for Pepper in the woods, there was no point in wearing anything fancy, although this had generally become his daily uniform. What was the point of a suit when he was no longer king and not entertaining anyone?

He ran down to the kitchen.

Lolly was polishing silver, but she got up, gave him a little bow, then went to get him coffee, like she always did. He didn't really need it after the amazing sleep he'd had, but he'd drink it anyway. For one thing, it was delicious. For another, Lolly was going to the effort.

Mrs. Applestock came in with a sack of flour. "Good morning, Your Lordship. How was your night? Biscuits aren't quite ready yet."

"Outstanding. And no worries about the biscuits, I'm up earlier than usual. Thank you for the food you sent up last night, by the way. I don't know what Elswood told you, but a little black cat showed up on my balcony. He ate every bit of the food you prepared."

"How wonderful. Cats are such smart creatures. They don't like just anyone, you know. They're picky. They only like people worth their time." She smiled. "Is he still around?"

"No, Pepper was gone this morning, but I'm hoping he comes back."

"Pepper?" Her brows lifted.

He laughed. "I had to call him something. And he was a little spicy. Will you get some real cat food next time you're at the store?"

"I'm going today. I'll make sure I add it to the list. What kind?"

"I have no idea. Whatever looks good. Get a bunch. Canned, the good stuff. And some dry."

Lolly was grinning as she set a mug of coffee and a little pitcher of cream next to him.

He fixed his coffee with cream and added some sugar. "Have you seen a little black cat around here?"

She shook her head. "No, Sire. But I'll keep an eye out."

"Good. Thank you. It would be nice to have a cat around here, don't you think?"

Her grin got a little bigger. "It would be."

He drank a good bit of the coffee, then got up, ready to head out and speak with Henry and Fenwick. "All right, I have to go. I'll be back later to eat."

Mrs. Applestock shook her head. "You certainly seem chipper this morning."

"I slept well. Amazing what that can do for you."

She nodded. "Indeed. What would you like for breakfast?"

"Eggs and bacon. Biscuits, of course. Maybe some hash browns. Sugar beans. Buttered mushrooms, too. The whole thing."

She laughed. "I'll get to work."

"Oh, one more thing."

"Yes?"

"Do you know where I can find Theodora?"

CHAPTER NINE

The sky had still been dark when Theo had tugged on her Gallow House livery and reported to Mrs. Baton's office.

Why on earth such an early start was required, she had no idea. None of the tasks Mrs. Baton had sent her to do yesterday after lunch with Robin had really needed doing. Theo had polished some very pretty crystal stemware that looked as if it had never been used, then she'd organized the walk-in linen closet, which contained more linens than she'd seen in one place in her life.

The linens had already been pretty organized, but Mrs. Baton had insisted each piece be taken out, shaken out, inspected for tears or stains, then if in good repair, refolded and stacked neatly.

Theo was no fool. It was all grunt work designed to keep her busy.

The end of the day had had Theo questioning her ability to keep such nonsense up for a year, but she had a feeling this was Mrs. Baton's way of testing her.

And Theo wasn't going to fail. Not with all that was at stake.

At least this morning she'd been able to join the rest of the staff in the downstairs gathering room for breakfast. Biscuits, cod sausages, scrambled eggs, and thankfully, lots of coffee. Good coffee, too. Goblin spiced coffee.

She'd nabbed a small apple and tucked it away in her room. Not that there wouldn't be food later, but old habits died hard, and having something *just in case* always seemed wise.

Now, she was headed to the library with her basket of cleaning supplies and the specific instructions that each book was to be wiped down, checked for signs of damage, and carefully reshelved. It was the linen closet all over again.

Mrs. Baton must think that cleaning books was some kind of grueling task. Theo smiled. Being in a library, even if she was just cleaning it, would never be tedious or difficult or grueling.

Ever since her mother had died and Theo had been forced to leave the academy for regular school, books had become her refuge. Each book felt like a prize she'd won. She cherished them. She'd even carried one of her favorites on this trip with her, just in case there were none available.

The thought of being without a book to escape into just didn't set well, and she'd had no idea if King Robin was a reader. Even if he was, there was no telling if she'd be allowed to borrow any of his books.

So she'd done the only logical thing. She'd brought one.

Now, she was about to see just what kind of a reader he was. His library would either be filled with books that were just for show or filled with books that were much loved and well read. She was curious to see which.

She followed the directions Mrs. Baton had given her, going up to the second floor of the house, down a long hall and counting off the doors until she came to the fifth one. They were double doors, actually, which she didn't remember Mrs. Baton mentioning, so hopefully she'd found the right location.

She opened the one on the right.

And sucked in a breath. This was definitely the library. It might be the only library a person would ever need.

Slowly, she entered the space as if it were holy ground. She'd never seen a library this grand. Not even at the academy. The first floor was open in the middle to a second floor that was just as packed with bookshelves, and each shelf housed more books than she could count.

It would take her days to clean and inspect each tome in this amazing room. She sighed, and a broad grin spread across her face. Spending days in here was just fine with her. Especially if she could sneak in some reading.

She closed the door behind her and inhaled. Was there anything better than the perfume of books? Old paper, well loved. Leather bindings, worn from reading. All that ink, slightly metallic and earthy.

She walked in a few more steps. Small reading spots were set up throughout the space. A big chair with an ottoman. A long leather couch. A rolled-arm chaise. Each had a table nearby with a lamp that would provide the right amount of light, although the tall windows that looked out over the garden did a pretty adequate job of that already.

In the very center of the room was a glass case. She couldn't quite see what was inside, so she went over, feather duster in hand so she'd look like she was working.

As she approached the case, the contents became visible, and her heart clenched a little. A large, hand-drawn map of Limbo and Livion. Beside the map, King Robin's royal wax seal rested on a little purple velvet cushion. Above that, the official announcement of his coronation. The gold ink had tarnished a little, and the paper yellowed slightly, but the words were still very clear.

How bittersweet. Had he done this to honor what had been? As a beacon of what he hoped to regain? Or as a reminder that his treachery had cost him everything?

She frowned. She struggled with the last thought. There was nothing about the man that seemed treacherous. And yet, she knew what the history books said. What was taught. He was a terrible man. An enemy to his kingdom.

But if that's what he truly was, why make something like this? This display felt like a loving memorial to what had been lost. Not a remembrance of a kingdom and a throne he'd purposefully betrayed.

She shook her head, trying to clear the conflicting thoughts and emotions. It didn't matter. None of it did. One year, and she was done. One year, and all of this would be behind her.

But…if he was innocent, it *did* matter, didn't it? The answer to that was a resounding yes. Because his innocence would mean Queen Vesta was the traitor. But how was she, Theo, supposed to change anything? She was a peasant. A commoner. The daughter of a man who owed more than he owned.

She was powerless. She always had been. Her fingers wrapped a little tighter around the feather duster. There was no point in even thinking about such things. She took a step back from the display.

And ran into a hard wall of warm body.

She gasped and spun around, thinking she'd been caught by Elswood. "I'm sorry, I—"

His Lordship stood behind her. He was in black track pants and a T-shirt, looking very casual. Still very handsome, unfortunately. And he smelled even better than the library, which was quite a feat.

He smiled at her. "Good morning, Theodora."

She curtsied and kept her head down. He was so near. Inches away. It seemed improper to be that close to him, and yet there wasn't a fiber of her being that wanted to move. After all, she'd already been on his lap. "Your Lordship."

Had he already been in the library when she'd arrived? Or was he just that quiet that she hadn't heard him walk up behind her? "I was cleaning. I'm sorry to bother you. I should get back to—"

"You're not bothering me. I was looking for you, actually."

She lifted her head. "You were?"

He nodded. "First of all, I signed the indenture."

"Thank you."

"You're welcome. Secondly, I was wondering if you could help me search for a little black cat that came to visit me last night?"

She blinked at him. At his strong jaw and eyes that were so very blue. Like the water at the center of a deep lake. "A cat came to visit you last night?"

"Mm-hmm. On my balcony."

"There must be a lot of stray cats around here, don't you think?"

"I'm not sure. I've never seen any before. Certainly not him."

"Him?"

"I'm not sure about that either."

"I'd be happy to help you look. Mrs. Baton expects me to be cleaning in here, though. I should probably tell her where I'll be in case she comes to check on me."

"Don't worry about Hyacinth."

Theo snorted before she could stop herself. "Her first name is Hyacinth?"

"Yes." He grinned. "I know, right?"

She covered her hand with her mouth and made herself breathe before she burst out laughing. She regained her control, then dropped her hand and nodded. "Okay, then, let's go look for your new cat friend."

"Great." He glanced down at her outfit. "But first, you'd better change if we're going to be traipsing around in the woods."

When she was in jeans and a T-shirt with a shirt over top as a light jacket, they set out to look. Thankfully, she hadn't run into Hyacinth. She smiled to herself. She had to stop thinking of Mrs. Baton by that name, or she was going to lose it the next time she saw the housekeeper.

They left the house a different way than when they'd gone to the mines. This time, they went through a set of French doors that led onto an enormous back patio. Beyond that was the garden she'd seen from the library windows.

Most of it was an enormous pavilion covered in creeping, flowering vines. The pavilion spanned almost the entire width of the garden area and was at least two-thirds of the length. At the very center sat a beautiful tiled three-tier fountain. Its basin was large enough to have fish in it. The burbling made a lovely sound.

All around the pavilion were more plants, many of which Theo recognized from Limbo. One in particular really caught her eye, however.

"You have nightberries." She looked from plant to plant. They stretched down the entire side of the pavilion. "A whole thicket of them." A fortune of them. But was that really such a surprise? He had been king.

He came close to one of the plants, touching the leaf. "To be honest, I didn't know. I don't come out here often, and when I do, it's not to look at the plants."

"Didn't you build this house?"

"Yes, but Vesta was in charge of the gardens. This must have been her doing."

What else had Vesta influenced in this house? Theo had to wonder.

He picked one of the berries and tossed it into his mouth. "I love these things."

"So do I. Not that I've eaten them very often." Anyone who'd grown up in Limbo loved them. Nightberries were amazing. Like a very sweet blueberry with a hint of honey. They were typically too expensive for anyone but royalty and nobility to enjoy them, but Theo had tasted them once as a child, thanks to her mother's access to the fruit in the royal kitchens.

There was also a black market for nightberries. After her mother died, Theo had made a little extra money to help her and her father survive by using her talents to steal the berries from the royal gardens and sell them, but her father had gotten wind of her side business and made her stop, fearing she'd end up in the clutches of the Overwatch.

For a little while after that, he'd quit gambling to ease their debt. His health had even rallied a bit. But neither change had lasted long.

Robin held a berry out to her. She took it and popped it into her mouth. The taste was exactly as she remembered it, sweeter maybe, and she was instantly reminded of her mother. She swallowed, smiling at him, something that was shockingly easy to do when she was around him. "Thanks."

He picked a few more, bouncing them into his palm. "Where do you think we should look for this cat?"

She looked around. "Cats sleep a lot during the day. He probably found a spot to curl up. A hidden spot. One that's also safe."

"Like under this thicket?"

"Exactly like that." She glanced at him. "I'm not saying we're going to fail, but the chances of finding a cat that doesn't want to be found are pretty slim. Especially when finding him would involve crawling under bushes covered with thorns. Not to mention filled with spiders and other creepy-crawlies."

He laughed. "Good point. You sound like you know a lot about cats."

"Not a lot. Some."

"Did you have one as a pet?"

She shook her head. "Pets weren't really in our budget. Although..." She smiled at the memory that came to her. "I used to feed the eels in the moat with stale bread my mother gave me. For some reason, they liked pumpernickel best."

Robin's grin broadened. "Let me guess, you used to pretend you were the princess who lived in the castle?"

She snorted. "No. I used to pretend I was the queen."

CHAPTER TEN

Robin laughed. He adored Theodora's sense of self. "Of course you did. How silly of me. Really, though, I should have known. You're not the kind of woman who takes a back seat to anyone, are you?"

Her smile flattened a bit. "I guess not, but I do anyway. And often. I have no choice. I was common-born."

He picked a few more berries. "So was I."

Her brows rose slightly. "You were?"

He nodded. "Did you think I was born into nobility?" He helped himself to another couple of berries, then walked over to one of the many carved wood benches and sat, patting the seat next to him.

She joined him. "Well, you ended up as king."

"Because of what I did during the war. Because my actions impressed the aging king enough to turn over the crown. Not because of who I was or the family I came from." How much of his history had been suppressed? All of it? He held out the handful of berries.

She took one. "I guess I never thought about it."

"Vesta came from nobility. I'm sure that contributed to her belief that she should hold the throne alone. That and the general belief of most fae that the throne was rightly theirs anyway."

"Not all fae believe that." Theo ate the berry, then tucked one leg under the other and twisted to face him better.

"That's why I said most. I know there are some decent fairies out there, but you'll excuse me if I'm a little bitter toward the lot because of my ex-wife."

Theo nodded. "Understood."

"Thank you." He offered her another berry. Truth was, he was a lot bitter toward the fae. He knew it was something he needed to get over, but that was easier said than done.

She took a berry but didn't immediately eat it. "So what would you have said to the people of Limbo if you'd been given the opportunity to defend yourself against the queen's accusations?"

Robin studied the dark purple berry between his fingers. The tiny geometric sections that made up the oblong fruit reflected the soft light. He tossed it into his mouth. "I appreciate you asking me that, but I'm not sure what good it would have done. I was given no trial. No chance to refute her accusations. Just drugged, poisoned, removed, and imprisoned. And as much as I would like for you to believe I'm innocent, that's something you need to decide for yourself."

"But isn't there something you can tell me that would prove it?"

He sighed and shook his head. "Not really. The orcs even sided against me, but then, why wouldn't they when I captured their king? They had no reason to defend me. Having me on the throne was a constant reminder of their failure."

She sighed. "Right."

He looked at her. "Anyone who was around when I was king should be able to tell you that Vesta's overthrow was hostile, except that I suspect very few are willing. Which I understand. She puts fear into people. And promises great things. It's a heady combination. Enough that the masses decide it's easier to go along with her than fight."

"I've never heard anyone question what she's done."

"Why would they? Those who oppose her have a way of disappearing. Or being so maligned that their own reputations are left shredded and their lives in ruins. Who would willingly bring that upon themselves and their family?"

"No one. Very few, anyway." She squinted at some point in the distance. "You had no chance, did you?"

"Not much." He took a breath. "None, actually."

"I'm sorry."

He looked at her, mostly because it sounded like she genuinely meant it.

She made a curious face. "Why are you looking at me with such a serious face?"

"Because I think you mean that."

"I do." She stole another berry from his hand, her

fingers barely touching his palm, but that was enough to make him aware of her. "I know what it's like to have things stacked against you and feel powerless. To be shown something wonderful only to have that thing snatched away."

There was sorrow in her eyes, but no self-pity. This woman was not only beautiful but remarkably strong. She was the kind of woman who should have been at his side. Not Vesta, may wood fleas infest her person. Theodora would have made an extraordinary queen. He nodded. "I know you do."

She answered him with a brief smile, then ate the berry she'd swiped. "I believe you."

"Good, because I really do listen when you talk about your past."

"No. I mean I believe that you didn't betray the kingdom."

His mouth fell open. "You do?"

She nodded, wiping a little juice from the corner of her mouth. "Until proven otherwise. Maybe I'm wrong. Maybe you're laughing at me on the inside, but you don't seem like the kind of man who'd do the terrible things Vesta claims you did."

He closed his mouth and made himself swallow. "Thank you."

It was impossible not to be shocked. And happy. But then, Theodora was a smart woman. And obviously a keen judge of character. She deserved better than cleaning his bookshelves for a year. Along with a sudden rush of affection for her, a new idea came to him.

"Can I ask you something?"

She nodded. "Anything. Although I reserve the right not to answer."

"Fair enough." He held out the last berry. She shook her head, so he ate it. "What's it like downstairs?"

She frowned. "What do you mean?"

"Is it comfortable? Your room? The living quarters for the staff? How is it all?"

"It's fine."

"So it's not comfortable."

She laughed softly. "My room is exactly what I expected. It's perfectly adequate for my needs. The gathering room where we eat is definitely big enough. Really, I haven't spent much time down there. This is only my second day here. Mrs. Baton has kept me plenty busy."

"Doing things that don't really need doing, I'd imagine."

Theodora bobbed her head back and forth. "You're not wrong. I think. I don't really know what it takes to maintain a house of this size and grandeur. Maybe the linen closet really did need to be reorganized, even if it looked perfectly in order. Who am I to say?"

He'd never seen the linen closet. "When you say your room is adequate, what do you mean?"

"I mean it has a bed, a chair, a dresser… What else do I need?"

He sat up a little straighter. "What about a lamp? A window? A television?"

"It has the first two. There's a television in the gathering room, but I haven't watched it. Not sure about the others."

"How are the others?" He had a feeling he knew the answer to this question already.

"Mrs. Applestock and Lolly are wonderful. They're exactly as you'd think they'd be. And as they appear to be." She let out a little snort. "So are Elswood and Mrs. Baton, for that matter, but I don't want to speak ill of anyone."

"Which means you have ill to say. You just don't want to say it."

She smiled but gave him no other response.

He could answer for her. "They're both very stern, serious people. I know that. But are they like that all the time?"

"So far." She shrugged. "I really don't see much of them, Elswood especially. Mrs. Baton gives me my orders in the morning, we all eat breakfast together, then everyone goes their way." She paused like she was thinking. "Henry's very nice. And I met Fenwick this morning at breakfast. He seems nice, also."

"They are both kind, considerate men. Hard workers." He sighed. "As for Hyacinth and Elswood, perhaps I should speak to them—"

"No." She stiffened suddenly. "That is, please don't. I don't think it would be well received. Or make any difference, except that they might assume I was the root of it."

"And that would make things harder for you."

She nodded. "Maybe we should go look for that cat."

Perhaps it was her declaration that she believed in his innocence, perhaps it was his attraction to her, perhaps it was something else entirely, but he was feeling a sudden urge to give her some happiness like she'd just given him. Whatever the reason, the desire to do something for her just would not be squelched. "Theodora, we're not going to find the cat."

"No, Sire, we most likely are not."

"Let's not spend our time doing that, then."

"All right." She got up. "I should get back to the library. Thank you for the berries."

"Please, sit down."

She hesitated for a moment, then sat. "As you wish."

"The rules of the indenture are broad. In fact, the only real stipulation is that you are to spend a year of your life in service to me. And service is a broad term."

She nodded. "That's how I understand it."

"This house doesn't need another member of the housekeeping staff. Or kitchen staff. Or any staff, for that matter. I don't need it."

She paled a little. "I promise, I am doing everything Mrs. Baton tells me to—"

"Forget Mrs. Baton." He took a deep breath. It was hard for him to say the next words, but the small amounts of time he'd already spent with Theodora had made his need abundantly clear.

"I would like you to serve your year as my companion."

Hard blinking answered him. Then a stern glare and a deep frown. "I am not *that* kind of woman, Your Lordship."

"I don't mean *that* kind of companionship." Although the thought of her in his bed was not unpleasant. At all. But he was going to have to explain himself more plainly. In language that pinpointed just how pathetic he was. "I mean as my friend. As company. As an actual companion." He stared out at the pavilion.

"Oh." She was quiet for a while, but he didn't want to look at her in case she was staring at him in revulsion for being so pitiful. "I could do that."

That turned his head. "You could?"

She nodded. "What kind of things would you want to do?"

"Well, for one thing, we could have meals together. I have dined alone for years, and I am sick to death of it. We could take strolls in the garden. Maybe one night a week we could watch a movie. Did you know there's a theater room in this place?"

"I didn't know. I suppose eventually I'd be sent to clean it, though. All right. I can do those things, although I might be tired from the day's work sometimes."

He shook his head. "There would be no day's work. All of that would cease."

"Oh? Well, that would free up my time considerably." A little half smile bent her mouth.

"What else would you like to do?"

He would like for her to be at his side all day. Not to do anything, but just to have the company. Asking for that might sound odder than what he'd already requested, though. He thought hard. "You could accompany me to the mine from now on."

"I could do that."

Something was going on in her head. He could see it behind her eyes. Some sort of machinations. He wouldn't blame her for wanting something out of this.

He decided to launch a preemptive strike. "In exchange, I'll provide you with something you want. Within reason."

Her brows went a centimeter higher. "I would like access to your library. To the books there."

"You like to read?"

"I love to read."

"Then that will be part of our day. We'll spend our afternoons there. Doing just that."

Her lips parted, and a second later, a brilliant smile lit her face. "That would be wonderful."

He nodded. "It would be." He loved to read, but being alone in that enormous space sometimes felt worse than being alone anywhere else. He had no one to share all those stories with, no one to talk to about them.

But that was a small request on her part, and he wanted to do more than that for her. "What if I arranged for one of the master lapidaries in town to give you lessons? There's a guild, you know. You said you weren't able to finish your studies after your mother passed. Is that something you'd still be interested in?"

Her hand went to her mouth, then down to her necklace. She shook her head, and when she spoke, she seemed a little breathless. "I can't believe—I absolutely would be. And that's very generous of you, but I am here to pay a debt, not leave you with one."

He spread his arms. "Does it look like I cannot afford lessons?"

"No, it doesn't look that way at all." She took a deep gulp of air. "Thank you. Lessons would be incredible. Life-changing."

"Then it's settled. You're no longer downstairs help." He got up. "Come on."

She stood. "Where are we going?"

"To move you upstairs."

CHAPTER ELEVEN

Becoming a lapidary, a trained stonecutter, would change Theo's life in a way nothing else could. A profession like that would not only keep a roof over their heads but could actually help pay down her father's debts. In the year's time that she had ahead of her, if she studied hard and practiced often, she could build on the rudimentary skills she already had and end up with enough training to apprentice with any of the gem cutters in Limbo. The apprenticeship would only pay a little more than she made working her current jobs, but once she proved herself, she'd be set.

This opportunity was beyond anything she could have hoped for. Anything she could have dreamed of.

She wasn't even sure Robin understood everything he was offering her.

Sadly, Theo already knew none of what His Lordship wanted would be well received. Mrs. Applestock and Lolly probably wouldn't care. Henry or Fenwick either. But Mrs. Baton and

Elswood would undoubtedly explode at the impropriety of it. That seemed to be their favorite word, after all.

Oh, they might not say much to Robin's face, but behind his back, they'd have plenty to chatter about. And then they'd make their feelings known to her in the way they treated her. She would bet on that with every single cent she had, if she were a betting person. Which she would never be. Even if she came into money.

But she held her tongue and followed him downstairs.

At the bottom of the steps, he stopped and turned to her. "Show me your current room. Please."

"Sure. This way." She led him through the hallways and down the last one to her door.

"Why the last one? All these rooms can't be in use. Did you pick this room?"

"No, it was given to me." She opened the door. "This is it."

He looked in but stayed where he was. Didn't make a difference. There was no more of it to be seen by walking through the door. "It's so…small. And plain."

She shrugged. "It's fine."

"It's like a prison cell." He frowned. "Where's the bathroom?"

She pointed over her shoulder. "End of the hall there."

Still frowning, he glanced at the door, then back at her room. "Who assigned this to you?"

She hesitated, hoping against hope that this wasn't about to take the turn she suspected. "Elswood."

Robin's frown deepened. He looked back the way they'd come. "Elswood! Where are you? Show yourself, man."

A moment later, he appeared at the end of the hall. He looked worried until he saw Theo. Then he grimaced and glared at her. "Whatever she's done, my lord, I can assure you—"

"She hasn't done anything." Robin pointed at Theo's space. "Do all the staff rooms look like this?"

Elswood peeked in as though he needed a refresher. "They're all very similar."

Robin crossed his arms. "Let me see them."

"All of them, my lord?"

"Is that a problem?"

"No, Sire, of course not." Elswood fumbled with the keys on his belt, finding the right one, and opened the door across the hall. The room was almost identical to Theo's but had no window. At least she'd gotten that much. There were also some stacked boxes and a few extra chairs in the small space. Nice to know she hadn't been given the catchall room. "As you can see, this room has no natural light, which is why we use it for storage."

Robin was silent a moment, then walked down the hall toward the kitchen. He stopped about halfway and pointed to a door. "Who's room is this?"

"No one's."

He went a few more steps toward the kitchen, this time stopping one door from the end. "And this one?"

"Lolly's, Sire."

"Fetch her back here."

"As you wish." Elswood disappeared.

Theo shook her head at Robin and kept her voice soft. "You don't have to do this."

"I think I need to. Other than to eat in the kitchen, I haven't been down here since the house was under construction." He looked unhappy. "I've assumed all was equal down here. I see that's not the case."

Elswood returned with Lolly. She had a dish towel thrown over one shoulder and a vegetable peeler in the pocket of her apron.

Robin smiled at her as she curtsied. "How do you like your room, Lolly?"

She looked slightly petrified. "It's very good, Sire."

"I promise, you're not in any trouble. Would you mind letting me see your room? This isn't any kind of inspection. I'm just curious about your accommodations."

She nodded, only slightly less nervous. "It's right here." She slipped past him and opened the door.

Theo took a look. It was twice the size of her room. Maybe more. Big enough to have a sitting area with a small couch and a television. She had two windows, a bigger bed, a closet, and *her own bathroom*.

Theo frowned, then realized Robin was scowling now.

"Thank you, Lolly." Robin looked at Elswood. "Let's see your room."

Elswood stiffened. "Mrs. Baton and I have larger spaces, Your Lordship. As is befitting our positions in the household."

"And that's absolutely warranted," Robin answered. "But it's still my household. I want to see your room."

Theo really wanted to see it, too.

Elswood's expression turned dour. "Right this way."

Without another word, he led them to a door and opened it. Theo gasped before she could stop herself.

It wasn't a room so much as an apartment because, from what she could see, the space had multiple rooms. It was also very well furnished. Gone were the tile floors and cream walls of the other staff quarters. Elswood's rooms had thick patterned carpets over hardwood floors, deep-green walls, fancy art in gilded frames, dark wood furniture, and a chandelier. And that was just in the rooms that they could see from the door.

"Judas," Lolly breathed.

Robin didn't say a word for several long moments. Then, still looking into the apartment, he spoke. "Mrs. Baton's looks the same?"

"She has decorated with, perhaps, a more feminine hand," Elswood replied. "But yes, her quarters are similar."

"Mrs. Applestock's rooms aren't anything like this," Lolly volunteered.

Elswood's scowl in the scullery maid's direction only lasted a second, but Theo caught it. "Her quarters are fine."

Robin turned, blocking the view into Elswood's rooms. He seemed taller and broader than he had a second ago. "I expect some differences in housing based on position and superiority, but that doesn't explain the extreme delta that exists between these rooms. Especially Theodora's room."

Elswood sputtered. "Your Lordship, she's merely an indentured worker, come for a year, nothing more."

Robin's gaze narrowed, but his tone remained calm. "That doesn't make her less than. And doesn't Lolly work as hard, if not harder than some of you? What about Mrs. Applestock?" He sighed. "I'm disappointed, Elswood. I want these inequities resolved. Am I understood?"

Elswood nodded. "Yes, Sire. As soon as possible."

"If something needs doing to make that happen, a wall taken down, a window added, carpeting, new furniture, whatever it is, make it known."

"I will, Your Lordship. Right away." Elswood straightened. "I'll start with Miss Middlebright's accommodations."

"No need," Robin answered. "She moving to the Lapis Room upstairs."

Elswood's jaw hung open. "Sire, that's a guest room."

"And from now on, Theodora will be treated as a guest, as she will be serving out her indenture as my companion. Do you have a problem with that?"

Elswood's mouth was still open, and Theo imagined he had all kinds of problems with that. His mouth snapped shut, and he shook his head. "Whatever Your Lordship wishes."

Robin looked at Theo, his expression softening. "How long will it take you to gather your things?"

"Not long." She went straight back to her room without waiting to be dismissed. Guests didn't have to wait for such things, did they? She threw everything into her tattered bag, except her Gallow House livery, which she left on the bed, and marched straight back to Robin. "Ready."

He smiled as he took her bag. "Let me show you to your new quarters."

Together, they left and walked upstairs. She hadn't expected him to carry her bag. It looked rattier than ever in his strong, elegant hands, but it was what it was. She waited until they were out of earshot to speak. "You know Elswood isn't happy."

"I know," Robin answered. "And I don't care. I'm greatly displeased that Mrs. Applestock and Lolly have been living in smaller quarters. Not once have they said a word. And they do a tremendous amount of work. They deserve more comforts."

He was angry. She didn't want to make his mood worse, so she kept her thoughts to herself.

Apparently, that wasn't what he wanted. "You don't agree?"

They turned down the hall, passing the library.

"I completely agree. I like both of them very

much. I think it's wonderful they're going to get more space and more luxury."

A hint of a smile played across his lips. "And how do you feel about getting a new room?"

"It's very generous of you."

He shook his head. "I don't think it's generous. I think it's as it should be." He paused in the middle of the hall. "Look at this house. It's enormous. Why shouldn't you sleep in a nicer space? Why shouldn't everyone have more room? But that's not really what I meant. I should have asked if you're comfortable being on the same floor that I am."

That hadn't occurred to her, but now she looked down the hall. She didn't know which set of doors led to his room. She shrugged. "I like being closer to the library."

He grinned. "Always a good thing." He walked backward a couple of steps until he came to a set of double doors. "The Lapis Room."

Double doors? For a guest room? Why that should surprise her in this place, she had no idea. But it was the room he wanted her to have, so she'd be happy about whatever was behind those doors.

He opened them and walked in.

She followed, doing her best not to lose her composure. The space was gorgeous. And large. Decorated in many shades of deep blue with accents of white, silver, and purple, the room was somehow both cozy and luxurious. It felt vaguely celestial.

He kept going through the sitting room and into the bedroom. He put her bag on the settee at the end of the bed and walked straight to a pair of French doors. "This is one of the best parts of this room."

He opened them, went outside, then turned to her. "Come have a look."

The room had a balcony. She joined him on it. Not just a tiny little span of a balcony either. It was long and wide enough to have a chaise lounge with a little table next to it. She went to the railing. Below, the garden with its enormous pavilion was spread out before her. She could just smell the sweetness of the flowers. Even a hint of the nightberries came through. "This is amazing."

"I have a balcony too. I spend a lot of time out there." He stood next to her at the railing. "Shadowvale can be a bit gloomy during the day, but in the evening when the clouds part, it's magical."

"This room..." Was going to be very hard to leave in a year. "Is just wonderful. Thank you for letting me use this space while I'm here."

"I'm happy to do it. Happy, too, that a guest room in this house will finally *be* used."

Chimes rang through the house, muted slightly on the balcony. Robin looked inside. "That must be Amelia come to see about the samples from the mine."

"The woman who built this town?"

"Yes. Come meet her."

Theo shrank back. "I don't think I should. I'm not really a guest. I don't—"

"Please. I would like you to meet her. And for her to meet you."

She glanced down at her clothes. Jeans and a T-shirt didn't seem appropriate.

He shook his head. "Amelia won't care what you're wearing, I promise."

Maybe not, Theo thought. But she suddenly cared how she was perceived. Perhaps because she was no longer being presented as Robin's servant, but his companion. She ought to look like that meant something to her. "Please, give me just a few minutes, and I'll be down."

He nodded as he headed for the door. "The main sitting room."

"I'll be there." Just as soon as she changed and ran a brush through her hair and did her best to look like someone worthy of the time and consideration the exiled king was giving her.

She shouldn't care about that. A day ago, she didn't. So why now?

Because she cared about him?

Was that possible? She realized it was. Completely possible. And incredibly stupid.

CHAPTER TWELVE

Robin looked forward to Amelia's weekly visits. Besides his trips to the mines, they were his main connection to the world outside the walls of Gallow House. Especially because, unlike his trips to the mines, Amelia's visits were much more social. Grent might be able to catch him up on the mine gossip, but Amelia knew everything that was going on in town.

She didn't mind sitting with him while she filled him in on it either. Not that she'd been such a social butterfly herself for a long time, but now that her niece had moved to Shadowvale, Amelia's newfound happiness was evident in not only her attitude, but her social life.

Which meant she had more to share with Robin. Because of her, he felt connected to the town. Even though he wasn't really.

Now he had Theodora to keep him company. But he didn't want her to feel as isolated as he did. Even if she was going to be here for only a year. There was no reason for both of them to suffer.

He strode into the main sitting room. Amelia was looking out the windows onto the garden. "So nice to see you, Amelia."

She glanced over her shoulder with a smile. "Hello, Robin. Your garden looks wonderful. I really need a cutting from that rosebush. I've always admired those deep-purple flowers, but they are particularly stunning at the moment."

"I'll make sure Fenwick gets you one."

"Thank you." She turned. "How is the mine?"

"Excellent. They're producing some outstanding new rough." He'd left the samples in the room earlier, knowing he'd need them. He took the bag from a drawer in the armoire and brought it over to the low table between the couches. "Have a look at this new opal they've tapped into."

He opened the bag and started pulling the samples out, starting with the opal. Mrs. Applestock would have a tray of goodies delivered via Elswood soon. Tea, finger sandwiches, little cookies, small cakes. All things Amelia liked. It was their ritual.

Amelia picked up the opal rough and examined it. "This looks very good. The fire is fantastic."

"I agree." But he had more to talk to her about today than the mines. "Someone new is staying with me."

She looked up from the opal. "Company? I must say that's unusual. It's not Vesta, is it? Can't be. You're smiling."

He laughed. "No, not Vesta. My guest is a woman from Limbo, though. Her father owes me a debt to be paid with a year's worth of service, but he's unwell, so she's come to fulfill what we call an indenture."

"Is that so?" Amelia smiled. "I'd love to meet her."

"Good, because I've invited her to join us. I want to introduce the two of you." He hesitated. "I decided that I want her to serve her year out as my companion. You know my situation."

"I do." Amelia smiled kindly, her gaze sympathetic. "A companion is a wise choice."

"More than that, I'd like to offer her the chance to train as a lapidary. You don't have a problem with that, do you?"

"Not at all. I know what an affinity goblins have for stonework. I think it's a smart move. Are you hoping to get her to stay beyond the year?"

He took a breath. He hadn't willingly given space to that thought. It was too soon to even wonder about that. But he already knew how much he wanted her to stay. Foolish, really. An impetuous impulse born of his loneliness.

She was only here out of obligation. And she had a father to return to.

He shook his head as he set the last few samples out. "I don't think that's a possibility. Her father will need her home."

"I see," Amelia said. "Shame. You could do with more than just permanent staff in this house."

And in his life. But Theodora wasn't that person. She couldn't be if she was leaving. And she couldn't stay. She wouldn't. She was too loyal of a daughter to abandon her father. "The thing is, I don't want my limitations to limit her as well. A year is a long time to be subjected to my constraints."

"And yet, you've managed for many years."

"'Managed' is a kind word. I've survived. Mostly because I've had no other choice. Theodora should."

"I won't argue with that." She smiled. "I must say you look better today than you have in a long while. Any chance that's because of her?"

"I…" Was it? How could he answer that? "I don't know. Maybe. I did sleep well last night for the first time in a long time."

"Glad to hear that." She narrowed her eyes. "There's something you want from me, isn't there?"

He took a breath. "There is. Do you think Emeranth would be willing to befriend Theodora? Show her around a little?"

"Did I hear my name?"

He turned to see Theodora walk in. She was in black leggings and an oversized shirt, her hair braided back at her temples in a traditional style, and she was smiling. Did she have gloss on her lips? He wasn't sure, but she looked beautiful. He stood. "Yes. You did. Theodora Middlebright, this is Amelia Marchand."

Theodora approached, then stopped and looked like she wasn't sure what to do next. "Ms. Marchand, His Lordship has said such wonderful things about you. It's an honor to meet you."

"Thank you, Ms. Middlebright."

"Please, call me Theodora."

"Join us," Robin said.

She sat on the same couch as him, but at the other end. She was still smiling, but there was tension in her expression. She was uncomfortable. Nervous, maybe.

Amelia said, "Robin was just telling me about your situation. I understand you're going to be here for a year."

Theodora nodded. "Yes, ma'am."

"Now, Theodora," Amelia began, "we can't have that. Call me Amelia. Please. I want us to be friends. More specifically, I'd love to introduce you to my niece, Emeranth. I think you'd get on well. She's a witch, like me. And I believe you're close in age."

Theodora glanced at Robin. "That's very nice of you, but I won't have much time for socializing."

He shook his head. "I'll make sure you have time. You should go out and see the town. Emeranth could show you around."

Amelia nodded. "You girls could go out to lunch. Em could even invite a few of her friends."

Theodora sat up straighter, still looking at Robin. "If that's what you want."

"What I want is for you not to feel like you're in the same prison I am." He sighed. "My life is not something I'd wish on anyone."

She interlaced her fingers, keeping her hands in her lap. "May I speak freely, Your Lordship?"

"Of course."

She cleared her throat softly. "I know you're unhappy because of the restraints on your freedom. I know you're lonely. No one could blame you for that. But don't you ever have parties? Don't you invite people in?" She looked around. "With all this space, you could have a party and probably invite everyone who lives in this town."

Amelia snorted. "She's not wrong, Robin. But you could certainly start with something small. A dinner party. A cocktail party. A garden party. You do have that beautiful, and may I add, unused pavilion out there. What do you think?"

Before Robin could answer, Elswood pushed in a tea cart. He stopped when he reached them, his narrow-eyed gaze flitting over Theodora. "I didn't realize Miss Middlebright was joining you. Mrs. Applestock only prepared enough for two."

Robin laughed. "I doubt that."

"There might be enough food, but I only have cups and plates for two."

Robin gave him a sharp look. "Then bring another set. Problem solved."

"Yes, Your Lordship." With a bow, he left.

The platters of food, teapot, cups, and plates were all still on the cart.

Theodora jumped up. "Let me help."

Robin made a little face. "You don't have to do this."

"Someone does. It might as well be me." She set the food platters on the coffee table, put a cup, saucer, and plate in front of Robin and Amelia, then held up the teapot. "Tea?"

"I would love some," Amelia said.

As Theodora was pouring, Elswood returned. This time, he had a tray. "I informed Mrs. Applestock that you've included Theodora, and she sent me with this."

He put the tray on the far end of the coffee table. It held the requested third setting, plus a plate of chocolate-dipped strawberries, shrimp salad sandwiches, and a cheese plate.

Robin spread his hands out. "See? She can't do anything in small portions."

"Then just imagine," Theodora said, "what she could do for a party."

Elswood's brows lifted, but he said nothing. Robin knew the butler's questions would come later, worked into some innocent conversation. Elswood had his ways of finding out what he wanted to know.

"I don't know," Robin said. "I'll think about it." But he already had. Many times. A party sounded like such a simple thing. A way to get to know people and expand his circle. It would bring him the friends and interaction he so desperately craved.

But as those friendships deepened, he'd be invited places. Places he couldn't go. And then he'd be stuck either making excuses that would eventually turn his new friends against him, or he'd be forced to confess that his cruel ex-wife had imprisoned him. Made him a pawn in her political game.

It was flat-out embarrassing to think about the whole town knowing how he'd been so cruelly betrayed by the woman who'd shared his bed.

Now they just thought he was a strange recluse who was bitter about losing his crown and kingdom. He could bear that.

Theodora took a cup of tea and went back to her seat. "You already have thought about it, haven't you?"

He looked up at her, unable to find an answer that wasn't a lie and knowing the truth wouldn't be well received.

She turned her cup on the saucer, then set both on the table. "If you wanted to throw a party, you would have already. So there's obviously a reason you don't want to. It's okay. It's none of my business. I shouldn't have suggested it."

"No," Amelia said. "It was a good idea. It still is."

"No," Robin said. "It's not. I don't need company at the expense of my dignity." He got up, suddenly overwhelmed by the burden of his life. "Now if you'll excuse me."

He walked out, aware of how small his actions were and how petty he looked. But while this life might not look miserable to anyone else, he was on the verge of losing his mind. And would be until his wretched curse was lifted.

CHAPTER THIRTEEN

"I'm sorry for ruining your visit," Theo said to Amelia. "I didn't mean to upset him. That's something I've been actively avoiding. If he rejects my indenture..." She exhaled. She was talking too much. It wasn't her way, but she felt like the important woman across from her deserved an explanation, though she didn't need to also hear Theo's problems.

Amelia stared after Robin, looking less than pleased. "He won't cancel anything. He likes you. He might even go so far as to realize he needs you."

Theo glanced at Amelia. "Forgive me, but I don't think that's true at all."

Amelia turned her attention to Theo again. Thankfully, curiosity had replaced the displeasure on the woman's handsome face. "How long have you been here?"

"Two days."

"Did you start out as his companion?"

"No. As general household staff."

Amelia nodded as if the picture was becoming

clear. "And in that short amount of time, he's changed the terms of your service, elevating you to upstairs, and decided that you should be trained in a useful skill. All of that, and you don't think he's come to any conclusions about how he feels about you?"

"Respectfully, all of that is because my mother was his pastry cook when he was newly crowned king. He's very sentimental about that time in his life, and due to that, he's also sentimental about her. I believe that being reminded about her passing and finding out what her loss did to me has left him with the feeling that he needs to do something for me. That's all."

Amelia pursed her lips and nodded. "I see. You're wrong, but I understand why you'd believe that."

Theo frowned. "You can't think I mean anything to him in such a short amount of time."

"I've known Robin for as long as he's lived here. This is the first time I've come to visit him that he not only looks well but seems genuinely excited about something. I'm pretty sure it isn't this new seam of opal, no matter how much fire it might contain." She smirked slightly. "He likes you."

He liked the little cat who'd come to visit him, Theo knew that much. "I don't know…"

"I do." Amelia helped herself to one of the small lavender cakes on the three-tiered serving stand. "Do you like him?"

"I…that is…it doesn't matter what I think of him. We're not equals."

"Why not? He's no longer king. The only reason anyone still calls him your lordship or sire is out of respect."

Theo shook her head. "But he was king. And I'm common-born." Though, so was he. He'd told her as much. The difference was she hadn't risen above that. And never would.

"Theodora, how do you feel about him?"

She took a breath, unsure why she felt compelled to answer this woman she didn't even know, except that she didn't want to cause trouble for Robin. "I like him more than I thought I would. He's surprisingly kind and generous and funny. He's also a little…"

Theo struggled to find a word that didn't paint Robin in a bad light.

After a moment, Amelia filled in the silence. "Sad?"

Theo nodded. She'd been reluctant to say it. "I think because of that, I feel for him. And I definitely didn't expect that. I came here mad. Angry that I had to spend my next year here, angry at my father, angry at Robin. Just angry about all of it."

"You don't seem so angry now."

"I'm mostly resigned to it, I think. But it's so different than what I thought it was going to be." She looked out the window toward the garden. "I'm not happy to be spending so much time away from my father, but that can't be helped."

"What would your father want you to do in this situation?"

Theo thought on that for a few long, introspective moments. "He'd want me to make the best of it."

"Did he give you any advice before you came here?"

"Not really. He just told me to be safe and not to worry about him. And to try to have some fun."

"But you can't turn off your worry that easily, can you?"

"No." Mrs. Oakhill, their next-door neighbor, had promised to look in on Theo's father every so often, but Mrs. Oakhill was getting up there herself. It was a help, but not enough to ease Theo's worry. Not when her father's track record of taking care of himself was sketchy at best.

"Then you'll have to do your best to follow the other guidelines he gave you. Be safe. Have some fun. Two out of three isn't bad."

Theo squinted at the woman. "What are you saying?"

"I'm saying Robin needs someone to spend time with. Someone who cares about him. I think that person could be you. Even if you have to dig deep to find that care. I'm not saying lie to him. Just try to understand his position." Amelia shook her head. "This life wasn't his making."

"You believe that Vesta did all this to him? That he's innocent of the crimes she's accused him of?"

Amelia nodded. "Absolutely. When I first met him, the taint of fairy magic on him was undeniable. Still is. It surrounds him and this place. And the more I've gotten to know Robin, the more I understand what a good man he is. What Vesta did to him, not just taking his throne, but the way she's limited his movements here, only further proves that she's the monster. Not Robin."

Did Amelia have any reason to lie for Robin? Theo didn't think so. But they were clearly friends. Still, Theo was glad to have someone else confirm what she'd already been thinking. "I want to help him. I really do. My mother liked him very much. At least, she liked her job in the palace very much. And I don't think she would have felt that way if he'd been the monster Vesta makes him out to be."

Amelia nodded. "That's an astute observation."

"So how do I help him?"

Amelia smiled. "You already are helping by spending time with him. But I also think your party idea deserves more of his attention. Don't let go of that."

"I won't. Anything else?"

Amelia put her hands on the couch as if she was about to get up. "I know his movement is restricted, but he needs to get out of this house. Going to the mines doesn't count. Maybe you can get him to go out for a walk? There has to be some room for him to move on his own grounds."

"We've talked about that, so a walk will be easy."

"Good. One more thing. You'll soon hear, if you haven't already, about a magical book hidden in the enchanted forest. A book with the power to remove the curse of the person who writes their name in it."

Theo gasped softly. That was just what Robin needed.

Amelia held her hand up. "Unfortunately, it won't work for fairy magic that was created in another dimension like Limbo. That magic is so strong and so powerful that not even I could break it."

"Then what would?"

She shook her head slowly. "Other than Vesta's own command, I don't honestly know."

"Is there any way to find out?"

Amelia tipped her head. "I can certainly research it again. I did, years ago, but came up empty. Doesn't mean I can't give it another shot." She smiled. "I do love a challenge."

"That would be wonderful."

"No promises." Amelia stood. "If you need anything, you call me. Mrs. Applestock has my number, as does Robin. In the meantime, I am going to see about my niece taking you into town for lunch."

Theo got to her feet. "Thank you. It was lovely to meet you."

"You, too. Be well, changeling."

Theo stiffened, and her mouth fell open. "I'm not—"

"You are, but don't worry. I won't tell him. But you'd better before he figures it out on his own."

"How did you know?"

Amelia laughed softly as she headed for the door. "Nothing stays secret from me for very long, my dear. Especially not magic. Especially not in my town."

*

Robin realized he'd lost his temper in a fit of self-pity. It was embarrassing, and yet he couldn't quite bring himself to do anything about it besides hide in his room. Theodora probably wished more than ever that she could go home.

The thought filled him with sadness.

He should apologize to her and Amelia. If Amelia was even still here. Regardless, he'd send her flowers. A big bunch of the purple roses she'd been admiring in his garden. Those, along with a note of apology, should get him back in her good graces.

As for Theodora, he wasn't as sure with her. But he could start with *sorry*.

He took a deep breath before leaving his quarters. She had every right to be upset, but he had a feeling she might hold back because of her situation. How awful that must be to have someone else in control of your future. But then, he knew a little about having someone else in control of your life.

He turned down the hall and toward the big curving staircase that connected the upstairs and the main floor. Theodora was at the other end of the hall in front of her bedroom door, about to go inside.

He lifted his hand in greeting as he walked toward her. "Did Amelia leave?"

Theodora nodded. "She did."

He grimaced and put a hand on the back of his neck. "Was she terribly mad?"

Theodora turned toward him. "No, not mad at all. But..." She stared at the marble flooring for a moment before looking at him again. "I owe you an apology. I didn't mean to upset you and—"

"You don't owe me anything." He closed the distance between them with a few more steps. She was about as perfectly beautiful as any woman he'd ever seen. "My reaction was uncalled for. I need to apologize to you and Amelia for storming out." He exhaled hard. "The idea of a party is wonderful. Having people around would be amazing."

She tipped her head slightly as if waiting for the rest. "But?"

She was even smarter than she was beautiful. Those green-gold eyes missed nothing. "But people tend to reciprocate when you issue an invite. They ask you to their house or out for dinner or to a movie or something that requires you to leave your house. How do I explain that I can't because I'm a pawn in my ex-wife's political games? That I was too dumb to see through her manipulations and realize that I was being played for a fool?"

"Your Lordship—"

"No." Enough ranting. Enough explaining himself. He shook his head. "I don't want to be a laughingstock. Call that ego or arrogance or whatever you want, but there it is. I have had enough humiliation. I don't want more."

Was the pain in her eyes on his behalf? That couldn't be.

"Oh, Robin. You poor—" She froze, her brows bending in distress, which did nothing to detract from her loveliness. "Forgive me, Sire. I didn't mean to be so familiar."

"Enough of that nonsense, too. I am no one's king. Call me Robin. To be honest, I hate being reminded of who I once was, but I've put up with it because Elswood has always insisted it's proper. Mrs. Baton, too." He snorted. "Proper can go to Hades."

It occurred to him that maybe, if Theodora stopped referring to him as sire and your lordship, she'd think of them as equals.

He'd like that very much.

Her distressed expression turned to amusement, and she laughed. The sound intoxicated him so much he leaned in and kissed her. Gently at first, but she tasted so good and her lips were so soft that his need for her increased, and his mouth grew insistent.

He wanted more of this woman. But then, hadn't some part of him known that the moment he'd laid eyes on her?

Her startled gasp broke them apart. He backed up, realizing just how bold and brash his actions had been. "I don't know what came over me. I didn't mean to—no, that's a lie. I *did* mean to kiss you. But I shouldn't have. I'm not sure what made me think that was acceptable. I promise it has nothing to do with you being my companion. It's just that you laughed, and you looked so beautiful that I lost my head, and…"

She wasn't saying anything. Just staring at him. Eyes sparkling, lips still parted. Perfect for more kissing.

He wasn't going to do that, unfortunately. "Are you all right?"

"You kissed me."

He nodded. "I did. I claim that fully. But you didn't answer my question. Are you all right?" He was starting to wonder.

"I don't know. I feel…tingly all over."

He raised one brow. He felt a little tingly himself. "I think that's pretty standard. If it's a good kiss, anyway. You have been kissed before, haven't you?"

Her fingers went to her mouth. "Not like that," she breathed out. Then her eyes widened, and she looked at him. "What did you do? Did you use magic? Or release some kind of incantation?"

He held his hands up. "I promise I just kissed you."

She put her hands to her face. "Then why do I feel like this?"

"Like what?"

"Like I might faint. And I'm not the least bit hungry. For food." Her mouth scrunched up. "Oh no. This isn't good. This isn't good at all."

Chapter Fourteen

It wasn't good because Theo *liked* him. Her body, traitor that it was, wanted more of his mouth on hers. Where was that coming from? And why?

Had Amelia done something? She was a witch, after all, and clearly a very powerful one if her magic created this town. Plus, she'd told Theo to be kind to Robin. And to help him have fun. How kind did Amelia expect her to be? And what sort of fun did she think Robin needed to have? And why didn't the idea of fun with him repulse her?

"Why isn't it good?" Robin asked.

She couldn't very well tell him that she didn't want to like him. That went against the whole point of being his companion. And it would hurt his feelings, something she unfortunately cared about. Plus, she didn't want to lie to him. She *did* like him. She just didn't want to like him in the kind of way that caused her insides to turn to jelly.

Because of all that, she remained as tongue-tied as if he were still kissing her.

A look of understanding crossed Robin's face.

"You're not single, are you?" He turned away before she could answer. "Of course you aren't. How foolish I am to think a woman with your wit and beauty would have no love interest at home?"

"No," she whispered.

He turned back to her, shaking his head. "I knew it. Why I ever thought otherwise, I don't know. I'm sure half the kingdom has made a bid for your hand."

Not hardly. She had a suspicion she wasn't going to be able to hide her reputation from him for much longer. She swallowed and spoke softly. "That's not what I meant."

"Whoever your special someone is, I hope they know how lucky they are." He frowned as if her words had just registered. "What?"

"I am single." She stared at her shoes. They'd seen better days. Like most of her wardrobe. "I don't have anyone. I spend all my time looking after my father and working."

That was all true. Just not the full story, but he didn't really need to know the rest of it, did he?

"You are a remarkable woman, Theodora."

No, she wasn't. She was angry and irritable and bitter about her life. Although perhaps being away from her life had lightened that part of her enough to make him blind to it. "I'm not that remarkable."

He smiled like he was happy to placate her.

She needed air. And space. She was too close to him. Too immersed in his world too quickly. "I was planning to come see you, actually. To ask if you'd like to go for a walk. I'd like very much to get outside." The walk had been Amelia's suggestion, but Theo was firmly behind the idea now. Outside, she could have space without making it seem like she needed it because of him.

"You know I can't go far."

"No, but you could show me around the rest of the garden. You must be able to go that far. Maybe into the woods a little?"

"These woods aren't really ideal for wandering. Too dangerous."

"They are?"

He nodded. "There are lightning bugs in there that will zap you. And a variety of poisonous flora and fauna."

She frowned. And yet, he lived here.

"You're wondering why I built the house here, aren't you?"

"I am."

His eyes narrowed slightly. "The woods were nothing like this when we chose this spot."

"'We' meaning..."

"Yes. *Her*. Anyway, the enchanted forest existed, as did this area known as Dark Acres, but the day that I woke up here after losing my throne...that's the same day the woods were suddenly surrounding the house. Before then, they had been much sparser and farther away."

"You're serious."

"Very. As I told you at the mine, this town has its own magic, but then, you came through the gate, so you must know that already."

She crossed her arms. "I didn't come through so much as I went over."

"Oh?" He laughed. "I've heard the gate doesn't always open for everyone who wants it to. Doesn't mean you aren't welcome. Just that you need to work for it a little more."

She rolled her eyes. "Like everything in my life." She instantly shoved that thought down and smiled. "So if not a walk, how about a drive in that beautiful car out there?"

He lost his happy expression. "I can't go far."

"That's all right."

He took a deep breath. "I mean it."

"How far can you go?"

He grimaced, and a long silence stretched out between them before he answered. "To the end of the driveway."

"But that's not even—really? That's it?"

"Yes."

A new thought suddenly came to her. "You said you have Henry drive you, though, right? So you must be able to go farther with him, then. Let's get him to take us somewhere."

Robin's grimace remained, and he shook his head. "Henry doesn't drive me. He drives Mrs. Applestock or Mrs. Baton or Elswood if they need to go into town. Doesn't matter who's behind the wheel when I'm in the car. It stalls at the border of my reach."

He looked so miserable. Without thinking, she grabbed his hand and squeezed it. "Come on, let's go for a walk and talk about something else. Show me the rest of your garden."

He held on to her hand, suddenly looking a little less miserable. "The garden Vesta built?"

"That might be true, but it's your garden now. You should get out there and enjoy it. Plus, we might see Pepper."

He got an odd look on his face for just a moment, then he nodded. "All right, let's go. This way."

They passed a lot of doors on the way down to the opposite end of the long hall.

"How many bedrooms does this place have?"

He snorted. "Too many. These aren't all bedrooms, though. One is a sewing room; another is a guest office. There's an upstairs sitting room. All rooms I don't use. But a lot of guest rooms, too. And then there's the rear stairs."

He manually opened a door at the very end of the hall. "These are really for staff, but since no one's ever at this end of the house, they don't get used much. Maybe not at all. I'm not sure. But they're the fastest way down to the garden from here."

"Good to know." She went through the door he was holding for her. "This place is kind of a maze."

"It's easy to navigate when you have nowhere else to go."

"I'm sure that's true."

They started down. He let her go ahead of him. "How was Amelia when she left? Are you sure she wasn't mad?"

Theo answered as she hit the landing and turned

to take the second flight. "She didn't seem that way to me."

"Good." He walked down the stairs behind her. "I think I'll send her a bunch of roses anyway. She was admiring the purple ones in the garden."

"I bet she'd love that."

"I think so, too." He went ahead of her a little. "Door, open." It did, and the back patio lay before them.

"That's really a thoughtful thing to do." She squinted at him as they went outside. There was no sun, but it was still bright. "You know, you're much nicer than I thought you would be."

"Door, close," he commanded, grinning. "What were you expecting? Or shouldn't I ask that?"

"Only if you want the truth."

They strolled toward the pavilion.

"I'm fine with the truth. I prefer it. So yes, I would like to know what you expected. But I also want to know what the people of Limbo think of me. Of what they think I did. Mostly, I want to know what lies Vesta has used to poison my memory. Besides my supposed plan to sell the citizens of the kingdom into orc slavery."

Theo stopped walking as they entered the vine-covered pavilion. The shade and the sound of the fountain were nice, and the air smelled sweet from the small white flowers on the vines. She didn't want to tell him about Vesta's lies. The very thought of how he'd react made her hurt for him. "Please don't ask me that."

He turned to look at her. There was pain in his eyes. "Are they all that bad?"

She looked away, unable to find the words.

"That's answer enough." He let out a sharp, bitter laugh. "Do you have any idea how deeply it cuts to know the kingdom I loved has been turned against me?"

She glanced at him. He was staring up, but she doubted he was looking at the clusters of tiny star-shaped flowers. He was smiling in a way that showed every bit of hurt inside him. Why had she started this conversation? "I'm so sorry, Robin."

"Why should you be sorry? You didn't do this to me."

She took a step toward him, something inside her unraveling. "I'm sorry because I hate the idea of you being hurt by the things I might say. No, I didn't expect to like you, but I do. I imagined you'd be this wretched, cruel old beast of a man who was going to make my next year unbearable, but you're nothing like that. You're young and handsome, and you've been kinder and more generous to me than anyone's been since my mother died."

She took a breath. "More than that, it's clear to me that your kindness isn't an act."

The pain vanished from his face as concern took its place. "Why haven't people been kind to you?"

She barked out the same kind of laugh he had just a few moments ago. That was what he'd heard out of everything she'd said? "Because..." Time to tell him the truth. He'd learn it eventually. "Because I am not kind to them. I'm not a nice person. I'm angry and bitter, and to be perfectly honest, I'm single because no sane man in Limbo wants to saddle himself with a woman like me."

Robin frowned as though he didn't understand. "You haven't been like that here."

"Because I can't afford for you not to like me. So I've been working on my attitude and curbing my tongue. But you've made it easy to be different, too. Maybe because you didn't know what I was really like, so you treated me like anyone else. Maybe because I'm away from all the reminders of how hard my life is. I don't know."

He came closer and brushed a strand of hair off her cheek. "Why are you like that when you're home?"

She took a deep breath. Then another one. "When my mother died, the light went out of my life. Everything that was good died with her. The darkness sucked me in, and I soon realized how easy it was to give in to the anger. Especially when I realized it made people afraid of me. Made them leave me alone. I liked that better than all the pity I got for having a dead mother and a gambling father, for losing my schooling, for having to go to work so young, for all the bad hands I was dealt."

His brow bent, but he said nothing.

She sniffed. "After a while, I didn't remember how to be happy anymore. And then, in a little while longer, I didn't care, because the anger owned me. It was what kept me going. What protected me. People let me be. They started calling me Moody Middlebright."

The pain was back in his gaze, but this time it was for her. "I understand very well how the darkness can pull at you. And how anger can be the easiest thing to feel. But I am so sorry for all the bad things that have happened in your life."

She shook her head. "You're the last person who should be apologizing to me. You've had your own troubles. More than your share, really." She sighed. "How are you not a raging storm of hate and resentment?"

"I was in the early days. Still struggle with it a lot." He smiled a little. "But I can't let myself go down that path very far, or I'm not sure I'd come back. It's dark and inviting."

She nodded. "I know."

He gave her a curious look. "Maybe your coming here was what we both needed."

"Amelia said I should try to get you to have fun."

"She did, did she?"

"Yep." Sharing her truth with him had made her feel lighter, a very unexpected side effect.

He came closer, leaving very little space between them. "You know what's fun?"

She looked up at him. Into his sapphire eyes with those long, beautiful lashes. "What?"

He cupped her jaw in his hands. "This." Then he pressed his mouth to hers in a long, slow kiss. He took his time, like she was a sweet to be savored. An indulgence that he wanted to explore.

She reached out for something to hold on to, a way to steady herself from the dizziness of sudden pleasure. Her hands found his trim waist, hard with muscle beneath the thin layer of his T-shirt. She tried to think about how this shouldn't be happening, but forming thoughts was impossible, unless it was to focus on him and the firm press of his lips and the warmth of his body under her hands.

She'd never been kissed like this. Not once. And if this was what kissing was really like, she wanted more of it. From him.

Thankfully, he seemed in no hurry to be done.

Minutes later, when he ended it, she was breathless.

His smile was languid and confident. "See? Wasn't that fun?"

She nodded silently. She understood the question, but words escaped her. All she could do was...*smile*.

CHAPTER FIFTEEN

Robin wanted to kiss her again. He wanted to spend the rest of the day kissing her. But he didn't want to scare her off either. At least she looked happy. Quite the opposite of the picture she'd painted of herself. Was he the reason for that change? Perhaps. But probably best to leave things there.

He took her hand and started to walk toward the woods.

After a few moments, she said, "I don't know what to say or think about all that."

"The kissing?"

"Yes."

"Is that because you don't want me to do it again?" He braced himself for her answer.

She laughed softly, and even in the lower light of the pavilion, he could see pinkness in her cheeks. "No. If anything, I want you to do it again, more than I should."

He grinned. Good to know they were on the same page where that was concerned.

"It just feels so strange," she continued.

"You'll get used to it."

She snorted, seemingly back to her usual self. "No, I meant kissing *you*."

"Why?"

She gave him an amused look. "You were king. *My* king, for however brief a time."

If only she'd been his queen. How very different would his life be now? "I understand how that might be a bit of a sticky wicket for you, but I would prefer that you think of us as equals."

She didn't say anything for a moment, but it was clear from the worry in her gaze that something heavier was on her heart. "That's a hard thing, but I'll do my best."

He had a feeling he knew the source of that worry. "And I'll do this. I'll promise that nothing you do and nothing that happens between us will cause me to void your indenture. I know you're concerned for your father's well-being."

"I am. Thank you."

"Does that make the thought of kissing me again easier?"

She smiled. "Maybe." Her smile got a little bigger. "So, how about that party idea?"

He groaned.

"You could start small. Just a little dinner party. Amelia and her niece."

He still didn't like the idea of the awkwardness that could follow, but he wanted to make Theodora happy. "If I invite Emeranth, then I should invite her beau as well. Deacon Evermore. He's sort of the law in this town. But five is an odd number for a dinner party, isn't it? I suppose I could invite his sister, Gracie, too. She's a friend of Emeranth's, and I imagine someone you could very easily be friends with."

"Sounds perfect. How about tomorrow night?"

"I wasn't saying—" He sighed, but there was no real emotion in it. He was far too wrapped up in the feel of her hand in his to be frustrated about anything. "I suppose that would be all right. I'll have to ask Mrs. Applestock if that's enough time for her to organize and prepare everything for the meal."

"I think Mrs. Applestock will explode with happiness if you tell her she's going to get to cook for six people. And that the meal is actually going to be served in the dining room."

He laughed. "You're probably right."

She inhaled suddenly, as if she'd just realized something.

"What is it?"

"This is going to be a fancy kind of gathering, isn't it?"

"It doesn't need to be. Why?"

She looked upset. "Because this is the fanciest outfit I have, and it's not remotely fancy."

"I'm sure we can do something about that."

"You don't understand. I don't have money for clothes." She frowned harder. "I don't have money for anything."

"I'm happy to give you the money for—"

"No. Please, I don't want money from you."

"And I don't want you to worry about this. We'll find a solution. I'll speak to Amelia. I'm sure she'll have an answer." He hesitated. "We could always have a cookout. Those are casual, right?"

Theodora made a face. "And ruin Mrs. Applestock's fun? As much as I detest hand-me-downs and previously worn things, I'm also used to them. Maybe there's a charity shop in town. I do have a few dollars."

"Like I said, we'll figure something out." He wasn't about to let her fret over something like clothing. Not when he had more money than he needed and a deep desire to ease her worries. She shouldn't be spending her money anyway, not when she was working as his companion. That felt like a job that ought to come with some kind of stipend. Especially for clothing.

"All right," she said. "This is farther into the forest than I thought we'd manage."

"What?" He immediately paid attention to where they were. They'd left the pavilion and the grounds of the house behind them a while ago and were now deep into the enchanted forest. Trees surrounded them to the point that he almost couldn't see the house. He stopped dead. "This shouldn't be possible."

"It shouldn't?"

He turned to look back at the house. "We're past where I can usually—how are we so far? Why wasn't I stopped? This is…" He shook his head. "I didn't even feel anything."

"How far should you have been able to go?"

"A few feet beyond the pavilion. Not more than that." He glanced at her. "The only thing that's different is you."

"But I haven't done anything. I don't have any more magic than the average goblin."

He suspected that wasn't exactly true, but right now, he didn't care. The fact that he'd gone beyond the confines of his prison for the first time in almost twenty years overshadowed all else.

He let go of her hand and tried moving a few feet in every direction. Nothing stopped him. He held his hand out to her again. "Come on. There's something I want to try."

Minutes later, he was behind the wheel of the Packard with Theodora in the passenger seat. He hadn't driven the car in ages, but it wasn't something he could ever forget how to do. He loved this car. He'd dreamed of driving it again someday. Really driving it. Not puttering to the end of the property and back.

Henry nodded at them. "Have fun, Your Lordship."

"Thank you," Robin said. "Oh, and no more of that lordship business. I'm not your king. I'm not anyone's king."

"As you wish, your—sir."

Robin laughed, gave the man a big smile, and stepped lightly on the gas. The Packard rolled forward, and Robin hoped against all odds that what had happened in the forest was not a freak thing.

He made it out of the courtyard and down the

drive. As he approached the end, he reached for Theodora's hand again. "Just in case we have to be touching for it to work."

She smiled and took his hand. "You already proved that wasn't the case."

"Humor me."

The car rolled past the property lines and out onto the main road. A shot of joy went through him that rivaled only the sensation of kissing the woman beside him. "It worked," he breathed.

"Um, *ow*."

He glanced over. Theodora was grimacing. "What's wrong?"

She lifted their joined hands. "You're squeezing kind of hard."

"Sorry!" He let go, then braced himself to be thrown back across the road and back into his prison. It didn't happen, but he still found it hard to believe he'd broken free of his restraints. He pulled the car over onto the side of the road and parked. "Is your hand all right?"

She nodded, smiling. "I'm pretty sure you didn't break any bones."

Her teasing tone amused him. "Good to know. And good to know for sure that we don't have to be touching for this to work. Are you up for a bit of a drive?"

"I have nowhere else to be." She got a little smirk on her face. "And nowhere else I'd rather be."

"Then let's see just how far I can go." He pulled back onto the road and headed for town.

The breeze blowing past was amazing. Seeing something besides the limits of his property was equally good. But having Theodora beside him, magical, beautiful, moody Theodora, felt like a gift.

He didn't know where he was going exactly, he just knew he wanted to drive until there was no more road left to travel. Wherever that took him. Maybe all the way to the gate.

As they went, he realized he didn't know much about the town he called home. He'd never been able to explore it. Sure, he'd seen a little in the very beginning, while they were building the house, but most of his time then had been spent at the house supervising things.

And he knew a little from Amelia, but hearing someone talk about a place was no substitute for visiting.

Now he had not only a chance to see it for himself but company to visit with. He gave Theodora a quick look. "I may never want to go back."

Her eyes were narrowed in his direction. "Is this your way of getting out of the dinner party?"

He laughed. "No, but now that you mention it, I guess I should send the invites before I talk to Mrs. Applestock. If people can't come, there's no reason to get her all worked up."

"Robin, when was the last time you had a dinner party?"

He had a feeling he knew where she was headed. "Never."

Theodora seemed to be barely suppressing a grin.

"People will come. I promise you, this isn't something they're going to miss."

"I suppose you're right. Plus, I can't see Amelia being unable to attend when she was all for it."

The car suddenly stalled and started to slow. He pulled off to the side before it came to a complete stop. He didn't know anything about cars, but he knew a lot about his curse. One almost slipped from his lips.

"What happened?" Theodora asked.

"I have an idea." He exited the vehicle, then walked forward with his arms out. He'd barely gone two feet when his hands touched the invisible wall he knew so well. "My barriers aren't gone. Just moved. For some reason."

The realization hit him like a crushing blow. He sat on the hood of the car, closed his eyes, and pressed his hands over his face.

He heard Theodora get out, then felt her hand on his shoulder. "I'm sorry."

He nodded but said nothing. His mood had gone from jubilant to vile in a split second, and he didn't want that to spill over onto her. This wasn't her fault.

"I know you're upset. I am, too. It's okay to be upset. This stinks." She hesitated. "Worse than an eel gone belly up in the Fangmore moat."

He snorted, despite his mood. Then he sighed and lifted his head. "I really thought the restrictions were gone."

She nodded. "I did, too. But maybe…this is just the beginning."

"The beginning of what?"

"I mean, maybe the barriers are degrading. Maybe tomorrow you'll be able to go a little farther. And farther still the day after that."

He gave her a long look. "You're awfully optimistic for someone with the nickname Moody."

She made a face at him. "I blame you."

He laughed, but it was short-lived and ended in a sigh. "I am very disappointed. Gutted, actually."

She leaned against the hood, slightly closer to him than she was before. "We could spend the rest of the day reading in the library. Or whatever you think would make you happy."

"Reading would be nice." He straightened. "I guess we should go back anyway. I need to tell Mrs. Applestock about the dinner party."

She smiled. "I'm really glad you're going through with that. You know, when you call Amelia to invite her, you might ask her what she thinks is going on with the barriers. You said she's a powerful witch. She must be to have created this town. She might have a way to test the magic. See if it's weakening."

"Not a bad idea." He smiled. And meant it. "Thanks, Moody."

She nodded. "Anytime, Your Lordship."

He shook his head in amusement. "We're probably going to have to push the car back a bit to get it to start again."

"No problem." She put her hands on the hood.

He did the same, and together they moved the car a few yards. "That should do it. Let's see if it'll start now."

They got back into the car. He turned the key. The engine sparked to life. He did a quick three-point turn and got them headed for home.

She was good for him, no question about it. If he'd been out for this drive on his own and run into the wall…he knew how dark his mood could get. And how fast.

But now he was actually looking forward to testing the barriers again tomorrow, instead of losing himself in revenge fantasies against Vesta.

Not that he still wouldn't love for her to tumble into the moat and get devoured by the eels, or have some other fortuitous accident befall her, but with Theodora around, he cared a lot less about what happened to Vesta.

All because his present was much more interesting.

Which made him think about a brand-new problem. What was he going to do when Theodora's year was up?

CHAPTER SIXTEEN

Theo felt for Robin so much that she ached inside. She hid it, though, for his sake, because he didn't need a pity party from her. He needed a distraction. It made her happy that when they returned the car to Henry, Robin had said they'd be back to take it out again tomorrow.

That seemed promising to her.

They went inside together and straight to the kitchen. Mrs. Applestock was up on a stepladder, wiping down the upper cabinets.

She smiled at them when they entered. "Good afternoon, Your Lordship. Theodora."

She climbed down and stuck the rag she'd been using into her apron pocket. "Hungry?"

Robin helped himself to one of the lemon muffins cooling on a rack. He peeled off the paper cup. "No, but I do have something I'd like to talk to you about."

"Oh?" She walked around to the same side of the island that he was on. "What is it, Your Lordship?"

He swallowed the bite he'd just taken. "I'd like to address everyone in the staff room, please."

"Right away, Sire. I was just getting ready to call everyone into the gathering room for lunch."

"Perfect."

She went over and pushed the first button on a wall panel. Soft tones followed. It was the first time Theo had heard the intercom system, although Mrs. Baton had mentioned it.

"Thank you, Mrs. Applestock," Robin said. He tipped his head at Theo. "You should have one of these muffins. They're really good."

She took one. "Is this our lunch?"

"Oh my, no," Mrs. Applestock said. "I made sandwiches. I was just going to put them out for the staff."

Robin finished his muffin. "Sounds good. I could eat something more substantial."

Mrs. Applestock frowned. "But you don't want the same lunch I made for the staff."

"Sure I do. Give me the platter, and I'll carry it to the gathering room."

She did as he asked, getting an enormous platter of sandwiches from one of the refrigerators. He took it and off he went.

Theo followed, with Mrs. Applestock behind her. He took the chair at the head of the table, which was already laid out with potato chips, a tray of cold vegetables, and pitchers of water and iced tea. Theo sat beside him. Mrs. Applestock sat on the other side, looking a little unsure.

He and Theo filled their plates.

Before long, Lolly, Mrs. Baton, and Elswood came in. Right behind them were Henry and Fenwick.

Robin gestured toward the remaining chairs. "Please, fill your plates, then have a seat."

Theo watched their strained expressions. It was her guess he hadn't addressed all of them like this in a long time. If ever. And certainly not while joining them for a meal.

Once they were all seated, he gave them an easy smile. Good start, she thought. Lolly seemed to find it reassuring, although Baton and Elswood didn't unclench in the slightest. Henry and Fenwick were busy eating.

Robin put his hands on the table. "Thank you for letting me interrupt your lunch. I have two things I'd like to discuss with you all. First, however, I want to thank you all for your service here. It is very much appreciated."

"Oh Judas," Lolly breathed out. "Are we getting the ax?"

Fenwick froze, a chip inches from his mouth.

"Lolly," Mrs. Baton hissed.

"No," Robin said. "I assure you that is not what's happening. I just wanted you to know I am grateful for your hard work."

Lolly slanted her eyes at Mrs. Baton, but aimed her words at Robin. "Thank you, Your Lordship."

Fenwick went back to eating.

"That's actually the first thing I want to speak to you about. The titles. It's time for them to go. I haven't been king in many years, and calling me sire and lordship and grace just seem foolish now."

Elswood's mouth fell open. Mrs. Baton tutted. Henry's mouth ticked up in a grin as he chewed. Mrs. Applestock smiled. "As you wish, sir. Is that all right? Sir?"

"Sir is fine. Or Mr. Gallow. Or even Robin."

"Sir it is," Fenwick said.

"Well, I never!" Mrs. Baton looked like she was about to become apoplectic. "That's highly improper."

Robin's smile seemed to thin. "It would be, if I was king. But I'm not. I'm not even nobility. I was common-born. And I'm done holding on to a past I will never regain."

Mrs. Applestock lifted one shoulder. "I don't think I'd feel comfortable calling you by your given name. Sir'll do for me, Your Lordsh—that is, sir, I mean."

"Excellent." He looked at Elswood. "Did you want to say something?"

Elswood shook his head. "It's your house. Your rules, Sire." He sighed. "But it's going to take a bit of getting used to."

"I can understand that." Robin's smile returned to full strength. "The next order of business is, tomorrow night I am having a dinner party."

Mrs. Applestock squealed with the kind of joy normally reserved for life-changing surprises. But then, Theo wondered if a dinner party wasn't exactly that for someone like her. "Oh, that is marvelous news. Marvelous. How many?"

"Six."

She clapped her hands. "Splendid. Formal? How many courses?"

His mouth bunched to one side. "Not too formal." He looked at Theo. "What do you think about the number of courses?"

She knew immediately that him consulting with her on this party was going to ruffle a few feathers. Namely Baton's and Elswood's. She smiled. "I think Mrs. Applestock can answer that better than I can."

"You're probably right." He turned to the older woman. "What do you think?"

She tapped her chin. "If you want to keep it simple, how about soup, main course, dessert. I can do a few canapes, too. Although I feel those can ruin a person's appetite sometimes."

"Three courses sounds perfect." He gestured at Elswood. "You'll coordinate the wine with Mrs. Applestock's menu?"

Elswood nodded. "I will."

"Henry, will you valet the cars?"

"Absolutely."

Robin went on. "Mrs. Baton, I'm sure the dining room is in perfect shape already, since it's never been used, but I'll leave the table setting up to you."

She nodded. "Thank you, sir." Then she smiled, something that caught Theo by surprise. "It will be lovely to see the good china and crystal put to proper use. What kind of flowers would you like?"

He shrugged. "Whatever's blooming in the garden. Fenwick, can you help with that?"

"Happy to, sir."

"Thank you," Robin said. "Which reminds me, please send a bouquet of the purple roses to Amelia Marchand with my regards." He planted his hands on the table. "Any questions before I let you finish your lunch?"

Elswood raised a finger. "May I ask, sir, what brought all this on?"

Robin glanced at Theo, his smile wide and bright. "I just realized it's time for a change." He stood, making all of them get to their feet, and picked up his plate. "If anyone needs me, Theodora and I will be in the library. Oh, and, Elswood, I realize this might make more work for all of you, especially with Theodora's terms of service changing, so please, if you need to, hire some extra help. Wherever it's needed."

Elswood gave him a little bow. "Yes, sir."

"Good. That is all." Plate in one hand and a drink in the other, he gave Theo a sweet look. "Shall we?"

She wasn't totally comfortable with such familiarity in front of the rest of the staff, but it was nice to see him so happy. "Are you going to make your calls to invite people before we go to the library?"

He nodded. "I should, yes. Let's go to my quarters. I'll use the phone there. And we can finish our lunch on the balcony."

"All right." His quarters? As in his bedroom. Where he slept. The idea sent the strangest sensation through her, like she was about to enter some secret, forbidden place. In a way, that was true. His private rooms were just that—private.

But it was more than that. She was about to get a glimpse of who he was when he was alone. A person's private space spoke volumes about them.

They went up the steps and past the library to a set of double doors at the end of the hall. He balanced his plate on top of his glass so he could open one. He held it for her to enter ahead of him. She went in. The foyer felt very much like him. Dark and serene, all deep blues and plums with hints of gold. Very royal and very masculine.

Immediately across from the entrance was the Gallow crest, lit by a gentle spotlight. On either side of the crest were sets of double doors. One set was already open.

He pointed through those doors. "The phone is in the living room right through here."

"Don't you want some privacy?"

He shrugged. "I don't mind. But I'll show you the balcony. You might as well eat while you wait on me. I'm sure I won't be long."

"All right." She walked with him into the living room, which wasn't much more than a massive sofa, a large ottoman, and an enormous television. "Great setup for movies."

He nodded. "It is. Which is probably why I never use the theater."

"But that must have a bigger screen."

"It does. I suppose we should start using it.

There's a popcorn machine and soda fountain in there, too."

"You could invite the rest of the staff. Might be fun for them. If you wanted to, obviously." Maybe that was overstepping. He might not want to spend time with the staff like that.

He gave her suggestion a few seconds of thought. "I love that idea. In fact, the night after the dinner party would be perfect. A little evening off after the extra work." He took her hand. "Although, a movie night for just the two of us has merit as well."

She smiled.

He tipped his head toward the next room. "Balcony is just through here."

So was his bed, an enormous nest of a thing with a swooping canopy that connected the four tall posters. He went right past it to the sets of French doors on the far wall.

He opened one pair, then turned. "My balcony. A little grander than the one attached to your guest room, but I do spend a lot of time out here."

She walked through. His balcony was the size of all of his rooms combined. "It's an amazing space."

"I think so, too." He hooked his thumb over his shoulder. "I'll just go call Amelia, and then after lunch, we can do nothing but read for the rest of the day."

"I'll be right here."

He went to make his call. She put her food and drink on the small table, then walked to the railing and looked out over the garden. It was a beautiful space. From above, the pavilion with its blossoming vines looked like a raft of flowers. They were so thick they hid the fountain, although if she listened closely, she could hear it. That garden was all that separated the house from the encroaching forest. She stared into the murky depths of the thick woods, intrigued.

At home in Limbo, the forest that surrounded the kingdom was her refuge. When life got too burdensome, which was often, she'd slip outside and wander into the woods until she found a spot just to sit.

Once, she'd gone starstone hunting. They were usually found in the very early morning after a hard rain. The rain had an effect on the sap of the elestia trees, and if the temperature was right, starstones formed. They were such pretty things. Like a translucent silver pearl. When faceted and polished, they were dazzling.

Working at a bakery meant her early morning hours were rarely her own, so that hunting trip had happened only once. Still, that single hunt had earned her a week's pay for the two stones she'd found. That money had given them a little breathing room with one of her father's collectors.

Her gaze dropped to the balcony as her thoughts turned to him. She hoped he was all right. That his health was good and that he hadn't given in to the urge to wager money they didn't have.

"Theodora?"

She looked up. "Sorry, lost in thought."

Robin came to her side, carrying his plate and drink. "I see that. Everything all right?"

"I was just thinking about my father. Could I write him a letter? You have a way to get mail to Limbo, don't you?"

Robin nodded. "We do. And you can write one in the library. Everything you need is in the rolltop desk by the reference section."

"Thank you." She felt better already. "Is everything set for dinner?"

"It is." He went to the table and put his meal down. "Amelia was thrilled and promised me that she'd take care of inviting Deacon and his sister."

"That's wonderful." She bit her lip. She still didn't have anything to wear that wasn't jeans or leggings. Hopefully, that would be fine.

One of his brows lifted. "Really? Because that's not what your face is saying."

"Nope, I think it's great."

He gave her a look. "Theodora."

"You should call me Theo. Theodora seems so formal, and now that I'm calling you Robin—"

He smiled. "Stop trying to change the subject, Theo. What's bothering you? Besides your father."

She sighed. "I'm just thinking everyone else is going to be dressed nicer than me."

"Ah, yes. We haven't done anything about that, have we?" He took her hand. "I have something to show you."

CHAPTER SEVENTEEN

Robin had a feeling Theodora might not like what he was about to show her, and he completely understood if that was her reaction. He didn't like it either. Despite that, he'd done nothing about it in all the years he'd lived here.

He led her back to the foyer entrance of his quarters and through the doors opposite the ones that opened into his personal space. He wasn't sure how many years it had been since he'd entered these other rooms. He knew Mrs. Baton kept the apartment clean, but other than that, he did his best to ignore its contents.

He opened the doors and walked through, Theo at his side. Gone were the deep blues and royal purples that he favored. Instead, these rooms were all about the pale greens and aqua blues that had been the queen's signature colors. He took a breath, then wished he hadn't. Her perfume still lingered faintly. "This was Vesta's side."

Theo looked around. "The space is gorgeous. I don't want to like it, but I do." She made an apologetic face. "Sorry."

"It's all right." He supposed it was very pretty. To him, it just reminded him of *her*. "She left a lot behind. Anything personal, I assume she took. What's here is mostly clothing, jewelry, shoes, some knickknacks, cosmetics, things like that. Anyway, I thought maybe some of the clothing might be useful to you."

Theo's brows went up. "Are you suggesting that I borrow some of the queen's things for the dinner party?"

"Absolutely. Why not? She clearly doesn't care. If any of it meant anything, she would have taken it with her."

"But these are…the queen's things."

"Does that matter? Because it doesn't matter to me. In fact, I should have thrown all of this out years ago."

"You would have thrown all of her stuff away?"

"In a heartbeat."

Her brows crept slightly higher. "Why haven't you? You obviously have no love for her anymore."

He snorted. "As if that was even possible." He surveyed the space. "I guess I've left it all because ignoring it was easier. And in the beginning, I might have thought she was going to come back and confess that it was all a bad dream."

How idiotic he'd been.

He shook his head, disgusted at himself. How had he ever cared for her? "I was so young and so foolish. I should never have trusted her."

Theo frowned as if it bothered her to see him upset. "Don't do that to yourself. Yes, you were young, but you were supposed to trust her. She was your wife. And the marriage was intended to bring the two kingdoms together. How were you to know she had other ideas?"

"I guess." Her concern was like a spring breeze, reminding him that there was still good in the world. He stared at the space before them. "I realize you may have different tastes from Vesta, but do you think you can find something to wear?"

"I'll have to see what's left, but I'm sure there will be something I can adapt. I'm all right with a needle and thread, if need be. And we're about the same size. Or we used to be."

"Used to be? Did she finally grow that two inches she always wished for?"

"Not vertically. Her Royal Highness has developed quite a fondness for butter cakes and pulled-sugar sweets. Her figure is a good deal rounder than it once was."

He couldn't care less what Vesta looked like now. "Maybe that's why she didn't come back for these things. Or send for them. They won't fit her anymore."

Theo shrugged. "Maybe sending for them or coming back for them would, in her mind, be admitting she needed or wanted anything associated with you. If that makes sense."

"It does."

"But I can't imagine she'd ever return here. Considering what she did to you, she should be too afraid to do that."

"I hate her with every living inch of my being, but I would never lift a hand against her. Unless she attacked first."

Theo pondered that. "I'd say she's already attacked you."

He couldn't argue with that. "True. But I would never try to harm her. I wouldn't hesitate to tell her what I think of her, though."

Theo seemed less interested in the contents of the room than she had just a second ago. "This is a very generous offer, and one I will take you up on, but I'd like to eat my lunch, then write that letter to my father before I look through the clothing. If that's all right."

"Of course it's all right. Let's eat, then we'll go to the library, and I'll get you what you need."

They finished their lunch quickly, then went to the library. In a few minutes, he'd shown her where the stationery was in the desk and which drawer held the pens. She got to work on the letter immediately, head down, pen clutched just so, the tip of her tongue peeking out of her mouth.

He settled into a nearby chair with the book he'd been reading, a biography on a scientist that interested him. Every once in a while, he'd glance up at her. Sometimes, she'd be writing away. Other times, the tip of the pen would hover over the paper while she seemed to be searching for the right word.

It was utterly charming.

At last, he looked up to see her standing next to

him, a sealed, addressed envelope in her hand. "All done."

"Put it in the chute. That goes directly to Mrs. Baton's office. She'll mail it. She handles all the mail."

Theo scanned the room. "Where's the chute?"

He pointed. "By the bellpull. Near the door."

"I see it. Thank you." With a smile, she started in that direction.

"And then are you going to look through Vesta's clothes?"

Her smiled faltered. "You're really sure you're okay with me doing that?"

"Absolutely. Are you okay with it?"

She squinted just a little. "I think I am. Honestly, I'm not sure. I guess I'll know when I get in there."

"Well, if you decide there's nothing there you can use, that's fine. But I do think it's high time I put Baton to work cleaning it all out."

Theo took a breath. "Okay. I definitely need something to wear to this dinner party, so I can't afford to turn this opportunity down. I'm sure I can make something in there work." She stuck her letter in the chute, then turned back to him and gave a little wave. "Off to see what's what. You know where to find me."

But she didn't go anywhere, and he realized she still had an air of trepidation about her. He suddenly understood what she must be feeling. Vesta had been his enemy for years, but until a few days ago, Vesta had been Theodora's queen. Under those circumstances, how could she not feel strange about digging through the woman's closet, no matter how long it had been since Vesta had cared about those things?

He closed his book. "How about I come with you and then go read on my balcony? That way, if you need me, I won't be far. Would that make you feel better?"

Theo exhaled, nodding. "I think it would. Especially if I have a question about something."

He stood and tucked his book under his arm. "Say no more. I completely understand. Let's go."

Together, they walked back to his quarters. In the foyer, he opened the doors to Vesta's side, leaving them wide open. "If you need me, I'm just a shout away."

"Thank you. This is really very kind of you, even if you say you don't care about these things."

"I don't. But you're still welcome. Have fun." He went off to read, wondering what Theo would make of Vesta's castoffs.

If Theo couldn't find anything in those deep closets, he'd have Henry drive her into town to go shopping. No companion of his was going to help host a dinner party feeling less than her best if he could help it. And he could.

There was something utterly surreal about standing alone in the midst of Queen Vesta's quarters. Theo would have been lying if she'd said there wasn't the tiniest element of fear involved. Vesta did that to a person.

But Vesta was a world away. And Theo's curiosity quickly squelched any remaining fear. She was bursting to explore. To see what Vesta had considered too insignificant to take with her. Part of Theo felt like she was about to read the woman's diary. There was definitely a personal, private nature to all of this.

Then again, these quarters represented the Vesta of nearly twenty years ago. Not exactly the woman who ruled Limbo now. And yet, that woman had been the one who'd poisoned Robin and turned his people against him. How different could she be?

Theo wandered through the sitting room. Unlike Robin's quarters, there were very few books here. A few of the coffee table kind, the big weighty things filled with pictures, but that was it. Robin, on the other hand, had a stack of books on his nightstand and another on the floor beside the bed.

Could it be that Vesta had taken her books with her? Or was it just that reading wasn't her thing?

Theo felt she knew the answer to that one.

She went to the double doors that probably led into the bedroom and opened them. Indeed, the bedroom lay beyond. All the same colors that were in the sitting room adorned the space, though a few shades deeper and with more touches of gold and crystals.

The bedroom was, in a word, gaudy. Mostly because of the bed. The tall, upholstered headboard was done in white velvet. The tufts were each accented with a glittering crystal surrounded in gold. The bed linens were shiny white satin finished with gold thread. And the coverlet, also white satin, was quilted with an enormous gold V embroidered in the center.

Theo put her hands on her hips. "That's not over the top at all."

With a bed like that, what on earth was she going to find in the closet? There was only one way to find out. She started looking around. There was a small balcony, nothing like the one accessible from Robin's side, but maybe his balcony was so large because they'd been meant to share it.

Another set of double doors stood at the far end of the room. Theo headed in that direction.

But there was no closet behind them. Instead, Theo found the queen's bathroom, which was as extravagant as the bedroom. Maybe more. In part because it had a soaking tub shaped like a swan and gold faucets at the tub, sink, and shower that also resembled swans. The floor was a mosaic of blue tiles in different hues, to look like water. Every so often, a green lily-pad-shaped tile broke up the blue. A few had pale pink flowers painted on them.

Vesta liked a theme.

Theo left the bathroom to look for the closet again. That's when she realized that the mirrors on the wall across from the bed might actually be doors. It seemed at least one of them was.

"Closet door, open." One of the mirrors swung

wide, and a light came on, illuminating the room beyond.

Theo went through. And stared in amazement. Vesta's closet was larger than the house Theo had grown up in. The same house she still shared with her father.

She walked in a little farther. Perhaps the closet just looked so large because it wasn't completely full. Which wasn't to say it was empty. Enough clothes filled the closet to open a small boutique. But it would have taken three times as much clothing, shoes, and accessories to call the massive closet full.

Besides the racks around the walls, a large square island of drawers sat dead center. On top of that was a display of hats on stands. Past that was a sitting area with two plush velvet chairs in the same aqua as the bedroom walls, a bench, a dividing wall that was all shelves of shoes and handbags, and a large three-panel mirror across from the chairs. In front of those mirrors was a raised platform. Apparently so that whoever was on the platform could see themselves better. It felt like something a queen would have.

Theo stood there a moment and had a long look around, turning slowly as she studied it all. She wasn't sure where to start.

Not because of the size of the space, but because she didn't really know what people wore to a dinner party at the home of a former king. A dress seemed like the logical option. But what length? What color? How formal?

Without answers to any of that, she stared at the array of clothing before her until the colors started to blur. There was too much choice. Being clueless about what was expected at such an event wasn't helping either.

Although, maybe she was putting the cart before the horse a bit. She didn't even know if any of these things would fit her. Probably the best idea was to find something she didn't hate and try it on.

She started looking through the rack closest to her. Thankfully, the majority of what was in the closet was dresses. The closet was also fairly well organized by style. Blouses were all together, as were coats, pants, skirts, etc. But the biggest category was dresses.

Vesta did wear them often. Theo thought back to all the times she'd seen the queen during her public appearances. Always a gown of some kind. Maybe that was a protocol thing? Theo wasn't sure, but it was working in her favor now.

She decided she'd start with the shorter ones since those were all in the front anyway. Day length, she thought those were called. But then, what did she know about such things? If there was nothing in the shorter dresses, gowns were at the end.

Most of what Theo picked through was spangled and embellished to the point she was surprised the fabric could hold up under the weight of the additions. Fairies were well known for their love of all things sparkly, although her mother had been rather conservative in that area.

Perhaps because their budget hadn't allowed for such extravagance. Or maybe wearing a uniform to work every day had tempered her desire for anything too excessive.

Either way, Theo's tastes were definitely on the simpler side as well. She paused at an emerald-green dress with gold braiding spiraling around the neckline and down the front. Glittering rhinestones accented the spaces between the braiding. She squinted, trying to see past the abundance of extras.

The dress had a good shape and was made of heavy silk, giving it structure. Might as well start here, she thought.

She stripped down to her underwear and got into the dress, then went to the three-paneled mirror at the back of the closet for a look.

She stepped onto the platform and smiled, despite all the nonsense sewn onto the dress. She hadn't seen herself in anything this fancy in...pretty much ever. But whether the dress fit well enough to work was what mattered, and it did.

The green was a possibility. It kind of matched her eyes, and with her dark hair, a jewel tone seemed like a good choice. Plus, her mother's starstone-and-emerald necklace went perfectly with it. Satisfied, she took the dress off, laid it over one of the chairs near the mirrors, and went back to digging.

Almost everything in Vesta's closet was over-embellished, too ruffled, or spangled with abandon. Thankfully, Theo felt confident that in most cases, the excess could be removed without harming the actual garment.

After what seemed like forever, she made her way through the day-length dresses and ended up at the gowns. She didn't think she'd need a long dress, but just in case, she picked through those as well.

About a quarter of the way into them, she came across a gown that stopped her in her tracks.

The strapless gown hung by ribbons from its hanger. The color shifted from steely blue to dusky silver in an ombré effect that repeated over and over. Same-color sequins dusted the fabric with subtle sparkle, reminding Theo of stars in the evening sky. The dress was absolutely beautiful and shockingly understated, which made it seem out of place in the sea of wild gowns.

Maybe that was why this one still had the tags attached. She reached for the little rectangle of white paper to look at the price.

She lost the ability to breathe for about two seconds. Nearly five figures? Was that right? Could a dress be that expensive? That kind of money could have given her another year of schooling.

She dropped the tag. Suddenly, not touching the dress seemed like a good idea. How did anyone leave such a thing behind? It had to be that Vesta had simply forgotten about it. But who forgot about a gown that had cost so much? Theo couldn't fathom it.

And yet, here the gown was, buried in a closet of things that had been abandoned nearly twenty years ago. Robin was right. None of this clothing meant anything to the queen anymore. Otherwise, she'd have come back for them. Or asked him to send them to her.

And if this dress had cost so much, what did that say about the rest of the things hanging here?

New anger sprang up in Theo. Perhaps because of the excess of it all. Of course, Vesta was the queen, and excess and royalty seemed to go hand in hand. What did a gown like this mean to her? Probably nothing. Or perhaps Theo's anger was because her own wardrobe barely filled two drawers. The inequity was staggering. But then, Vesta didn't have a father who gambled away most of the money required to maintain even a minimal standard of living.

A new thought came to Theo. One that felt rebellious and a little wrong, but also like something that needed to be done. This dress didn't need to be left untouched and unappreciated. It needed to be worn.

Theo grabbed the gown's hanger and pulled the dress free.

CHAPTER EIGHTEEN

Robin had read the same page three times. Actually, he'd *tried* to read the same page three times. Each attempt he'd only gotten about halfway through the first sentence before his mind wandered to Theo.

She'd been in Vesta's quarters for a bit now. It was pretty quiet over there, too. Not once had she called for him or come over to see him about anything. Did that mean it was going well? Or was she on the verge of giving up, completely put off by the idea that she wear something that had once belonged to the queen?

Either way, his curiosity demanded he find out. He put his bookmark between the pages, set the book on the small table beside the chaise, and went to check on her.

When he got to the doors, he knocked softly, even though they were already open. He didn't want to startle her or catch her undressed. "Theo?"

She called back, "In here."

He stuck his head into the room but didn't see

her. She sounded muffled. Was she in the closet? He took a single step into the sitting room. He could just see the open closet door. "Just wanted to see how you're doing."

She peeked out from the closet. "I'm, um, okay, I guess. Probably a little overdressed at the moment."

"Oh?" He could see her only from the neck up. The rest of her was in the closet. "Can I see?"

She hesitated. "I guess so. Please don't laugh. I'm not wearing this for the dinner. I just wanted to try it on."

"Okay." He couldn't wait to see what she'd picked.

She stepped out into the bedroom, and he lost the ability to speak because of how beautiful she looked. He couldn't even close his mouth, which currently hung slightly open with all the grace and dignity of a swamp dweller.

"Isn't it pretty?" She did a quick twirl, holding up the dress just enough for him to see the heels she'd chosen. "I know, I look silly, but this dress is just so spectacular, and it still had the tags on it, so—"

"Silly is the last word I'd use for how you look right now. Amazing would be my choice." The strapless dress showed off her shapely shoulders and arms. And bust. It hugged her figure down to the waistline, where the skirt flowed out around her. She looked as regal as any noblewoman he'd ever seen. "You're *not* wearing that for the dinner party?"

"I think it's too fancy, don't you?" She stopped twirling, looking very confused. "You really think this looks nice on me?"

"Not nice. Amazing. You're beautiful in it. But you make that dress. Without you in it, it would just be another evening gown."

"That's very kind. Thank you. I've never worn anything like this in my life." Then she laughed as she glanced toward the closet. "I've never worn anything like most of those dresses in there."

"Vesta liked a certain style of clothing, that much I remember."

Theo nodded. "She definitely went for the flashy stuff. But I've never been a dress girl either. Which brings me back to this one. Don't you think this is too formal? What are you going to wear for the dinner?"

He hadn't thought about it really. "I guess a suit with a dress shirt? No tie. That would be too formal. So yes, the dress would be, too." Such a shame. She needed to be seen in that dress. Seen and admired. Maybe he should host something grander than a dinner party.

Had there ever been a ball in Shadowvale?

She frowned at the closet. "That's what I figured. It's fine. There's a lot in there, and I have a few other things that will probably work. Like I said, I just couldn't resist trying this on. Especially because it still had the tags on it." Her brows lifted conspiratorially. "Do you have any idea how much this dress cost? I probably shouldn't have it on at all."

"No idea. Vesta spent money like the kingdom had an unlimited supply." Which was almost true. The kingdom was wealthy enough because of their mines, much like Shadowvale, but that didn't require Vesta to spend it all. Ruling responsibly was apparently not her style. Shocking, that.

Theo's voice was low and serious. "Nine thousand dollars. And that was twenty years ago."

His brows lifted. "That is quite a sum. Chances are it was given to her, however. Lots of those clothes were."

"Really?"

He nodded. "That's how being royal works sometimes."

"So those who need the least are given the most." She rolled her eyes. "That's just great."

"Well, the dress is yours now." He couldn't imagine another woman in it. No other woman could do justice to it the way Theo did.

For a moment, she looked shocked. Then she spoke. "Thank you. But what on earth will I do with it? I don't have any place to wear a dress like this."

"Wear it for a stroll in the garden for all I care, but it's yours. When you look like that in something, you should have it. And that's that." But already, a new idea was percolating in his head. If this dinner party went well, there was no reason not to attempt something bigger and grander.

He sat on the bench at the end of the bed. It was the same hideous white velvet as the headboard. "Now, if you're not going to wear that to dinner, what do you think might work?"

Her brows lifted. "You want to see the dresses I'm considering?"

He sat back, resting his elbows on the bed. "If you want to show them to me, I'd be happy to have a look."

Her smile broadened. "Okay. Give me a few minutes to change."

She disappeared into the depths of the closet. A short time later, she reappeared in a heavily embellished green number.

He took a moment to choose his words carefully. "I like the color. And the dress fits you very nicely. But..." He waved his finger at the gold braiding that looked like some kind of wayward sea creature attempting to devour her neck. "That's a *lot*."

"Yeah, I know. It needs some decluttering. Most of them do." She spread her arms. "Otherwise, it's not too bad. Thankfully, most of the sizes are compatible." She glanced down at the simple black pumps she had on. "And some of the shoes are too small, but I've found a few pairs that work."

"You know," he said, "you would look good in a flour sack."

With a little laugh, she put her hands on her hips. "Maybe I should see if Mrs. Applestock has one."

He grinned. "She might. But how about you try the next dress on instead?"

They spent another hour or so like that, and he would have been willing to stay longer, watching her parade out in Vesta's abandoned things. The queen had never looked as good in them, and in the end, Robin gave all of it to Theo. Not just the things she'd tried on, but everything that Vesta had left behind.

He put her in charge of getting rid of it, too. Whatever she didn't want, she was to let Mrs. Baton know it needed to be cleared out.

"I can do that," she said. "But would you mind if I let her, Lolly, and Mrs. Applestock have a look through, too? There might be something in here they could use."

"Lolly I could see, but Mrs. Applestock is a bit rounder and shorter, and Mrs. Baton is too tall and grumpy."

Theo laughed. "Grumpiness doesn't affect size."

"No, but can you see her in any of those exuberant things?"

"Not even remotely, but much like I plan to do, she might be able to remake some of them. And Mrs. Applestock might like a handbag or a hat. Possibly a blouse."

He shrugged good-naturedly. "Do whatever you like. It's your project. When you're not working on your lapidary lessons. Which start next week, by the way. I've set it all up with the local guild in town. Henry will drive you to their hall, and you'll do your lessons there."

She took a breath and put her hand flat on her stomach. She was wearing a navy blue dress with giant red and pink silk flowers on it. "I can't believe that's actually happening. I'm so excited to get started. Thank you."

"You're welcome."

"Sir?" Elswood's voice rang out in the foyer.

"In here, Elswood."

The man came in. Not the briefest hint of curiosity showed on his face, but Robin had to assume he was wondering what was going on. After all, Robin hadn't set foot on this side of the apartment in at least a decade. Probably longer.

Elswood gave a short bow. "Dinner will be ready in an hour, sir. Does that suit you?"

Robin hadn't realized how late in the day it was already. "That's fine, but I'd like it served in the family dining room this evening. Two place settings, you understand."

Something—whether it was the dinner's location or the addition of a place for Theo—caused a modicum of a rise in Elswood's brows. "I understand. Very good, sir. I'll let Mrs. Baton know. Also, if I may?"

"Go on."

"As per your suggestion, two new staff have been brought on. A second housekeeper and a footman. We may only need them part time, but Mrs. Baton and I thought it wise to at least get them trained and ready."

"That's fine." Robin looked at the mantel clock. The time seemed right. Baton must keep it wound. "We'll be down for dinner in an hour."

Elswood nodded. "Very good." Then he bowed and left.

Robin made a note to remind the staff that he didn't want them bowing to him anymore. But that could be done later. Right now, he had news to share. "Theo?"

She popped out of the closet, back in her jeans and T-shirt. "Yes?"

"You have about fifty-five minutes to put that ball gown and shoes back on and do whatever else you need to to get ready for dinner." He stood. "I'll meet you by the Gallow crest then. I have to get myself dressed, too."

"Is it dinner already? I feel like we just had lunch."

"That was almost five hours ago."

"Really? Time flies." She made a face. "Wait a second. You want me to wear a ball gown to eat in the kitchen?"

He smiled. "We're not eating in the kitchen. We're having dinner in the small dining room. Just you and me. In nice clothes." He shrugged. "Why not?"

She blinked twice before answering him. "All right. Fifty-five minutes."

*

Dinner with Robin in a dining room sounded lovely.

But she didn't need fifty-five minutes to put that dress and those shoes back on. Maybe with the extra time, she'd do something with her hair. Maybe dig through the rest of Vesta's stuff for some earrings or a bracelet. Both good ideas.

Which didn't explain why she was just staring at herself in the closet's three-panel mirror. Was this a date? It sounded like a date.

But no. Definitely not. She was Robin's companion. He just wanted company for dinner. But that didn't explain why she was putting on a ball gown and heels and why they were eating in one of the dining rooms.

Because that bit sounded very much like a date.

She'd gone on a date once. Three times, actually. All with Pinter Crossgrove, an apprentice fishmonger. He was, as her father had joked more than once, a good catch. Despite the fact that he was an apprentice, the shop was his father's, so eventually he'd own it.

Fishmongers made good money. Pinter was a decent-looking fellow and had nice manners. Plus he'd been able, as her father had also joked, to overlook Theo's crabbiness. So she'd gone out with him, thinking she'd eventually get used to the constant scent of salt and sea.

But Pinter had wanted a wife, and Theo couldn't leave her father. Nor could she expect Pinter to take her father in, because that would mean taking on her father's debts. Those burdens were hers and hers alone.

So as nice as Pinter was, things between them had disintegrated quickly. All for the best, she'd told herself.

But her inability to make things work with him somehow made her tarnished goods in the eyes of the other eligible men in town. At least those who'd been willing to put up with her attitude for a date.

Or maybe they'd realized the truth about the

breakup. Theodora Middlebright came with a heavy paternal burden.

What man wanted that? None, apparently. And that realization had added to Theo's bad attitude and bitter outlook. Her nickname had taken on new strength after her breakup with Pinter.

Tonight was different, though. All Robin wanted was company. She could do that. And if things seemed to be going in the direction of a date, then she'd gently remind him that no matter what happened, she would leave in a year.

Back to Limbo. Back to her father. Back to her life.

In that moment, she understood perfectly what Robin had meant when he'd said this house had become his prison. He was bound by magic. She was bound by duty.

CHAPTER NINETEEN

With that unpleasantness still whirling through her head, Theo made herself put the magnificent dress back on. Then she slipped her feet into the simple black heels she'd found and went off to the bathroom to see about a brush.

She found one in a drawer of other beauty utensils. Most of it, including the brush, looked unused. How long had Vesta actually lived here? Theo was starting to wonder. Maybe she'd ask at dinner.

She dug around a little more and found a pair of jeweled hair clips. She perched on the vanity stool and did the best she could with her hair. She ended up with a couple of simple braids, pulled back and clipped together. Overall, a very nice effect. Certainly nothing like a lady's maid or a hairdresser could have pulled off.

More searching and she came up with some cosmetics, again almost all untouched. She broke the seal on a few and found them in decent shape even after so much time. She didn't want much anyway.

Just a touch of liner and a swoop of sparkling gray over her lids. The cake mascara worked fine after wetting the brush, and the rouge, something she barely touched, was enough after one swipe.

The pot of sheer silver glitter was open and a little messy, but that didn't stop her from dabbing the slightest bit of it along the points of her ears. She turned her head side to side in the mirror. Maybe she didn't need earrings after all.

Finally, she found a sealed pot of rose gloss for her lips, and she was done. She'd never imagined a day would come when she'd be wearing the queen's clothes, shoes, and makeup.

She wondered what her mother would think. Probably have a good laugh. Then tell her to have fun.

Theo touched the starstone-and-emerald necklace. "I plan to, Mama."

Surprisingly, her fifty-five minutes were almost up. She stood, gathered her skirts, which made the loveliest rustling sound when she walked, and headed for the foyer to meet Robin.

He was already there. And so handsome, her breath caught in her throat. In his dark suit and steely blue shirt, he looked every inch the warrior king.

She smiled when she was able to breathe again. "Your shirt matches my dress."

"That's why I picked it." He shook his head as he looked at her. "You look stunning. I mean...I thought you were beautiful the first time I saw you. But if you polish stones as well as you polish up yourself, you'll be a master stonecutter in no time."

She laughed, lightheaded from his compliments. "Thank you. You look very regal." She swallowed down a knot of nerves. "And very handsome, too, if I might say so."

"You might. Thank you."

"No blade?" It was the only thing he seemed to be missing.

He held his arms out. "None. Do you think I need one?"

"No. I don't have one either. Feels odd. But I suppose they're not as required in the house."

"No." With a little chuckle, he bowed and held out his arm. "Shall we?"

"Yes. Be warned, though. I may hold on tighter as we go down the stairs. I can walk in heels all right, but it's still a bit like being on stilts."

"Would you prefer we take the elevator?"

"No, the stairs are fine." There was something very dramatic about walking down an elegant staircase in a ball gown. And if she didn't do it now, when would she ever get the chance again?

"All right. Hang on to me, though. I'm here for you." He smiled. "I mean that."

"Thank you." She took his arm, wrapping her hand firmly around it. He was warm and solid, and she couldn't imagine a more perfect moment.

Well, perhaps if this was really her life, that would have been more perfect. If this was really her man and really her house. If this whole reality wasn't going away in a year.

They started for the stairs.

Her life in Limbo had taught her that dreams often remained figments of the imagination, and it was best not to get too attached to them. That's how a person ended up hurt and disappointed.

Fortunately, she was long past the dreams of her youth. And she knew better than to get attached to something that wasn't hers. At least she liked to think she did. She expected that no matter how hard she tried not to fall in love with this place or this way of life, it was still going to happen.

A year's time was a long stretch to get used to something. To think of it as yours.

She glanced up at Robin. At his strong jaw and kind eyes and ready smile. It would be so much worse if she fell in love with…

She wrenched her gaze away. That was not a thought she was going to have. Not a feeling she was going to entertain, not even for a second. Those words couldn't be allowed in her head. It was the sort of youthful foolishness a schoolgirl might give into. But not an adult woman.

He went carefully down the steps as if making sure she'd handled each one before moving on. That's who he was. Gentle and considerate. Once again, not the monster Vesta painted him to be.

How was she supposed to not fall for him?

Theo needed a distraction. She squeezed his arm a little tighter and smiled with all the nerves and excitement inside her. "What's for dinner?"

"You know, I have no idea. I'm sure Mrs.

Applestock has come up with something good."

"I'm sure she has. She's a wonderful cook."

"She is. We're lucky to have her."

We. As if Theo was somehow a part of this world.

They reached the bottom of the stairs without incident. Thankfully.

Robin turned them down a hall Theo hadn't traveled yet. At the halfway point, he walked her through a set of open doors and into a charming little dining room. The table was set for two, although it could have easily held four.

"How pretty," she said as she looked around.

The walls were pale rose above the chair rail and sand below. Gold and crystal fixtures finished out the space, but despite the chandelier, the room had a cozy feel to it. Maybe because of the brick fireplace on one wall. Or maybe because there wasn't so much gilt and glitz in this room. It felt more like a home and less like it had been designed to impress visitors.

Robin let go of her arm so he could pull out a chair for her. "This is the small dining room. Or the family dining room. That's what I thought it would be used for. Family dinners."

Which meant he'd imagined having children with Vesta. He'd envisioned a future for them. A man who planned to betray his kingdom wouldn't think that way. She put on a bright smile. Kind of interesting how easy it was to smile around him. "I love it. It's much more intimate than the big dining room I saw. Although that space will be spectacular for the party tomorrow. This is just perfect for a casual dinner, though."

He smiled back as he joined her at the table. "I'm glad you think so." He looked around. "At first, I used to eat in here every night, but then after a while it felt sad to eat here alone."

"So you moved to the kitchen."

He nodded. "Or sometimes I just ate in my quarters. On the balcony. I still do that a lot. Or I did until you. Although the balcony is really nice for that. In fact, we should have dinner out there some night. Unfortunately, it makes more work for Elswood."

She tipped her head. "In what way?"

"Well, he's got to carry the tray up and down the steps."

Her brow crinkled in amusement. "You know that besides the elevator there's a dumbwaiter, too?"

"Hmm...." He snorted. "I guess I forgot about that. But in my defense, when would I ever use it?"

She laughed. "You really need to explore your own house some more."

He sighed and shook his head. "It's a good thing you came."

A soft sound, like rubber wheels on marble, preceded Elswood's entrance. "Good evening, sir, and...Theodora."

Theo nodded, but Robin greeted him. "Elswood. What's on the menu?"

Elswood clasped his hands behind his back. "Tonight's dinner is a cold marinated vegetable salad followed by salmon with dill sauce, fingerling potatoes, summer corn cakes, sweet peas, and for dessert, pear and pistachio custard tarts with freshly whipped cream."

"Oh my," Theo said. "That sounds delicious."

"It does," Robin agreed. "And I'm suddenly hungrier than I realized. Bring it on."

Elswood bent forward slightly. "Wine, sir?"

Robin looked at Theo. She shrugged. Wine wasn't in her budget, so she never drank it. "I'll try a glass."

"Excellent," he answered before turning to Elswood. "Wine it is."

"Very good." Elswood went back into the hall and returned with a bottle. Theo realized there must be a serving cart out there. He filled a glass with white for the both of them. Then he excused himself and came back with their salads.

Definitely a serving cart.

After that, they were left alone. At least until the next course.

Theo looked at her forks. All three of them. Sometimes at home, because of how little time she had between jobs, she ate standing over the sink. Or while walking to work.

"Start with the farthest one out and work your way in." Robin winked at her. "That's what Elswood taught me."

She glanced out the door. "Elswood taught you?"

Robin nodded. "I told you I was common-born. My mother was a weaver, my father worked the mines. I was destined for them myself, I'm sure. Except then I caught the orc king, and the rest, as they say, is history."

She picked up the farthest fork. It was smaller than the middle one, which was the tallest of the three. "Do you ever wish you, I don't know, didn't catch him? Have your life take a different path?"

Robin finished the piece of zucchini he was eating. "I used to. All the time. But after a while, even the strongest piece of rope frays."

"Meaning?"

"Meaning I gave up on that. What's the point of wishing for something that can't ever happen? I can't undo my past. Daydreaming about it wasn't making me feel any better either. So I stopped."

"What about your parents? Are you able to keep in touch with them?"

"They saw me crowned, but my father, Benmore, died shortly after in a mining accident. I suspect everything that happened with Vesta would have killed him anyway. The stress of it, I mean. My mother, Pryn, still lives in Limbo. She's moved to the highlands."

That was an area in the hills, and because of its remoteness, the people who lived up there tended to be loners, loons, or artistic types who didn't want the restrictions of a more urban setting. A number of well-known goblin musicians lived in the highlands. And a few notorious rebels, too. "That's an interesting area."

"I guess I should take the move as a hint. She

hasn't talked to me since I was exiled. I write to her once a week. She's never answered."

That cut Theo to the quick. She couldn't imagine how that hurt Robin to be ignored by his mother. But she also couldn't imagine how a mother could do that. "How do you know she's moved if she hasn't talked to you or answered your letters?"

"I got a change-of-address card not long after I arrived here. To be honest, I think it was sent by whoever moved into our old house."

That was kind of them. "I don't mean to imply anything or place blame on anyone, but are you sure she's getting the letters?"

He shrugged one shoulder. "I have no reason to think otherwise. I should probably stop sending them. Obviously, she doesn't want to hear from me."

Theo didn't want to believe that. She pushed a slice of carrot around with her fork. "Just because she doesn't write back doesn't mean she's not reading them."

"True. But then, why doesn't she answer?"

Theo looked up at him as a hard truth hit her. "Maybe she does."

The furrows in his brow matched his frown. "What do you mean?"

She shook her head. "I mean maybe Vesta is interfering with the mail." With a sigh, she continued. "Being here has opened my eyes to some things. I believe Vesta is controlling so much more than what the people of Limbo know or understand, from our history to our news. Why couldn't she be stopping your mother's letters from getting to you? Or yours getting to her?"

His chest rose and fell, and darkness filled his eyes. "Of course she could be. I just didn't want to think Vesta could be that cruel. Dumb of me, I know, but you're right." He dropped his fork and stared out the windows onto the garden.

Anger practically rose off him in waves.

Theo felt terrible. Especially because the interference with the mail might be happening in his own home. Now was not the time to add that possibility to the mix, however. "I'm sorry. I shouldn't have said anything."

He shook his head but didn't stop gazing at the garden. "No, you were right to take the scales from my eyes. I've always suspected, but I didn't want to believe it. Now, hearing you say it, I know that has to be what's happening."

She set her fork down, her appetite gone.

He was practically seething. "That wretched fairy. I should have known better than to trust her. Or any of my advisors who pushed me into that cursed marriage. Limbo should have remained its own separate kingdom. There's a reason we kept our distance from the fae for so long. They can't be trusted, that's why."

Theo stayed silent, wondering once again what he'd do if he knew she was half fae. Now was clearly not the time to come clean about that. In fact, the only thing she could think to do was change the subject. "Would you like to go out for a walk?

Maybe a little fresh air would help."

After a moment, he nodded. "That's not a bad idea. I seem to have lost my appetite anyway."

"Me, too." Impulsively, she stood. "Maybe it would come back after a walk, though."

He finally looked at her, a hint of calm penetrating the anger in his eyes. "Maybe." He tossed his napkin on the table and stood. "Elswood."

The man appeared so quickly that Theo knew he'd been close enough to overhear their conversation. "Yes, sir?"

"Dinner is postponed. Give Mrs. Applestock my apologies."

"Yes, sir." Elswood gave Theo a quick slant of his eyes that she couldn't quite read.

She knew it hadn't been full of warm fuzzies. Elswood didn't like her, and she wasn't sure if it was because of her change in station or he was just protective of the exiled king. She hoped it was the latter.

Robin held his hand out. "Come."

She took it and let herself be led, praying that nothing else happened to upset him.

CHAPTER TWENTY

Robin was aware of how foul his mood was. It hadn't turned this dark in a very long time. But what else could be expected when the reality of his life was once again laid bare? Nearly twenty years gone, and Vesta was still finding ways to torment him. He stood at the edge of the patio. The sprite moss that clung to the pavilion's arches gave the whole thing a soft glow. He stared beyond it and into the forest.

Theo remained patiently at his side. She was tense, her brow bent with worry. Because of him.

He did his best to soften the tone of his voice. "I'm not angry at you or what you said. I'm angry at myself. For once again being a fool. For Vesta continuing to make my life a misery and my being unable, *again*, to do anything about it."

His hands clenched as new rage swelled in him. "She should *not* be able to keep my mother from me."

"No," Theo said with quiet strength. "She should not."

A deep, guttural sigh went through him. "I don't

want to talk about it anymore." Talking about it wasn't going to make either of them feel better.

"Okay. What would you like to do?"

He kept his eyes on the moonlit forest. When he was a child, the woods had been his safe place. "Walk." He made himself smile, even though he knew it was a weak effort and probably looked more like a grimace.

"Sure." She held out her hand.

He hesitated, then took it. "Thank you. I know I'm not the best company right now."

"Would you rather be alone?"

That turned his head around. "No. Please, stay with me."

She nodded. "Of course."

In the moon's silver gleam, she looked very much like a goblin queen. It was easy to imagine her wearing a crown. She was ethereally beautiful. The tips of her ears sparkled in the evening light, and her eyes seemed as large and luminous as starstones.

His desire for her became unbearable. He cupped her face in his hands and kissed her. She felt like the only safe place in his life. The only thing he could trust. "Theodora," he breathed her name against her lips.

"Yes?" she whispered back.

"I adore you. I am so glad you're here with me." If he'd still had a kingdom, he would have given it to her.

He felt her smile. "I'm glad I'm here with you, too."

He pulled her tighter, kissed her harder, held her closer, and it still wasn't enough. When he ended the kiss, he kept her in his arms, his forehead pressed to hers. Not even the wine they'd left behind in the dining room was this intoxicating. "I already cannot stand the thought of you leaving me."

She stayed quiet for a moment. "I'll have to go back. I have no choice."

He nodded. "I know. Your father." Her loyalty was part of what made her so good. He pulled back so he could see her face. "I wouldn't want you to leave him. That's why I think you should bring him here. Stay with me. Both of you. You could continue your schooling. And I promise he will get the best care possible."

Her eyes widened, but he wasn't sure what that meant. Had he overwhelmed her? Of course he had. Another forced smile bent his mouth. "Don't answer now. I know you need to think it over and talk to him about it. I understand. But will you at least consider it?"

She nodded. "I will. I'll write him another letter first thing tomorrow."

That was all he could ask. "Thank you." He took her hand again. "Let's walk and not worry about conversation for a while."

"Okay."

He squeezed her hand. "We can have our dessert when we get back."

That made her smile. "Those tarts did sound nice." She held up her finger. "But first..." Still holding his hand, she reached down with the other to slip off her shoes. She set them upright on the patio. "These aren't meant for forest walks."

"Will you be all right in bare feet?"

She grinned a little brighter. "I'm a goblin, aren't I?"

He laughed. "Indeed you are. And so am I." He let go of her hand and pulled off his shoes and socks. He shucked his jacket and tossed it on a nearby chair, then rolled up his sleeves. "There. Much better."

She smirked at him, like she was trying not to laugh.

"What? You don't agree?"

She looked him over from his feet up. "No, I agree. You look a little less royal now. I like it. I liked the way you looked before, too, but I like this just as well. Maybe more."

"Good. Because this feels a lot more like me." He grabbed her and pulled her in for another kiss. "I like the way you look, too. Barefoot in a ball gown. Makes you seem like some kind of wild, untamable creature who's just escaped the clutches of a terrible monster."

With a laugh, she twisted out of his grasp and danced a few steps into the garden. "Maybe I have. Maybe that terrible monster ought to see if he can keep up with me."

He frowned in mock protest. "I'm the monster?"

She shrugged. "I don't know. Are you?"

With another laugh, she hiked up her skirts and took off under the pavilion.

He shook his head and let out a whoop of sudden excitement as he took off after her. "I'm not only going to keep up with you, I'm going to catch you," he called. And then he was going to kiss her again. A lot.

"Maybe." She called back with a light, teasing tone that only spurred him on. "But maybe not."

The subtle glowing sprite moss in the pavilion caught the sequins on her dress and made them sparkle like distant fireflies as she ran past the fountain.

He gave chase, keeping pace with her until she darted into the woods. More sprite moss lit the way, along with a variety of luminescent mushrooms on the ground. He picked up speed. He had no choice. If she went too far, he'd be powerless to continue. His barriers might have moved, but they were still there.

It was nice to run, to feel the earth under his feet and the breeze against his face. He felt like a kid again, joyful and carefree. There was a lightness in him that hadn't existed in years. A lightness that was all Theo's doing. She pushed the darkness back and lifted his mood.

He hoped she took his offer seriously, but there'd be plenty of time to discuss that tomorrow. He was nearly on her heels now. He reached out, and the tips of his fingers just touched the fabric of her skirt where it billowed out behind her.

She looked over her shoulder, saw him, and picked up speed with a little gasp. She laughed immediately after. "You're not going to catch me that easily."

He smiled. She was right. He wasn't. He liked the chase too much. Except at some point, he *would* catch her so he could kiss her again.

They had to be at the very reaches of his boundaries. If she didn't turn soon, he might hit a wall. He opened his mouth to say something, but a snarl filled the air, cutting him off. A shiver of alarm went down his spine. He reached for his blade even though it wasn't there. A quiet curse fell from his lips.

Theo came to a fast stop, and he almost barreled into her. He put his hands on her shoulders to keep from knocking her down. "Hey, what—"

"Don't move," she whispered. "We have company."

The sulfuric stench hit him as he looked at the path ahead. An enormous hellhound blocked the way. The beast's head was at shoulder height with Theo. Muscles rippled beneath its black fur. It pawed the ground, claws furrowing the earth with deep grooves. Movement behind the beast made Robin realize the creature wasn't alone.

A trio of red-eyed monsters stared them down. Saliva dripped from their toothy mouths as a low warning growl vibrated through the air. And he'd foolishly left his blade behind tonight. They both had.

Robin kept his mouth next to Theo's ear and spoke as softly as he could. "You need to get behind me."

"I don't think moving is a good idea."

"Probably not, but I don't see what choice we have."

"Do you trust me?"

He frowned. Not that she could see his face. "Of course, but why—"

She took a step forward, putting space between them. The air around her shimmered like the ground radiated heat.

Then Theo disappeared.

And a fourth, much larger hellhound stood in her place.

Chapter Twenty-One

She'd had no choice. Neither of them had weapons, and hellhounds had no natural enemies, except for other hellhounds. Other bigger, more powerful hellhounds.

So that's what she'd shifted into. Doing that in front of Robin terrified her, because it meant revealing herself as a changeling, which instantly exposed her fairy blood. But being torn apart by the hellhounds frightened her more. She just prayed Robin would understand why she'd been quiet about her fairy half. Now was not the time to worry about such things, however. Not with three bloodthirsty beasts bearing down on them.

In hellhound form, she snarled at the group, pawing the ground just like they had, lunging forward with the same kind of threatening postures. She curled her lips back, showing off her fangs. When they faltered, she took a step forward. Inch by inch, she drove them back, until at last, they turned tail and, whimpering, ran off into the depths of the forest.

She snapped her jaws a few more times and let out a couple more deep growls for good measure. As soon as they were no longer visible and the sounds of them crashing through the forest faded, she shifted back to herself.

After a deep breath, she turned to face Robin. His expression opened a pit in her stomach. He looked shocked and upset. The darkness had returned to his eyes. She swallowed. Maybe she was reading him wrong and that was because of the hellhounds, not her revelation. "Are you all right?"

The steeliness in his gaze only increased her feeling of sickness. "You lied to me. There's no way you could have done what you just did unless you have fairy blood in you."

She'd hadn't lied. Lying implied she'd denied what she was, and she'd never done that, but what good would that discussion do now? Instead, she chose her words carefully, trying to keep her voice and her body language cool and calm. "Robin, I didn't tell you because I knew you wouldn't like it. I know you hate fairies because of Vesta, but you have to know not all fairies are bad. I saved us from those hellhounds. You have to see the good in that."

"A fairy who lies. Why should that surprise me?"

"Robin, please. I didn't lie. You never asked me if I was fae."

"You should have told me." Disgust curled his lip. "You're a changeling." He said the word like it tasted bitter.

"Yes, I am." She couldn't very well deny it now.

She didn't want to either. There was a part of her that was very much done hiding the gifts she'd gotten from her mother.

"How much of you is fae?"

She lifted her chin slightly. "Half of me."

He shook his head. "I rescind my offer for your father to come here. I don't need another fairy in my house."

So much for that. "I didn't get my fae blood from him. My mother was a fairy. The same woman who helped bake your coronation cake. The woman whose oatmeal cookies you loved."

Robin's eyes rounded a tad, and his lip curled. "A fairy in my kitchen. Was she a part of the plot to poison me? Was that how the toxin got in my soup?"

Theo frowned at him and his brash insinuation, and her anger started to outweigh her desire to remain civil. "Absolutely not. My mother would never have done such a thing. She was a pastry chef! She had nothing to do with the regular food. Besides that, she loved that job and thought very highly of you. Although I'm starting to wonder if she misjudged you."

"She thought highly of me? How much did she think of Vesta?" Theo opened her mouth to reply, but Robin kept going. "How much do *you* think of Vesta? You were so reluctant to try on her things. Is there a reason for that?"

"Because she rules the kingdom I live in. And I was only reluctant at first," Theo reminded him.

Then she held out her arms. "As you can see by the dress I have on, I got over that."

His scowl didn't go away. "I want nothing more to do with you. You're a liar, and you can't be trusted. I'm sure you're working for her."

"None of that is true."

"It is to me. We're done."

The sickness she'd been feeling earlier came rushing back. Her stomach churned, and she almost couldn't get her next words out. "Are you canceling my indenture?"

He stared at her for a long, hard second. "No. I won't punish your father for your sins. But you'll return to general staff. This house is large enough that I never need to see you again. I'll make sure Baton and Elswood understand."

With that, he turned abruptly and strode away, leaving her alone and feeling like she'd just had the air sucked from her lungs.

Every good thing that had come her way since she'd arrived at Gallow House was gone. No more time with Robin, no more schooling, no more opportunity to better herself once she returned to Limbo.

Why had she ever thought the outcome would be different? Her life so far had been a series of bitter disappointments. Why would she expect a change of scenery to make a difference?

*

Robin's head ached, but his heart hurt worse. He gripped the balcony railing as if his life depended on it, and maybe it did. At times, the pain made him dizzy. He pushed away and went to collapse on the chaise.

His sweet, dear, beautiful Theodora was a traitor. A fairy. Half, anyway, but what did that matter? It was clear now that his instincts had been right, and her presence in his home had been another calculated move on Vesta's part.

It all made sense. The story about her father being too ill to serve the indenture was probably true. Or maybe it wasn't, but it had gotten her in the door. Even saving him from the hellhounds seemed logical, because if he was dead, Vesta couldn't torture him anymore. Although, by shifting in front of him, Theo had exposed her true heritage. That part didn't fit the story, though she'd had little choice in the moment. But what did it matter? He was so gullible to be duped first by Vesta and now Theo.

Because she had taken him in, head and heart. And he'd certainly bought into believing she was a good, loyal daughter.

It had made him like her. No doubt the point.

And, oh, how he'd liked her. Too much. And too soon. But thinking about her only reminded him of the sweetness of her lips and the warmth of her soft body under his hands as he'd—

"Sir? You called?"

Robin looked up to see Elswood standing nearby.

"Yes." Robin sighed. He needed to tell Elswood about Theodora, but he didn't have the energy for that discussion. Not right now. It would keep until morning. "I'd like my hot toddy early. And I'd like it to be a double."

"I'll bring it right up." Elswood bowed and left.

Robin was glad to be alone again. Except that he wasn't glad, not really. He'd much rather have had Theo at his side. If only things were different.

It seemed clear that she'd been placed in his house by Vesta. Somehow, Vesta had found out about Theo's father's indenture and had persuaded Theo to come in his place so that she could report back on how Robin was doing and what he was up to.

What had the queen promised her? Riches? A position in the royal court? Care for her father—if he really was sick? Whatever it was, Robin doubted Vesta had delivered on the promise yet. Theo seemed to have very little. And had seemed genuinely appreciative of the good that had come her way.

Like the lapidary training, which would no longer be happening.

Robin closed his eyes. It was all too much. He'd been pulled out of his loneliness and given a taste of joy, only to have it snatched away in an instant.

Why had she shifted in front of him? That was the one part that didn't work with the rest of the narrative that she was here to spy on him. She'd exposed herself as a changeling and all the risk that came along with that to save them from the hellhounds. That was a selfless act. And one that she had to know could cost her dearly.

Just like she had to know that he would know only someone with both fae and goblin bloodlines could become such a creature. It was common knowledge. So why do it?

One answer came to mind.

Theo had no connection to Vesta, and she'd kept her secret only because he'd made it clear how he felt about the fae.

Was that possible? He almost didn't want to answer that question. Not after the anger that had poured out of him and the terrible things he'd said.

A soft meow made him open his eyes. "Pepper. Perfect timing. I could use someone to talk to."

The little black cat jumped off the railing and padded over to sit a few feet away from the chaise.

"Hi there." Robin was too down to manage more than a halfhearted smile. "If you'd shown up a few minutes ago, I'd already have your dinner ordered. Now you're going to have to wait." He patted the chaise. "Come on. Hop up and get comfortable."

The cat stared at him, then, after a second, did just that. But he stayed at the foot of the chaise.

"What's wrong? We're not friends all of a sudden? Or do you get friendlier after your dinner is served?" Robin laughed softly, but his mood soon won out. "I don't know that I'm going to be very good company, Pepper. Today was not a good day."

The cat sat very still and stared at him.

"Someone did something nice for me. Better than nice. Saved me from a pack of hellhounds. And I reacted very poorly." That was an understatement.

Pepper lay down and tucked his front feet under his chest like he was settling in for a chat.

Robin reached out and gave the cat a little scratch under the chin.

Suddenly, a new thought came to him. If Theo could transform herself into a hellhound, what else could she become?

He grabbed Pepper, turned him around, and had a look under his tail. Pepper hissed and let out a yowl, but it only took a second to confirm that Pepper was indeed a boy. Legend said a changeling couldn't alter their gender, no matter what they became. "Sorry. I had to see for myself."

He put the cat down, and Pepper took off for the railing.

"Hey now." Robin got up and went toward the little animal, trying to make things right. "I wasn't going to hurt you. I just—"

The cat went up and over the railing and disappeared.

Robin sighed. But he'd gotten what he deserved.

A knock rang out from his door. Apparently, his mood was so bad even Elswood was knocking now. "Come in, Elswood."

Robin went to the railing to see if he could spot Pepper, but finding a black cat in the dark was—

"It's not Elswood."

He spun around to see Theo standing at the door to his balcony. The ball gown was gone, replaced by the same jeans and T-shirt she'd had on earlier. Worn black flats covered her feet. "What are you doing here? I told you I don't want to see you."

"I know. And I promise I won't bother you again after this. I just wanted to say that I am absolutely not working for Vesta in any way. I'm sorry you think that, and I'm sorry I didn't tell you right away what I am. I've kept it a secret all my life. Fairies aren't exactly well loved in Limbo. At least they weren't when I was growing up, and my mother taught me that some things are better kept hidden. But as soon as I realized how much you detest the fae, I should have said something. You deserved to know who's in your house."

"I don't detest—"

She took a breath and kept on going like she hadn't heard him. "Also, I realize this means you'll want to cancel the dinner party, since you didn't want to do that anyway, but for what it's worth, I think you should still have it. And I want to say that even though you hate me now, I don't regret what I did. I would have felt much, much worse if those hellhounds had harmed you."

His emotions were a mess, but he knew one thing. "I don't hate you."

She blinked at him as the words seemed to register. "You don't?"

He couldn't hate her. Because, as angry as he'd been, he was calm now and had come to the realization that he couldn't so easily stop liking her. "No, I don't. But I'm not happy you lied to me."

"I didn't lie." She took a few steps toward him. "You never asked. But I didn't offer up the information, so let's call it a draw."

That almost made him smile. He liked very much that she didn't back down or shy from conflict. It took courage to face him in this moment. "Okay. A draw." He ran his hand through his hair. The braids at his temples needed to be redone. But what was the point of keeping up with tradition when that world no longer existed for him? And yet, this world was so empty. He needed things to change. "I would like to still have the dinner party."

Her lips parted. "You would?"

"Well, not *like*. But you're right that I should still have it. I need to have it." He stared out into the night. Pepper was out there somewhere. Pepper, who was clearly not Theo in another form. Pepper who might actually be his only friend, which was sad. "I can't keep living like this."

"I would agree with that," she said softly.

The clearing of a throat got his attention. Elswood stood in the doorway with a tray carrying Robin's hot toddy and cookies. Without saying a word, he put the tray on the small table next to the chaise and left.

Robin wondered how much he'd heard. He glanced at Theo. She looked completely unsettled. "I'm sorry for the things I said. And the conclusions I jumped to."

"Thank you. Does that mean I'm forgiven?"

He had two choices. Trust her or not. He held out his hand, decision made. "Yes. If you forgive me, too."

CHAPTER TWENTY-TWO

The sick feeling in Theo's stomach finally went away. "Of course I forgive you." She took his hand. "How could I blame you for not trusting me? You've only known me two days. And with your history, I'm surprised you'd ever trust anyone again."

He pulled her close and wrapped her in his arms. "Thank you for understanding. I want things to be good between us again."

She leaned into him and shook her head. "I want that, too." He was the first real friend she'd had in a long time. Her lack of friends was her own doing, but it was a hard thing to undo with her reputation. Running barefoot through the woods with him had been so much fun, the kind she'd thought she'd never have again. She wanted more of that. More of him.

"Good. I'm so glad that's settled." He kissed the top of her head before pulling back. "Will you stay with me for a bit? You can share my hot toddy and cookies."

"Okay. What's a hot toddy?"

He smiled. "You know, I'm not completely sure

what Mrs. Applestock puts in that concoction. I think there's whiskey, a squeeze of orange, some honey, spices…" He shrugged. "It's very tasty. I have one every night before bed. She started making them to help me sleep."

"You need help sleeping?"

He nodded as he went to the chaise. "Usually, yes. Come sit with me."

"Well, since you said there are cookies…"

He laughed as she settled onto the chaise next to him. "Here, try this first." He picked up the large earthenware mug and held it out to her. "See what you think."

"Smells good." She put her hands over his and took a sip. It was strong, but delicious. "I can see how that would help you sleep."

He grinned and took a long swallow, then put the mug back on the little table. They settled in, had iced oatmeal cookies, and looked out at the starry sky without saying much for a while. In part because they were eating, but also because the silence was perfect in the moment.

When the cookies were gone and the hot toddy half empty, he spoke. "Thank you for saving my life. No one's ever done that for me before. Not that I've been in that kind of situation before, but what you did was still something remarkable. You're kind of fearless."

She snorted softly. "No, I'm not. I was scared out of my mind. But I didn't know what else to do, and we'd left our blades inside. I just acted."

"Did you think about what my reaction would be?"

She nodded. "Yes. For a split second. I was worried about that, but there wasn't time to dwell on it."

"You obviously had every reason to worry." He let out a long sigh. "But you did it anyway. To save me."

She lifted one shoulder. "To save us. Don't make me out to be more of a hero than I was."

He stared at her, amusement in his gaze.

"What?"

"You're just something, that's all."

"Is that a compliment?"

He laughed. "Yes." Then he put his arm around her and went back to silently watching the stars for a bit.

She got a little closer and relaxed into his embrace. Maybe this was even better than running barefoot through the forest.

"What else can you change into?"

She suppressed a smile, then realized he couldn't see it anyway. "Pretty much anything. Living, that is. I can't become a table or a chair."

"Good to know. That's quite a skill set. Could your mother do that?"

"No." Maybe he didn't know as much about changelings as she'd assumed. "She was full-blooded fae. Only someone with the right mix of goblin and fairy blood has a chance of becoming a changeling. We're apparently very rare."

"I've never known one. Until now."

She leaned forward suddenly so she could see his face. "Please don't tell anyone. It's not something I share. Ever. My mother always warned that it could be used against me."

He shook his head. "I won't say a word. I promise." Then he put his hand to his heart. "Thank you for trusting me with this. Although I know you didn't really have a choice."

She leaned against him again. "I guess I could have let us become hellhound food."

"I'm forever in your debt for not going in that direction." He pulled her in closer.

Happily, she snuggled in. He was very comfortable. Before long, she felt herself drifting off. Reluctantly, she shook off the weariness and sat up, twisting to face at him. "Tomorrow is going to be a busy day. I should go to bed."

His half-lidded gaze made him look as drowsy as she felt. He nodded. "All right. Don't forget to write that letter to your father about coming here."

"You're positive you're still good with that?"

"Yes. I'm sure."

"Then it'll be the first thing I do." She hesitated, then leaned in and gave him a quick kiss.

He caught her and pulled her close, making the kiss not so quick. When he spoke again, there was a mix of pleasure and reluctance in his voice. "See you in the morning."

"In the morning. By lunch at least. My morning might be busy."

"What else do you have to do besides the letter to your father?"

"I need to work on whatever dress I'm wearing for dinner." She had one more project in mind as well. She scooted off the chaise before she could change her mind about leaving, because staying with him would be all too easy.

"Sleep well."

"You, too." Then, with a smile, she slipped out the door and down the hall toward her room, though that wasn't her destination.

She was tired. Exhausted, really. All of the emotion and tension of the evening had left her feeling like a wrung-out rag, but she wanted to write the letter to her father now and make sure it got in the mail immediately.

Because first thing tomorrow she had something else she wanted to do. Something special. A little surprise she thought would put a smile on Robin's face. Just thinking about it was making her smile. Such a rare thing for her. But it was becoming more common lately.

She went into the library. Moonlight shone through the windows, and for a moment, Theo felt as if she was standing in the middle of an ancient cathedral. She left the lights off. There was enough to see by, and she didn't want to ruin the beautiful atmosphere of shadows and light.

Once at the desk, she turned on the small lamp there. Then she took out the supplies she needed, sat down, and jotted a quick note to her father about

Robin's offer. She tried to keep it as neutral as possible so that her father's decision would be his own, but she knew some of her enthusiasm came through.

How could it not? A life here would be beyond anything they had in Limbo. More comfort for both of them. Less work for her. And a chance for her father to spend his last days away from the heavy burdens of his debt.

Plus, she didn't see how he could gamble here. Not if certain precautions were taken, like spreading the word that no one was to engage him in such activity.

She thought it was very likely that, once she finished her schooling, she could easily get a job with the stonecutters here that would allow her to pay off the remainder of his debts in five years or less.

She finished the letter, sealed up the envelope, stamped it, addressed it, and sent it down the chute.

With that off her mind, she finally went to bed. But even as she lay there, her thoughts wandered to Robin. She understood why he had trust issues. She also understood that if she broke his trust again, regaining it would be exceptionally difficult.

In fact, it might not happen at all.

For the second night in a row, Robin slept with the ease of a cat in the sun. He woke with a smile on his face and Theo on his mind. It was early, and he knew she was busy, so he languished in bed, enjoying the feeling of being well rested. It wasn't something he got to appreciate often. Maybe his days of sleeplessness were behind him now.

Maybe the distraction of Theo was all he'd needed.

That thought only made his smile bigger. He yawned. As comfortable as the bed was, the thought of coffee appealed even more. Then his stomach rumbled, and he was reminded that with everything that had gone on last night, dinner hadn't happened beyond the salad.

Oatmeal cookies and half a hot toddy were no replacement either.

He got out of bed and went straight to the shower. He swore he could smell coffee and biscuits, but was that actually possible two floors away? He wasn't sure. Probably just his appetite working overtime.

A hot shower, a quick shave, then he pulled on his uniform of track pants and T-shirt and headed downstairs.

The delicious aromas intensified the closer he got to the kitchen. It wasn't just coffee and biscuits, though. There was another note to the aroma that was vaguely familiar and a little sweet. He couldn't quite figure it out. Maybe Mrs. Applestock was working on a menu item for tonight's dinner party? Whatever it was, he planned on stealing a bite.

He walked into the kitchen and found Theo in an apron and thermal mitts taking a large tray out of the oven. A smudge of flour clung to her jaw. "Well, hello there. What are you up to?"

She jumped, nearly dropping the tray. "You scared me. And you're not supposed to be up yet."

He grinned. There was something incredibly charming about her when she was a little miffed and slightly bossy. He took a seat at the island. "I'm not? Did I forget that I asked for a wakeup call?"

She frowned at him. "I thought you'd sleep in is all. I was going to surprise you."

"With?"

She put the tray on the marble countertop between them. "Nightberry scones. My mother's recipe. Of course, at home we always made them with currants because that was what we could afford, but in the royal kitchens…" She shrugged.

"I remember those." He closed his eyes and inhaled. The aroma made sense now. And it brought back so many memories. All good. Happiness filled him. He opened his eyes. "That is an outstanding surprise."

Mrs. Applestock came in with a basket of ingredients. "They smell divine." She looked at Robin and shook her head like she was disappointed in him. "All these years, we've had these delicious things growing in the garden, and you never said a word."

"I really didn't know," he tried to explain. "Sorry."

Mrs. Applestock went oddly still. "I didn't mean to scold you, sir. I just—"

"No, you're right." He laughed as he nodded. "We've wasted time. And berries."

She smiled. "I was thinking about doing a nightberry tart for this evening."

"I love that idea." Introducing Amelia and her niece to one of his favorite things would make the evening that much more special.

"Good," Mrs. Applestock said. "Miss Theo here has given me her mother's recipe. I didn't know her mother had been one of your pastry chefs. Imagine that!"

He nodded as Lolly put a cup of coffee in front of him. "Caralynne was a very skilled baker. One of the best."

Theo beamed. "Thank you."

"Thank *you*." He added sugar and cream to his coffee. "You must have gotten up pretty early to pick those and get the scones made."

She smiled. "I thought it would be a nice surprise."

"It's the best one I've had in a long time." Certainly better than the one he'd had in the woods last night. He pulled out the stool next to him. "Will you join me for a scone?"

Theo nodded. "Sure."

"Mrs. Applestock, Lolly, please stop what you're doing and have a scone. You have to taste these, too. In fact, we should get Mrs. Baton and Elswood in here." Suddenly, he got to his feet. "You know what? Let's just take all this to the staff dining room. The coffee and the scones, I mean. Can we do that?"

Shocked faces looked at him. Mrs. Applestock spoke. "We can do anything you like, sir."

"Good. Let's get Henry and Fenwick in here, too, if we can." He glanced at Theo. "Unless you don't want to share the scones? I don't want to ruin anything you had planned."

Smiling, she shook her head. "You're not ruining anything. They're meant to be eaten. And I made a lot. Oh! That reminds me!" She spun around, opened the oven again, and pulled out a second tray.

The scones were a little more golden brown than the first batch but seemed fine to Robin. He moved to stand closer to Theo. "Thank you. This really was a wonderful surprise."

She looked up and into his eyes. "You're welcome."

A little flour decorated her left cheekbone, too. He wanted more than anything to brush it off, but Theo might not welcome the intimate contact in front of Mrs. Applestock and Lolly. There'd be no denying his relationship with Theo was more than just companionship if they saw that. Although they had to know something more was going on between him and Theo, didn't they?

He needed to distract himself before brushing flour off her cheek was the least of his transgressions, because kissing her seemed like an even better idea. He rubbed his hands together. "What can I do to help?"

CHAPTER TWENTY-THREE

Theo couldn't quell her nerves. She'd already met Amelia, but that didn't seem to make any difference. This was a dinner party, and she desperately wanted it to go well for Robin. The one possible crack in the porcelain was her. She was the weak link. The most uncultured and unschooled. He'd had to point out which fork to use when, after all. She didn't have the manners that these people did for a situation like this. Or the upbringing.

She was a common-born peasant. Robin might have been common-born, but he'd also been king. And even though he hadn't held the throne long, he'd been living in this house with that magnificent library for years. She knew how books could change you for the better.

They were her one saving grace, perhaps. But she'd never had access to the number of them that he had.

At least she'd had a well-educated mother who'd shown her by example how to be gracious. But was that enough?

She gnawed on her bottom lip as she paced through her suite. Why had she pushed him to do this?

For the thousandth time, she checked her reflection in the full-length mirror in the bathroom. She'd gone with the emerald-green dress. After removing all the gold braid detailing and about half the scattered rhinestones, it had turned into something that felt appropriate for a semi-fancy dinner party. A little sparkle, but not too much.

She wasn't the hostess, after all. Just another guest.

But there was one other thing that she liked very much about the dress. It made the wearing of her mother's starstone-and-emerald necklace seem intentional.

That was her only jewelry worth wearing anyway. For her hair, she'd done a single open-weave lace braid at each temple, then pinned them back. She'd applied a little bit of makeup, just like she had the night before. Her shoes were the same black heels as well.

Enough looking in the mirror. There was nothing left for her to do. She glanced at the time. Nerves had driven her to get ready too soon. Dinner wasn't for another hour. She wrung her hands and searched the room for something to do. Maybe she'd try to read. That would be a good distraction. She'd brought a few books back from the library last night, too.

A knock on her door made her jump. "Yes?"

"Theo? It's Robin."

She exhaled in relief. He'd be an even better distraction. She opened the door. He was still in track pants and a T-shirt. "Hi."

He looked her up and down, his brows rising and an appreciative smile bending his mouth. "You look *beautiful*. Very sharp. Green is your color."

"Thank you." She did a quick little curtsy. "You look…comfortable."

He laughed. "Yeah, I'm going to get dressed in a minute. But, uh, can I come in?" He looked oddly sheepish. "I have something for you."

"Of course." She moved out of the way.

He dug into his pocket. "I need some help, too."

"Oh? What with?"

"First…" He held out his hand. In it was a small black velvet box. "These were supposed to be a birthday gift for Vesta. Obviously, she never got them. Which I'm happy about. I know now she wouldn't have liked them anyway. Not gaudy enough for her tastes. But I'm hoping you'll feel differently."

She stared at the box, not quite able to take it. The last gift she'd gotten had been for her birthday, and it had been the letter T carved from a piece of scrap wood her father had scavenged somewhere. He'd inlaid a few small river rocks into the surface. It was lovely. Her father's carving skills were very good.

But this was jewelry. And whatever was in the box had most likely cost serious money.

More than all that, the gift was coming from Robin.

"Go on," he said. "Take it."

She inhaled, hoping fresh air in her lungs would bring her the fortitude she didn't feel. She took the box. The velvet was so soft. The box felt almost weightless.

"If you don't like the gift, that's perfectly okay. I just thought maybe you'd want something to wear tonight. Or whenever."

She hoped it wasn't a necklace. She wasn't going to replace her mother's with anything else. Tentatively, she opened the box.

The tiniest gasp escaped her lips. "Oh," she breathed out. Not a necklace. Earrings. Petite, dangling earrings. Each one was comprised of three starstones—a round one, a marquis and a pear shape—each set in gold. They were linked together like a chain so that the smallest movement set them dancing. "They're the most gorgeous earrings I've ever seen."

"I thought they would go with your necklace, too."

"They will. Perfectly." Suddenly, she realized her foolishness. He wasn't actually giving these to her. They had to cost a fortune. This was a loan, plain and simple. "Thank you for letting me borrow these. They're just the finishing touch my outfit needs."

"I'm not letting you *borrow* them. They're my gift to you. For you to keep."

She stopped looking at the earrings to look at him. "I can't accept these. They're too much."

"Now, Moody..." He grinned. "You saved my

life. That makes them not enough, but they're all I could come up with on short notice."

"But you don't need to—"

"Nope. Not going to listen to any of that. Besides, I want you to have them. I can't think of anyone I'd rather they go to than you. And they complement your necklace so well. Please. Take them."

She looked at the earrings again. They sparkled like diamonds, but starstones gave off a distinct silvery glitter that diamonds didn't possess. He wanted her to have them. If she said no, she'd only upset him. She couldn't do that, not right before dinner. "They're magnificent. I can't thank you enough. They're honestly the nicest thing I've ever owned. Besides my mother's necklace."

He looked incredibly pleased. "Put them on."

She took them out of the box and slipped them into her ears, then went to the small mirror by the wall that led into the bedroom. She turned her head side to side. "They're stunning."

"So are you."

She smiled, heat rising in her cheeks. "You're making me blush."

He shrugged. "It's the truth. You are."

She had to change the subject, or she was going to pass out from embarrassment. "What, um, did you want help with?"

"Oh, right. Could you fix my braids?" He tugged at the one at his right temple. It looked like it had been fresh a week ago. "They need redoing, and I'm not that great at it." He stuck his hand into his pocket and pulled out two ornate silver braid caps. "I brought these. I can never get them to work."

"I'd be happy to rebraid your hair." Then she realized what an intimate thing he'd just asked of her. As king, he'd no doubt had someone to do his hair for him. But he wasn't king. And she supposed he didn't want to ask Elswood. Or Hyacinth.

But braiding his hair meant close, personal contact. Her hands in his hair. And she'd already said she would. There was no turning back now. Not with those starstones dangling from her ears. It was the least she could do for him. "Do you want to sit here in one of the chairs? I'll go get my brush."

"Sure, thanks." He settled into the closest chair.

She went to her bathroom to get her brush and some smoothing oil, something else she'd found among Vesta's abandoned things. Theo had already used a little on her own hair. It made the iridescence shine even brighter.

She came back to find him taking out the old braids. He held up the small elastics that had been holding the ends. "I should save these, right?"

"Right. I know you brought those caps, but they go over the elastics."

"They do?" He rolled his eyes. "That explains why I could never get them to stay on."

She grinned. He'd definitely had help when he'd been king. "All right, what kind of braids do you want?"

His brows lifted. "Um…what kind did I have?"

"Simple three-strand."

"That's fine, then. Wait. Yours are fancier. What do you have?"

"Open lace, but that's more of a woman's braid. Plus, it might be too much with those caps. How about a three-rope twist? You probably had those when you were king." She couldn't quite read his expression. "Too much? I could do a simple two-rope twist."

He shrugged. "Whatever you think. Surprise me."

She squinted, trying to picture what braid would look best on him. Then she smiled, tight-lipped because she had an idea. "All right."

She brushed his hair, which was soft and gorgeous and made her envious, even though she knew she had nice hair, too. For a moment, she almost ran her hands through it with abandon, but she stopped herself. That might be a bit too far.

It might also lead to something that would make them late for dinner.

Instead, she focused on the job at hand. She brushed his hair, again, probably a little more than necessary, then separated out the temple pieces and worked a little of the oil into them. She plaited two tiny three-strand braids, then twisted them together in a rope. He closed his eyes as she worked. Finally, she added the silver caps to the ends. The end result was two slim but complicated-looking braids. A very nice job. Regal, even. Certainly worthy of the man who'd once been king. "There. All done."

When he didn't immediately respond, she realized he'd dozed off. She took that as a compliment. She shook his shoulder gently. "Robin?"

"Hmm?" He blinked himself awake.

"Your braids are all done. You want to look in the mirror?"

"I think I feel asleep."

She smiled. "You did."

His grin was sheepish. "Sorry."

She shook her head. "It's very relaxing to have someone working on your hair. Nothing to apologize for. Come on, have a look and see if what I did is all right."

They went to the ornamental mirror on the wall, and he peered in. He nodded. "Those are perfect. I can't even imagine how you did those. So much better than I could have done myself. You're pretty good at braiding."

"A lifetime of doing my own hair. Well, after my mother passed, anyway." She tipped her head at his casual clothes. "I don't want to nag, but you should probably get dressed."

"You're right. I should." He didn't make a move for the door, though. "Thanks again for the braids."

"Thanks again for the earrings."

A slightly wicked gleam played in his eyes. "Maybe they were worth a kiss?"

"Maybe." She almost laughed. "Okay, definitely."

As he leaned in, she put her hands on his chest. With the heels on, she was closer to his height.

He didn't linger, probably because time was ticking. "How about I meet you at the top of the stairs in twenty minutes?"

"Oh. I was going to go down and see if Mrs. Baton needs any help."

"Or you could just come to my quarters and make sure I put the right suit on."

She didn't believe for a minute that he needed her help with that decision. She smiled. "Okay."

Fortunately, he already had a suit laid out. She suspected Elswood had done that for him. It was deep midnight blue with a crisp white pinstripe. He put a brilliant white dress shirt with it, and then, as a nod to her dress, added an emerald-green paisley pocket square. The last thing he added was a bejeweled dagger to a leather shoulder harness. It was mostly ceremonial, but she had no doubt he kept the blade sharp.

He looked so handsome and so utterly royal that she felt like she might faint. Or kiss him.

He held out his arms. "What do you think?"

"I think you look so good I almost can't bear it." She sighed happily. "I wish I'd seen you with your crown and scepter and the monarch's cape of royal purple around your shoulders. No wonder Vesta had to lie and cheat and use poison to get you off the throne. You were born to be king."

His expression turned bittersweet.

Had her words brought up bad memories? That certainly hadn't been her intention. "I'm sorry. I didn't meant to upset you. It's just so rare that a person's insides and outsides are so well matched. I mean, look at Vesta. She's considered the most beautiful woman in the kingdom, but now I know

243

her insides are as rotten as the swamp of despair."

He chuckled. "If she's considered the most beautiful woman in the kingdom, it can only be because you're here with me."

Her cheeks flushed with heat, and she shook her head. "I don't know how to respond when you say things like that."

He took her hand. "You don't have to respond at all. Or you could just say thanks or even 'I know, Robin.'"

She laughed. "I'm not going to say I know."

"Maybe someday you will. I hope my words sink in. I don't think you've heard compliments often enough."

She'd never heard them. Except from her mother and father, but that was what parents did. They told their children they were smart and beautiful, no matter what the truth was, right? "It's going to take some getting used to, that's all."

He kissed her knuckles. "We should go down. Our guests will be here soon."

"*Your* guests."

"Our guests." He tipped his head in her direction. "I know you've only been here a few days, but to me, you've already earned your place as lady of the house."

"You can't mean that."

He cupped her face in his hands, his gaze achingly sincere. "Theodora, I can't hide my feelings for you. I realized after our argument that the reason I reacted so strongly is that I am falling in love with you."

"You can't mean that either." Except nothing in his tone or expression made him seem dishonest. Her own heart beat faster at his words, as if it had only then come to life. "We haven't known each other long enough to..." She couldn't finish. Because it would have made her a liar. She just wasn't ready to speak her feelings.

"I do mean it. And if I feel this way now, how much deeper will I be in another week? Or a month? There's no fighting it. And I don't want to. I am gone. And I don't care. I've lived a lonely, purposeless life for too long. No more. Not now that I have someone to love and take care of and spend time with."

He kissed her softly. "It's all right if you don't feel the same way. I know this is fast. I know it might be too much. But I've wasted so much time I don't want to waste another day. You must understand that?"

She nodded. "I do."

Yes, she understood. But she also wondered if he would have felt that way about any young, available woman who'd come to his house. Was he falling in love with *her*? Or with the *idea* of her?

She hoped he really did still feel the same in another week or month, because her feelings were definitely all about him. And if his feelings changed, finishing out the year was going to be incredibly difficult.

Especially after she'd just invited her father to move in.

CHAPTER TWENTY-FOUR

Robin and Theo stood in the foyer to await their guests. He'd never met Amelia's niece, Emeranth, but he had met her boyfriend, Deacon, on one occasion many years ago. Deacon was a raven shifter, as was his whole family, but they all had their individual curses, too. His curse, such as it was, allowed him to take on other people's curses. Amelia had thought he might be able to give Robin a break from his imprisonment.

That hadn't been the case, however. Try as Deacon might, he'd been unable to move the invisible wall that surrounded Robin even an inch.

The failure had prompted Amelia to surmise that fairy magic created in a different realm was uncrackable. She'd vowed to keep trying, but her tone had said what Robin had already been thinking: Don't expect anything to come of it.

But tonight, none of that mattered. Tonight had Theo by his side as he stepped boldly toward a new start. He'd realized that part of why he'd responded so poorly to her secret about her fae blood was because he cared so much for her.

He loved her. And he wanted to think that the woman he loved wouldn't keep anything from him. But he also knew that he'd given her every reason to think hiding it was the right choice.

Now, there were no more secrets between them. More than that, he was ready to take this next step to improve his life, whatever the consequences. Maybe that was the reason his boundaries had suddenly expanded.

He'd made the choice to be happy in the life he had. Of course, that was easy to do with Theo around. She was like a beacon of light in his dark world. He couldn't get enough of her, and she made him want more from the life he'd come to accept.

No more of the status quo being all right. It was time to press forward and strive for a bigger life.

This dinner party was just the beginning. As his social circle grew, he hoped his magic boundaries would continue to as well. Maybe someday, they would disappear altogether. Wouldn't that be something? And what would Vesta's response be then?

A car pulled up outside, ending that line of thought.

He was glad they'd come to the foyer. Maybe it wasn't proper etiquette, but it felt too impersonal for Elswood alone to greet their guests.

Elswood was at the ready, however, to answer the door.

Theo glanced at Robin, her smile a little tight. She was clearly nervous. "They're here."

"They are." He smiled back at her. "Did I tell you how beautiful you look, my love?"

He'd never seen a woman who captivated him more. He could see some of Caralynne in Theo. Mostly the way her eyes crinkled when she laughed.

If he were capable of it, he would have used his power to bring Theo's mother back. It was obvious that Theo missed her dearly.

The bell rang, and Elswood opened the door. "Good evening, Ms. Marchand and guests. Welcome to Gallow House."

"Thank you for having us," Amelia responded. She found Robin immediately and handed him a bottle of wine tied with a purple bow. "A little something for you."

"You didn't have to do that." Robin took the bottle, nodded in appreciation, then handed it off to Elswood.

"I couldn't come empty-handed." She smiled at him. "Don't you look nice, Robin. And, Theodora, that dress is very becoming."

"Thank you," Theo said shyly.

Robin put his hand on Theo's back. Amelia's caftan was an explosion of peacock colors. A few actual feathers decorated her turban. "You look beautiful, as always, Amelia."

With a smile, she touched the arm of the dark-haired young woman who'd followed her in. "This is my niece, Emeranth. Em, this is Robin Gallow and his companion, Theodora. Robin, you know Deacon, but I'm not sure you've met his sister, Grace."

"I haven't. It's a pleasure to meet you, Grace." He shook both of their hands.

"Thank you for inviting us to your beautiful home. Call me Gracie, please. Everyone does."

Robin nodded. "Thank you for coming. I realize venturing into the Dark Acres isn't everyone's idea of a good way to spend their evening."

The pretty blonde laughed. "I wouldn't have missed it."

He introduced Theo. "As Amelia mentioned, this is my companion, Theodora Middlebright."

Theo nodded and shook their hands as well. "Please call me Theo."

Emeranth smiled. "Theo it is. And you have to call me Em. Your hair is just too gorgeous."

"It is," Grace agreed. "You have to tell us what you use to get it to shine like that."

Theo laughed. "That's a goblin thing, I'm afraid. See Robin's hair? He has it, too." She nodded at the butler. "So does Elswood."

The two women glanced around. Em shook her head. "Well, how about that? I guess I'm out of luck." She laughed. "Maybe there's a spell I can learn."

"Oh, are you a witch, too?" Theo asked.

"I am."

It pleased Robin to see the three women getting on so well. Theo needed friends, and he couldn't imagine any better than Amelia's niece and Deacon's sister.

Tonight was going to be very good. He could feel

it. Why on earth had he waited so long to do this? Because he hadn't had Theo at his side. Feeling more royal than he had in ages, he gestured toward the dining room. "Shall we go in to dinner?"

As soon as they were close to the table, Theo saw that someone, Mrs. Baton maybe, had put little cards at each seat with their names on them. Assigned seats? Was that standard at a fancy dinner party? She wasn't sure. But she didn't like that she and Robin had been separated.

Although maybe that was how it was done. Theo wished she knew. Probably time to get an etiquette book from the library next.

Robin was at one end of the table, while Theo was at the other. At least she could see him over the low centerpiece of flowers and gem-encrusted candlesticks. She recognized all the flowers from the garden outside. She supposed the purple roses were a nod to Amelia. There was even some of the vine that covered the pavilion woven through. The little white flowers gleamed like stars. She liked the arrangement very much. Whoever had made up the centerpiece had done a good job.

On either side of Robin were Amelia and Deacon. On either side of Theo were Emeranth and Gracie. That kept family together on each side of the table. That seemed right. Except Em and Deacon were a couple.

Theo started to think maybe couples weren't supposed to sit next to each other at fancy dinner parties. A second later, she smiled. Had she just thought of herself and Robin as a couple? That was new and interesting. She liked it, though.

Elswood and the new footman took care of filling wineglasses.

Deacon held his hand over his glass. "I'm more of a beer man, myself."

Robin looked at Elswood. "Bring the man a beer. We have that, don't we?"

Elswood frowned. "I don't know."

"I'm sure Henry has beer," Robin countered.

Deacon lifted his hand as if to say stop. "Don't go to any trouble. Water is fine."

Robin shook his head. "It's no trouble."

"No, sir," Elswood said. "Not at all."

Robin seemed immensely happy to Theo. And very much at ease. But then, big dinners and fancy parties must have been regular occurrences when he was king.

She liked watching him. Not just because he was incredibly handsome or because he'd declared his affection for her, although neither of those things hurt, but rather because he was so charming and carried the evening like he'd been born to the noble life.

Quite a feat for someone who was as common as she was. It gave her hope that she could do all right as well, shake off her nerves and behave like a civilized being. She really didn't want to make a mistake that would embarrass Robin in front of his guests.

But Em and Grace were so nice that they'd already put her mostly at ease. Having people be kind to her was new. Of course, these women didn't know her reputation, and they hadn't been subjected to her mean side, nor would they be.

Theo was done with that part of herself. At least while she lived here. If she had to go back to Limbo, which was a possibility if her father didn't want to move, she'd have no choice but to become Moody again.

It was her best protection against that world.

The new footman finished filling everyone's glasses, and Elswood brought Deacon a beer.

When everyone had their beverages, Robin raised his glass. "Here's to new friends." His gaze was on her as he smiled. "And new beginnings."

They all drank to that.

Theo took more than a little sip of her wine, just to take the last bit of edge off her nerves. They were fading, but she still worried she'd do something stupid.

Gracie set her glass back down. "That green really suits you."

"Thank you," Theo answered. She almost blurted out that it was a hand-me-down from the queen that the queen knew nothing about, but she caught herself at the last moment. Probably wise. Like her mother had always taught her, she needed to listen more and speak less. She chose her words carefully.

"Your dress is very pretty, too. Both of your dresses are."

She imagined they were brand new from one of the shops in town. She'd seen a few on her walk here.

Em leaned in like she had a secret to share. "There is the most amazing secondhand store in town. We have got to take you." Then she got an oddly worried look on her face. "I mean, if you like that sort of thing. I know thrift shops aren't for everybody. There are some nice boutiques in town, too."

Theo laughed harder and louder than she'd meant to. "I'm sorry, but..." She shook her head. "I am *definitely* a thrift shop kind of person."

"You are? I didn't think someone like you would be into that."

"Someone like me?" Who did they think she was?

Em glanced at Robin before answering. "Aren't you...like a princess or something? Sorry, I don't know what goblins call their nobility."

Theo's mouth came open, but for a moment, she couldn't say a word. Finally, she found her voice. "I'm not a princess. I'm not even nobility. I'm just a regular citizen of the realm like everyone else."

"Oh." Em looked at Gracie. "She's one of us, then."

Both women laughed, and Theo's last remaining nerves disappeared. *One of us.* Had that ever been said about her before? Theo tried not to grin like a fool as she spoke to Em. "About this thrift shop. You can't tell me the dress you have on came from there?"

"This?" Em plucked at the sleeve of her black, off-the-shoulder dress. It was incredibly sophisticated. Like something a movie star might wear. "It sure did. So did my shoes and my earrings."

"Oh," Gracie said. "Stella's Bargain Bin is the bomb." She tapped the shoulder of her pale pink gingham shirt dress. "This was eight dollars. And Stella threw in a pair of sunglasses and a bracelet. It was some kind of buy-one-get-two deal."

Theo blinked. "I didn't even know that was a thing. I definitely need to go there." Her grin finally broke free. "This dress is a kind of a hand-me-down. It was left behind by…" Her smile disappeared as she looked at Robin. Maybe this wasn't her information to share.

He looked right back, his eyes filled with amusement. "It's all right." He looked at Gracie and Em. "My ex left behind quite a lot of clothing and such. Fortunately, Theo was able to put some of it to good use. As you can see."

"That was the queen's?" Gracie's words were half whisper, half exclamation.

Theo nodded. "Her shoes, too."

"Was that her necklace?" Em asked.

"No." Theo smiled again. "That belonged to my mother."

"It's incredible. I've never seen a diamond like that before."

"It's not a diamond. It's a starstone."

"Starstone?" Deacon suddenly chimed in. "Do we mine that here? That name isn't familiar to me."

"Nor to me," Amelia said.

"We don't mine it here," Robin answered. "It's not a gem that exists outside of Limbo, the goblin realm. Not that I've ever heard about, anyway."

Amelia's brows lifted as she turned to Robin. "Is that so? Why haven't you told me about this stone before?"

He shrugged. "I don't know. I guess...it never occurred to me."

She looked at Theo. "May I see one closer?"

"Here." Theo unhooked one of her earrings and handed it to Em, who handed it to her aunt.

Amelia lifted the magnifying glass at the end of the long chain around her neck and inspected the gems. "These are remarkable. Very much like diamonds, but that silver gleam is almost extraterrestrial."

She passed the earring back before speaking to Robin again. "Do you have any starstone rough?"

He shook his head. "No, I don't. I have a handful more that are polished, though." He pulled his ceremonial dagger from the sheath at his side and handed it to her. "The narrow band of gems set just below the pommel. Those are all starstones."

"They're lovely, but they won't work. I need a piece of rough."

Theo cleared her throat softly, her hand on her necklace. "The starstone in my necklace is only polished on the front. The back is still rough."

Amelia seemed to think for a moment, then nodded. "That ought to be sufficient."

Robin leaned in. "Sufficient for what?"

"Well, if Theodora would be willing to part with that stone, I believe I could do something rather remarkable with it."

Interest shone in his eyes. "Such as?"

She turned the dagger in her hands, looking at the stones with great interest. "Such as make Shadowvale the second location these beauties are found."

Theo clutched her necklace a little tighter. The thought of giving up a piece of her mother's necklace made her feel slightly ill. "I, uh—"

"That won't be possible," Robin said. "Theodora can't part with that stone."

Relief flooded her. She nodded in agreement, amazed that he'd stepped in so quickly.

"Ah, well. Perhaps I can try with one of the cut stones you already have, then."

"Absolutely," Robin said. He smiled at Theo before looking at Amelia. "Hopefully it'll work just as well."

CHAPTER TWENTY-FIVE

Robin considered the evening a success, even though it wasn't over yet. The rest of the dinner was spent the same way it had begun, with endless conversation about a wide variety of things. The topic of starstones came up repeatedly, but he made sure to keep it away from Theo donating her necklace.

He knew very well that would be too much to ask of her. He'd seen instantly by the look in her eyes that the very idea upset her. And why wouldn't it? That necklace clearly kept the memory of her mother close.

Thankfully, there were other topics of conversation. Mostly the food, which was amazing. Mrs. Applestock had prepared a standing crown rib roast of pork with onion gravy, apple and sage stuffing, potatoes au gratin, glazed carrots and parsnips, piping-hot yeast rolls with butter, and of course the dessert that would soon be served, the nightberry tart.

Not that any of them had room. They'd all eaten

far too much, but it was virtually impossible not to when the food was so delicious. The menu and Mrs. Applestock were highly praised. So much so, he thought the woman deserved some kind of bonus.

He also overheard enough snippets from the other end of the table to know that Em and Gracie were planning a day out with Theo. Shopping and lunch and a tour of the town. He made a mental note to be sure she had whatever funds she'd need for that adventure.

Elswood entered the dining room, pushing the silver serving cart. In the center sat the evening's finale, the nightberry tart. The glazed berries gleamed under the chandelier. The serving platter was decorated with more sugared berries and sprigs of rosemary. A silver serving bowl filled with fresh whipped cream accompanied the dish, along with an urn of fresh decaf coffee, goblin style.

The tart was sliced up, topped with whipped cream, and served to much oohing and aahing. Then there was quiet as they all dug in.

"Robin, what on earth is this delicious thing?" Amelia shook her head as she went back for a second bite. "I've never tasted anything like this."

"Nightberries. They're a goblin favorite." He smiled at Theo. "I didn't even know they were growing in my garden until Theo pointed them out. This tart is her mother's recipe."

Amelia looked at her. "I am so very glad you came to Shadowvale."

Theo grinned. "Me, too."

Deacon lifted his cup. "This coffee's pretty tasty, too, and I'm not one to like fancy coffee."

Robin laughed. "It's not fancy coffee. That's just how we make it."

Deacon nodded. "I see. Like the vampires and their chicory."

Robin knew that was how coffee was served in New Orleans, a place he'd only read about. He supposed the vampires favored that style, although that was purely speculation. Regardless, he nodded. "Yes."

"The coffee is good," Amelia said, turning back to Robin. "But you must get me cuttings of these plants. I need to try my hand at growing some of these. I've already started rooting a few of those purple roses you sent over."

Em set her fork down. "You should really tell Nasha about these berries."

Deacon turned to her. "You're the barista over there. You should figure out this coffee blend. I could drink this again."

"If Robin will give it to me, I'll happily add it to the menu," Em said. "But I'd still love to see what she could do with these berries. Not that this tart isn't amazeballs, but Nasha has a way with baked goods. I mean, obviously."

Robin shook his head. The name was familiar, probably from one of Amelia's stories, but he couldn't recall who Nasha was. "Remind me who she is again?"

"You know," Em said. "Nasha Black. She owns

the Black Horse Bakery in town. That's where I work. I'm the head barista there. Anyway, her father is one of your neighbors here in Dark Acres, although I'm not sure where his house is. If there's a place with a stable, that's probably it. He's one of the Four Horsemen of the Apocalypse, so he'd need a spot for his horse, naturally."

He shook his head again. "I'm sorry, I don't know her or her father, although I have heard horses going by. I've never been to the bakery."

Too late, he realized what he'd said.

To their credit, Deacon and Amelia said nothing, but Em and Gracie looked at him as though he'd lost his mind.

Em snorted softly. "You've never been to Black Horse? It's only the best bakery in town. I'm not just saying that because I work there either. How long have you lived here and you haven't visited?"

Gracie nodded. "They made my birthday cake. It was the most delicious thing you'd ever want to put in your mouth. Well, outside of this tart." She laughed. "I can't believe you haven't been."

Theo looked almost as uncomfortable with this conversation as she had concerning the one about her mother's necklace. He took a little breath and made himself smile. If he was really going to make a new start, he had to be able to tell people the truth. No matter how humiliating it was. "I can't really leave my property."

Amelia put her hand on his arm as if to stop him. "You don't have to—"

"No, it's all right." And it really was, in that moment, sitting with these people who'd suddenly become dear friends after breaking bread together. "Some of you already know this, but I can't go much beyond my property because that's the curse my ex-wife put on me."

"It's unbearably cruel," Theo muttered.

"What?" Em looked at her aunt. "You must be able to do something. We could take him to the grove, or Deacon, you could—"

"Child, don't you think I've tried? Don't you think Deacon's tried?" Amelia frowned. "The queen who cursed him is a full-blooded fairy, and her magic was created in another realm. Nothing I've done has worked. Deacon couldn't do anything either."

He heaved out a sigh. "Did everything I could think of, too."

"That's just awful," Gracie breathed. She looked like she might cry. Robin had heard she was tenderhearted. Instantly, he felt bad.

"It's all right," he said. "Believe it or not, the boundaries have begun to loosen a bit lately."

Amelia looked at him. "What? When did this start? How loose are we talking?"

He explained what he and Theo had discovered, how they'd actually driven off the property. "It was really something. Gave me hope."

"So just yesterday, then?"

He nodded. "But I went for a drive again today and—"

"You did?" Theo asked. "Without me?"

He shrugged one shoulder, smiling sheepishly. "I knew you were busy working on that dress. As much as I wanted you along, I didn't want to take up all your time."

She shook her head. "You should have asked. How far did you get?"

He couldn't keep the smile off his face. "I'd say half a mile farther, at least."

"Wow. That's great." Theo pressed her hands together. "Did you try walking around outside? Or the path to the mines?"

"No, just the drive."

"But that still proves you don't need me along for it to happen. I'm obviously not the reason the boundaries are shifting."

Amelia held her hand up. "Wait now. I wouldn't be so sure about that."

"Oh?" Robin glanced at her. "What makes you think that?"

"Well, for one thing, the timing is suspicious." Her eyes narrowed. "There was something I came across in my research, but I couldn't see a way for it to happen naturally, so I never said anything about it." She sat back. "I still shouldn't. Forget I said anything."

"Aunt Amelia," Em started. "You can't drop a bomb like that and then not follow through."

"Agreed," Deacon said. "That's a fire that needs putting out."

Amelia frowned, her mouth bending in a hard line. "My telling you could have a negative effect."

"On me?" Robin asked.

Amelia looked at him, then Theo, then back to him. "Yes. But on Theodora, too."

He couldn't imagine how that was possible. "How on earth would she be affected?"

"I can't explain it without—I just don't think I should say anything." Amelia picked up her fork and pressed it into the remaining tart crumbs on her plate, gathering them up. "I'm sorry. Let me think about it for a day or two. Then maybe I'll tell you."

Robin wondered if he might get it out of her in a private conversation. It could be that she just didn't want to share the information in front of everyone. He let it go. "Whatever you think is best, Amelia."

"Thank you." She folded her napkin and set it alongside her plate. "This dinner has been a delight, but we should go before we outwear our welcome. It was kind and brave of you to open your home, Robin. Thank you so much for your hospitality. I hope soon to extend the same to you."

Everyone started to rise and say the same things. Robin was a little sad to see them go, but at the same time, thrilled the evening had gone so well.

And that he would get to be alone with Theo now.

He and Theo walked their guests to the door, said more goodbyes, then, in a matter of seconds, were alone again.

She smiled up at him. "That was a great dinner party."

"It was. I am so glad you made me do it."

She laughed. "I didn't make you have that party."

"Well, you strongly encouraged me. How about that?"

With a smirk, she nodded. "All right. I'll accept that much."

He pulled her into his arms. "I ate enough for three people."

She leaned her head on his chest. "I'd say I'm so full I won't need breakfast tomorrow, but I know that would be a lie."

"I wish I felt like going for a walk in the garden."

"Me, too. All I really want to do is kick these shoes off, get out of this dress, and fall into bed."

He chuckled. "Your room or mine?"

She swatted him playfully.

He grinned. "I wouldn't mind getting out of this suit."

"I can't believe you didn't tell me about the boundaries moving again."

"I meant to, but then I fell asleep while you were doing my hair, and I just forgot. You want to go for another drive with me tomorrow?"

"Absolutely. I really hope we get even farther."

"Me, too." He held out his arm. "Come on, I'll walk you to your room. And I know after a meal like that, we should take the stairs, but how about we take the lazy option and go by elevator instead?"

"My feet vote yes on that." She took his arm.

He'd never been happier. Sure, it would have been nice to know what Amelia had found that might be influencing his prison, but he'd call her tomorrow and try again. It didn't matter in the moment, however.

Because the moment was perfect. He'd had company in his house, and it had been wonderful. He'd had conversations with people who weren't paid to talk to him. And now, after a successful evening, he had the woman he was crazy about on his arm.

Life couldn't be better.

Theo hissed and leaned heavily on him.

He stopped. "What's wrong?"

"Nothing, I'm fine. I just think these shoes aren't really the right size after all. Maybe I'll take them off here. We're almost to the elevator, right?"

He scooped her into his arms, cradling her against his chest. "Almost."

"Robin!" His name was clearly spoken in protest, but her smile went all the way up to her eyes.

He ignored the protest and focused on the smile. "Your mother's tart was a huge success."

She wrapped one arm around his shoulders. "It was. That was nice. Are you really going to give Amelia cuttings from the plants?"

"Sure, why not?"

"Just wondering. Will you tell the woman at the bakery about them, too?"

"I suppose. Is there a reason not to?"

"No." She laughed. "I think it would be kind of amazing if nightberries became commonplace in Shadowvale. They should be enjoyed by everyone. Not just people with money or a title."

She went silent as they reached the elevator.

He pushed the button. "What's on your mind?"

"Just thinking about Amelia wanting to start a mine of starstones. How would that even work? They're not a mined stone. They come from elestia tree sap."

"I don't know. I should explain that to her. But don't worry about it. She won't ask again about your mother's necklace."

The elevator doors opened, and he carried her on. She gave him a look. "You could put me down, you know."

"I know." He bent a little to push the button for the second floor.

She snorted, then shook her head. "What if I did give her the starstone? Would I be...compensated?"

The seriousness of her tone told him how much her father's debt must be weighing on her. Especially if she was even considering such a thing. "When Vesta and I came here to build this house, we gave Amelia some uncut stones. Opals, amethyst, tourmaline, iolite, sapphire. All kinds. She created the Dragonfly mine with that rough. Because of our contribution, I get twenty-five percent of the mine's profit."

Theo's eyes rounded. "Is that a lot?"

"In a year's time? It's more than the kingdom of Limbo is worth."

CHAPTER TWENTY-SIX

With Robin's good-night kiss still lingering on her lips, Theo carefully took off the earrings he'd given her and put them back into their box for safekeeping. She took one long look at them before closing the lid. Starstones really were beautiful.

Then she shucked her evening clothes and shoes, scrubbed her face and teeth, and slipped into her nightgown. Not a moment of that time went by without her thinking about what he'd told her.

His share of the mine's profits for a year were more than the kingdom of Limbo was worth.

The idea of that kind of money was staggering. Not because of how much it was but because of how it could change their lives. It could absolutely pay off her father's debts. More than that, it could buy him the kind of care he desperately needed. And it could allow him to live in comfort for the remainder of his days. He'd be worry-free, too, knowing that Theo had the means to take care of herself.

But only if she was willing to give up the most precious thing of her mother's that she had left.

She stood at the bathroom sink, staring at the necklace. She hadn't taken it off since the day after her mother had passed.

Her father had told her it should be put away in a safe (like they even had one of those), that it was too valuable to be worn every day, that she was too young to look after such a thing. Maybe that was all true, but she'd worried if it left her neck, she'd never see it again. He'd sell it, then gamble the money away. Or maybe he wouldn't even bother to sell it, just toss it on the table as his bet. She loved her father but hated his addiction. And so she'd stubbornly argued with him and kept the necklace with her at all times.

Looking back, she wondered if he realized what would happen to the necklace if he ever got his hands on it. If he understood his own weakness. Maybe that was why he hadn't tried harder to take it from her, because he could have if he'd really made an effort.

Whatever the reason, she was glad the necklace had stayed with her. On that day after the worst day of her life, it had made her feel like she had a part of her mother with her.

She flattened her hand over the pendant, pressing the gems into her skin. It still made her feel that way. But she was an adult now, and in the scheme of things she understood it was just an object. Her memories wouldn't suddenly disappear because the original starstone was gone. She could certainly replace that with glass.

She also had to consider what her mother would want her to do. Theo took a long, deep breath. The answer to that question came easily.

Take care of her father.

A tear slid down Theo's cheek. She knew it was the right thing, but why did the right thing make her so upset? Why, once again, would she have to sacrifice? It wasn't fair. But then, not much of her life had been.

The truth was, she was smart and capable and able to take care of herself. She could live the rest of her life without all that money. But her father couldn't. Not for long, anyway.

She brought the pendant to her lips and kissed it. "Tomorrow, Mama." She'd tell Robin in the morning that she would give the pendant to Amelia. Maybe by then she'd have found some peace about it.

A yawn suddenly hit her. She was tired. Being social was exhausting. So was the weight of responsibility. She turned the light off and headed for bed, ready to sink into that luxurious mattress and forget everything for a while.

But a knock on the French doors stopped her in her tracks. Robin? With the darkness outside and the sheers over the glass, she could only assume. She glanced down. She had no robe, and this nightgown was a little too threadbare to be decent. She grabbed the throw off one of the chairs and wrapped it around herself.

Then she opened the door to see what he wanted. "Robin?"

"Does he often call on you late at night? And do you always refer to him with such informality?"

Theo gasped as she saw who'd just spoken to her, then her knees bent on instinct, and she dropped down. "Your Highness."

What in Hades was Vesta doing here?

"Get up."

Theo rose, still not believing that Vesta was on her balcony. Whatever reason had brought the queen here, it wasn't a good one. That was pretty plain. She could feel herself quivering ever so slightly. Nerves or fear, she wasn't sure. Maybe both. She stayed silent, though, waiting on the queen to speak first.

She didn't have to wait long. "You didn't answer my question."

"I'm sorry, Your Highness. What did you ask me?"

"If my *husband* often calls on you late at night."

They weren't married anymore. Theo knew that. Everyone in Limbo knew that. In fact, Vesta had several royal companions who did a lot more companioning than Theo was doing with Robin. But obviously, Vesta meant to start something. "No, Your Highness. Never. But I am here as his indentured servant. It would certainly be within his rights."

"You called him Robin. Seems awfully informal for a servant."

That wasn't a question, so Theo didn't answer it.

Thankfully, Vesta moved on. Her finely penciled brows arched. "Does he house all of his indentured servants in guest quarters on the same floor as his own?"

Vesta's second thinly veiled suggestion that something else was going on nudged Theo's nerves in the direction of outright anger. But it wouldn't do to get angry with a woman like Vesta. The power she wielded made her far too dangerous an opponent to take on. "I wouldn't know, Your Highness."

Vesta hesitated, then strolled to the edge of the balcony, put her hands on the railing, and stared out at the garden. She wore a long turquoise gown of silk with a wide jeweled gold belt that matched the lace edging the sleeves and hem of the dress.

The strands of jewels woven into the braids piled high on her head complemented those in the belt. More jewels dripped from her ears, neck, and fingers. Even her slippers were jeweled. And the tips of her ears were painted with tiny gold designs. After a moment, she spoke. "This house is breathtaking, isn't it? I designed these gardens. Did you know that?"

"Yes, Your Highness." Short answers were probably the best. Short answers with as little additional information as possible.

Vesta looked over her shoulder. "So he still speaks of me, then?"

Theo briefly thought about shoving the queen over the railing, but they were only one floor up. The fall would cause injury, for sure, but not enough to make it worth the effort. "Yes, Your Highness."

Theo said a little prayer that Vesta's visit would

be short and not include a trip to her old quarters. If it did, Theo prayed Vesta wouldn't remember exactly how things had been left, considering that Theo currently had a lot of the clothes in the closet separated into piles.

Vesta turned suddenly and leaned back, hands wide on the railing. "I have a kingdom to run, so I'm going to keep this short. You work for me now, do you understand? You will be my eyes and ears. As such, you will write me a letter daily telling me everything he does. *Everything*. I already know you're good at writing letters, so don't pretend otherwise."

That explained so much. Like how Vesta had found out Theo was here. Vesta had read the letters Theo had sent home to her father. Or at least the one. If Vesta had read the second, with Robin's offer for him to relocate, she'd probably be angrier than she was now.

Well, Theo was feeling a little angry herself. Especially because she suspected either Elswood or Baton were responsible for getting the letters to Vesta. "No, I don't understand. Why do you want—"

"You dare question your queen?" Vesta's eyes narrowed as a cold, calculating gleam lit them. "All you need to know is what you have been told. You will report on everything he does. Or your father will be placed in the darkest, dampest cell in my dungeons. That won't be very good for his health now, will it?"

No, it wouldn't, but Theo was in no mood to agree with the fairy menace before her. She clenched her teeth in an effort to quell her rising rage. "A letter every day. I understand."

Vesta smiled. "That's a good girl. Now, since I don't have time for a letter about today's events, why don't you answer a few questions for me? Has he done anything unusual lately?"

Like throwing a dinner party? Or kissing her? Professing his love for her? Giving her starstone earrings worth a fortune? Theo thought those probably qualified as unusual, but she wasn't about to share any of that with the woman who'd just threatened her father. "I've only been here a few days. I don't know him well enough to know what would be unusual for him."

A muscle in Vesta's jaw twitched. "It's very easy to forget to feed a prisoner in the dungeons. Days might go by even."

More threats. Theo's fingers dug into the throw she was clutching. It was that or put her fist into Vesta's nose. How familiar that rage was, even though she hadn't felt it in a few days. "I spent most of the day working in the kitchen." That wasn't a total lie. Theo's anger spilled out just a little, raising her voice. "I can't tell you about what I don't know."

"Keep it down, girl."

"Yes, Your Highness."

"Did he say anything about going anywhere?"

"The first day I was here, he went to the mines."

Vesta sighed. "Anywhere else? Did he go into town?"

"He doesn't go into town. Or anywhere, really." Was that what she was after? Trying to find out if her bespelled boundaries were still secure? Interesting. That could mean she'd sensed something was off with her magic here but didn't know more than that. Valuable information. And something Amelia might be able to use.

Vesta smiled and nodded like that was the answer she'd wanted. "Keep a record of that. I want to know if he leaves this house or ventures out anywhere besides the mines. I want to know where he goes. And how long he's gone for. And if he goes to visit anyone. If he does, I want to know who that person is. In fact..." Vesta raised a finger as though an idea had just come to her. "You should try to go with him."

Theo frowned and played dumb. Vesta probably thought very little of her IQ already, so why not? "Why would he want me to go along?"

"Yes, why?" Vesta looked her up and down. "You aren't the most appealing thing, are you? Even so, it shouldn't be hard to sway him. Just fawn all over him and laugh at his jokes. Then make him think you're desperate to share his bed. That will do it. Men are simple creatures with simple needs. Robin is no exception."

Was that what Vesta had done? Lied to Robin about her affection for him? Shared his bed and made him think it was love? "Yes, Your Highness."

"Good. I'll expect the first letter tomorrow."

"How should I send it?"

Vesta made a face. "The same way you sent the letter to your father. Give it to the housekeeper. Or whoever you give them to."

The last sentence came too late. Vesta knew Baton was the one delivering the letters. But Vesta definitely hadn't read the second one yet. The second letter would change everything. Theo decided to test her theory. "Won't that take longer than a day to reach you?"

Vesta sighed as if Theo was impossibly dumb. "Yes, but I will still expect tomorrow's report as soon as possible."

"Yes, Your Highness."

Vesta leaned in. She smelled of sandalwood and roses and desperation. "Remember, little goblin. If I don't get a letter every day, your father's future will turn very dark indeed."

Theo wanted to ram her head into Vesta's face. Instead, she nodded. "Yes, Your Highness."

"Tra-la-la." Vesta waved her hand at Theo. "Off to bed with you now. You have a busy day tomorrow."

"Yes, Your Highness." Theo slipped back inside, leaving the door slightly ajar, then she dropped the throw and quickly shifted into the form of a lightning bug. Immediately, she flew out through the cracked door to see where the queen went.

Vesta traipsed down the stairs and into the garden. Theo followed, buzzing along a safe distance behind. With a quick glance to either side, Vesta hitched up her skirts and dashed beneath the pavilion. She went straight to the beautiful tiled fountain, took one more look around, then stepped up onto the ledge.

She whispered a few words. "*Peri peri nixie ta.*"

The water lit up with a soft blue glow. Vesta jumped into the fountain and disappeared without a splash.

Outside of a few pet words of her mother's, Theo had never learned to speak fae, but she didn't need to in order to understand what she'd just seen. The garden Vesta had built contained a portal to Limbo.

And it was controlled by fairy magic.

Still in lightning bug form, she flew straight to Robin's balcony. This couldn't wait. Vesta would read the second letter very soon, and Theo knew her father would pay the price. She couldn't risk whatever might happen next.

She hovered above the chaise. There was no sign of Robin on the balcony. He must have already fallen asleep, which meant he was in bed. She landed and returned to her human form, realizing too late she was only in her nightgown. Modesty would have to wait for another day.

She went to the French doors that led into his bedroom and peered in. Despite the darkness, she could just make out a Robin-shaped form under the covers. She knocked softly, not wanting to startle him. "Robin," she whispered. "Wake up."

He moved, but that was it. She knocked again, a

little harder this time, and raised her voice. "Robin. Get up."

He moved some more and this time sat up. He blinked with the kind of sleepy slowness of someone roused well before they were ready. He looked a little grumpy. She didn't blame him. Being woken up too soon had that effect on her as well. He squinted at the door. And looked like he might lie down again.

"*Robin*." She tapped her fingers on the glass.

He squinted harder, then tossed the covers aside and padded to the door. He opened it, revealing he was in boxer shorts. And nothing else.

She almost forgot why she was standing there.

"Hey," he said sleepily. A slow grin spread across his face as his gaze raked across her body. And the thin nightdress covering it. "This is a nice surprise."

She crossed her arms over her chest. "You won't think it's so nice when I tell you why I'm here." She shook her head like she was trying to make sense of something. "I just had a visitor on my balcony."

"Who?"

She sighed. "Vesta."

CHAPTER TWENTY-SEVEN

Robin used up every curse he knew. Twice. And one of them three times. But none of them adequately expressed what he was truly feeling about his ex-wife paying a visit to Theo. That blasted woman had no right to be here.

He strode back to his bed, grabbed the robe off the bench at the end of it, and handed it to Theo without looking at her. "Here."

Not that he *didn't* want to look at her. The nightgown she was wearing left little to the imagination, and his imagination had already been working overtime where she was concerned. This was not the time for such pleasurable pursuits, however, and he sensed she was uncomfortable.

"Thank you."

He stared at the wall while she put the robe on. "What in Hades did that woman want?"

"For me to tell her everything you're doing."

He turned. Theo was finishing the knot in the robe's tie. Still beautiful, even in something too big for her. "She didn't just expect you to do that because you're a dutiful citizen of Limbo, did she? Let me guess. She threatened your father? Or you?"

Theo nodded, the hard light in her eyes a mix of sorrow and anger. "My father mostly. And do you know how she found out about him? And about me being here? Baton."

He frowned. "Wait. Baton's working for her?"

Theo shrugged. "Seems that way. Vesta wants me to write her a daily letter detailing your actions. When I asked how to get those letters to her, she told me just to keep giving them to the housekeeper."

Robin pondered that. "I know Hyacinth isn't the warmest of people, but that doesn't mean she's on Vesta's payroll. It could be Vesta's got someone on the other side who receives and then delivers the correspondence when it arrives. That person could know it comes from the housekeeper."

"True. And if your mother isn't getting her letters from you…"

"We don't know that for sure. It still could be that she's just not answering me."

Theo hugged her arms around her torso. "I suppose. I guess I didn't think the letters through entirely."

"You could still be right. At this point, we're probably better off not trusting anyone." He sat on the end of the bed, using the bench as a footstool. "What else did Vesta say? Did she do anything? Did she come into the house or stay on the balcony? Tell me everything."

"Well…" Theo climbed up and sat beside him.

She started at the beginning and explained everything that had occurred. At the end, she shook her head. "I think we need to do two things and do them very quickly. One, we need to tell Amelia that Vesta doesn't appear to have control over her magic here, just the sense that it had changed in some way."

"Agreed."

"And two, I need to go through that portal and bring my father here before he becomes Vesta's prisoner. I'd say we need to bring your mother, too, but given that you've had no communication with her in so long, I don't know if she'd be open to that."

"I don't know. I'd love to bring my mother over, but now might not be the time." If she really wanted nothing to do with him, his attempt to move her to Shadowvale could be disastrous in many ways. "And listen, I know you're worried about your father, but you can't go through that portal. You have no idea where it ends up. What if it's in the middle of the Fangmore courtyard? There is a fountain there. Or there used to be. Regardless, you'd end up in the dungeons quicker than your father."

Theo frowned. "Not if I go through in another form. I could be a fish. And then transform again once I know the coast is clear."

"And if she's filled that fountain with eels? I won't have you become a late-night snack for one of those slimy buggers."

"Then I'll go in as an eel." She slanted her eyes at him. "This is my father's life we're talking about."

"I understand that, but you can't go without a plan. How will you get back?"

"Same way I get in."

"Not if that fountain is in the castle. You might get out of there, but there's no way you'll get back in."

"Then…I'll transform myself into Vesta. No one would dare stop me then."

"How will you explain the lack of Overwatch protecting you? Especially with an old man in your company?" He shook his head. "It seems very risky to me."

Her shoulders slumped. "I know it's risky, Robin. But leaving him there is riskier. I can't let her do something that will shorten what little time he has left."

"No, you can't." He knew she was hurting. But losing her would destroy him. "Let's go see Amelia first. Maybe, with this new information, there's some help she can give us. Maybe she can give you some kind of protection spell. Or a charm that can make you invisible. Something. It's worth a quick trip."

Theo looked at him. "You think you can make it to her house?"

He raked his hand through his hair and swore again. "Probably not. I'll call her and see if she can come here. In the meantime, you go get dressed. Be quiet, though. I don't want to wake anyone else. We don't need the interference."

"I'll be quick. And quiet." She headed for the balcony, slipping out of his robe and leaving it behind on a chair.

He watched her go, the dim light from outside enough to silhouette her body through the nightgown's thin fabric. It left him temporarily unable to do anything but stare.

His concerns rapidly returned, though. He couldn't let her go to Limbo alone, but he was helpless to move beyond Vesta's boundaries. And how would that work with the portal? Was it some kind of safe zone that he could slip through? Vesta would think he would continue being clueless about it even being there. Could that mean she'd left it unblocked? Or had she included a barrier of some kind on the off-chance he discovered it? What would that be? Would he be caught halfway, stuck in some magical prison between two worlds?

That wasn't a happy thought. But maybe Amelia could venture a guess. *Amelia*. He got off the bed, remembering what he was supposed to be doing.

Outside on the balcony, Theo was at the railing. She disappeared suddenly. Then a streak of red light zipped away from his quarters and disappeared into the night. Smart to travel as a lightning bug. No one would ever suspect.

He pulled on track pants and a sweatshirt, then went to his nightstand for his phone. He rarely used it except to call Amelia. She and Deacon were the only numbers in his contact list, actually. He dialed her, hoping by some chance she was still awake.

"Robin?" Her clear voice filled his ear. Almost like she'd expected his call.

"Oh good. You're awake."

"Something's happened."

"Yes. Vesta was here, and we believe Theo's father is in danger. Can you—"

"I'll meet you under the pavilion in ten minutes."

She must be using magic to get here as he was pretty sure she lived farther away than that. "Thank you. Will you please tell me whatever you wouldn't tell me at dinner? It might help."

A moment of silence passed. "I hesitate to share this, because it could go wrong very easily. But considering what's happened, I will tell you what I've learned. Like with most magic, the one thing that can often counteract a powerful spell is real, true emotion. Usually one contrary to whatever emotion was strongest when the spell was cast. What do you think Vesta was feeling when she put that curse on you?"

He thought for a second. "Hatred. Of me. Of my people."

"And what would counteract hatred?"

There was no hesitation this time. "Love." He took a breath. "Are you saying that because I've learned to love again, the boundaries are lifting?"

"No, child. I'm saying that because someone else has begun to love *you*, Vesta's magic is losing its grip. A castle of sand has no defense against a wave. Love is weakening Vesta's hate."

"Theo," he whispered.

"Yes," Amelia agreed. "But you cannot tell her, because knowing such a thing will only make her try to love you harder, and that could have disastrous results. Do you understand?"

"Yes. Thank you."

"You're welcome. Ten minutes." She hung up.

He sat on the bed, looking at his phone. It went dark in his hand, and still he stared at it. His shifting boundaries were proof of Theo's love for him, even if she wasn't ready to acknowledge those feelings. What an amazing woman she was. With his entire being, he wanted to shout her name and run to her, but she'd want to know what had brought that on, and he couldn't tell her.

So instead, he sat there a moment longer, taking in the incredible gift he'd been given. Theo. If only she knew.

Then another thought came to him, pouring over him like an ice-cold rain shower.

If she went to Limbo through the portal, would that mean his boundaries would return? Moving through the portal wouldn't change her feelings, but she'd no longer be in this realm. He had no idea what effect that might have. But as much as the thought of being trapped again without her rattled him, he knew she had to do something. She couldn't let her father fall into Vesta's clutches.

Vesta would never let the man go willingly. And Theo would never forgive herself if she didn't at least try. Just like she'd never forgive Robin if he asked her not to go. He hung his head. But her going alone felt like a suicide mission.

He couldn't have that either. Then he'd never forgive *himself*.

So whatever it meant to his own personal safety, he

would be at her side. He put his phone back on the nightstand and went to his closet, flipping on the light. Set in the center of the back wall was his armory. He opened the floor-to-ceiling cabinet, revealing an array of weapons, most bladed. Whatever happened this evening, there was a good chance that being heavily armed was the right way to go.

That also meant track pants and a T-shirt weren't going to cut it.

In another cabinet in the closet, he found his battle leathers. Thanks to Elswood's attentions, they'd been kept oiled and in excellent shape.

A few minutes later, he walked out of the closet, dressed and armed and more ready than ever to take on Vesta. Many years had passed since he'd fought for his life against the orc king, but tonight was different.

Tonight he was fighting for the life of the woman he loved. The woman who loved *him*. And the life that lay ahead of them.

He smiled, nodding slowly. That was exactly what he'd prepared himself for. The defense of the woman who, without even knowing it, was setting him free. That and a future with her.

When this was over, and she and her father were safe and Vesta was no longer a threat, Robin was going to shower Theo with so many wonderful things that those starstone earrings would look like a carnival prize.

With his hand on the dagger tucked into his belt, he went out onto the balcony to wait for Theo.

Very little time passed before a lightning bug flitted into view. He stepped back as it flew over the railing. Just in case it wasn't Theo. But then the air shimmered, and Theo appeared.

She was in jeans and a T-shirt, a dagger strapped to her thigh. He suspected there might be another one or two hidden somewhere on her person. Probably in her boot. She looked him up and down. "You look…"

"Please don't say ridiculous. It's been a while since I've worn these."

"I was going to say intimidating. And the kind of handsome that gives me blush-worthy thoughts."

He smirked. "Well, then. Good to know. I can put these back on anytime you like. But right now, we need to get down to the pavilion to meet Amelia. She should be here any minute."

"Okay. Stairs?"

"Yep." With her at his side, he started down toward the garden. "You know…we should get you some battle leathers made."

She snorted. "I don't think they'd be ready in time for what's about to happen."

"I mean for future purposes."

She cut her eyes at him. "You think there's going to be more fighting in my future?"

"I meant for…recreational reasons."

She squinted at him. He winked back. Her eyes rounded. "Oh. *Robin*."

"What?" He laughed softly as they reached the patio. "I am a man, you know. With needs. Simple needs. I believe Vesta mentioned that. And you're supposed to be taking advantage of that, so you really ought to get on it."

She snorted again. "You're terrible." She shook her head. "I'm glad you can laugh at a time like this. Actually, I'm glad you can make me laugh."

They walked into the pavilion, and Amelia came toward them from the other side. They met at the fountain, which seemed fitting. "Good evening. Tell me what's going on."

"First," Theo said, "I want to give you this." She reached back, unclasped the necklace, and held it out to Amelia.

"Theo," Robin started.

She glanced at him and shook her head.

The witch took the necklace. "You're sure? You know the starstone will be gone forever."

Theo nodded. "It's okay. Assuming the compensation is about what Robin told me he's getting for the mines. I'll need that to provide a way for my father and myself in our new life here."

"It will be the same compensation," Amelia answered. She tucked the necklace into the pocket of her caftan. "Now, tell me what's happened."

Theo gave her the short version. "So you can see, I need to get my father out of there immediately. And I need to be able to take care of him here."

Amelia nodded. "Indeed."

Robin straightened. "It's not safe for her to go back to Limbo alone, but I'm not sure I can get through the portal with Vesta's boundaries in place. What do you think?"

Amelia walked to the edge of the fountain and stared into it. After a moment, she looked at Theo. "If you open the portal, will it be open on the other side? Will it be obvious that someone's activated it?"

Theo bit her lip for a second. "My best guess is no, it won't be, because Vesta wouldn't want anyone else aware of what she was doing."

Amelia pointed at the water. "Open it."

Theo spoke the words she'd heard Vesta use. "*Peri peri nixie ta.*" The water glowed blue. "It's open."

Amelia stepped closer. "Robin, put your arm in as far as it'll go. Tell me what you feel."

He stripped off his leather jacket, going down to just his vest, then knelt at the edge and put his hand in. "Water mostly." He leaned in, sinking his arm past the elbow. "No, wait." He smiled. "Air. I feel air."

Amelia's smug expression was completely understandable. "I'd say she didn't bother including the portal when she set your boundaries."

CHAPTER TWENTY-EIGHT

Wild energy coursed through Theo as she and Robin stood before Amelia to accept a quick spell of protection and obscurity. The last part wouldn't make them invisible, just less likely to be noticed.

Theo was happy for any extra help they could get. Returning to Limbo held all kinds of dangers, mostly from Vesta, but if Robin was recognized…that was going to open up a whole new crock of eels. "Wait."

Amelia's hands were out in front of her, and she looked like she'd been about to cast the spell. "What is it?"

"Can you do something about Robin's looks?"

He frowned at her. "I thought you liked the way I—"

"I think you're very handsome, but this isn't about that. This is about someone recognizing you. If that happens, the Overwatch is going to be on us like spots on a griddle bug."

He grimaced. "Good point." He looked at Amelia. "What do you think?"

"There is something I can do, but it might not feel so good while I'm doing it."

He shrugged. "Get it over with, then."

She came closer and put her hands on his face, then she closed her eyes and whispered a string of words Theo didn't understand. Robin grunted twice in discomfort. In the shadows, it was a little hard to make out what was happening, but when Amelia took her hands away, Robin had a full beard and moustache. Not the attractive kind either.

He looked like he'd been living in the forest for a couple of years with a broken twig as his only grooming device.

Theo did her best not to laugh. "No one is ever going to look at you and think you were once king."

He hissed out a breath. "Great, but for the record, ouch."

Theo patted his arm. "It was for an excellent cause." She smiled at Amelia. "Thank you."

"You're welcome." The witch raised her hands again. "Now for the rest."

A minute later, after more words Theo didn't understand and a sprinkling of dust taken from a red leather pouch, Amelia brought her hands down. "Listen now. My magic is strong, but not impenetrable. I don't know how long it will last when carried to another realm."

Robin adjusted one of the daggers tucked into a sheath at his thigh. "Vesta's magic has lasted just fine here."

"Yes, but I'm sure she was on this plane when she

put the curse on you. That's very different than taking magic between worlds. If I'd cast my spells in Limbo, I'd have no doubts about how long they'd last."

"Understood," he said. "We don't plan on being there any longer than we have to."

"That's for sure," Theo said.

"Get going, then." Amelia took a seat on the bench nearest the fountain. "I'll be here waiting."

"Really? That's kind of you." Theo tipped her head. "Or are you worried about something you haven't mentioned?"

Amelia crossed her legs at the ankle. "Just that wretched woman coming back here." She smiled. "But if that happens, I'll take care of her."

Theo would love to see that.

Robin snickered. "Thank you, but you don't have to—"

"You still owe me nightberry cuttings." Amelia waved her hand at them. "Now go."

Robin grabbed Theo's hand. "Ready?"

She stepped up onto the fountain's ledge. "Ready."

He joined her. And then they jumped into the water.

A wash of blue filled Theo's vision, then it went dark, then deep blue, and they were standing in the middle of the Fangmore Castle fountain.

Thankfully, it was about the same time in Limbo as it was in Shadowvale, which meant it was late enough in the evening that most people were in bed.

Not the Overwatch assigned to castle duty, however.

Robin pointed to the walkaway on the far side of the courtyard where a soldier was on patrol. Then he tugged on her hand as if to say they needed to move.

She agreed with a squeeze and let him lead. After all, he'd been in the castle courtyard before. She hadn't. When they'd ducked into an alcove, he spoke, his voice a whisper. "Which way to your house?"

"Two streets back from Bakery Row at the end closest to Blight Swamp." It wasn't the nicest of neighborhoods, but after tonight, it would just be a memory. Hopefully. "If we take the long way around Center Street, we're less likely to run into anyone."

He nodded. "Treasure Lane still stays open late, I take it."

"It does." Treasure Lane, on the other side of Center, was the quickest way to her house, but it was also home to most of the bars and gambling dens in Limbo. Because of that, Treasure Lane would be full of anyone with a little coin and a desire for fun. There were too many people there to risk traveling it.

"The long way it is, then."

"Do you know a way out of the castle that's not obvious?"

"I do." He smiled. "Servants' gate."

No doubt the same one her mother had used all those years ago. "Go on. I'll follow."

Carefully, they made their way out of the castle. There was only one guard at the gate, and he was half asleep, chin on his chest. He didn't bother to look up as they passed.

Even so, she held her breath on the bridge over the moat. Beneath them, the slide and slither of the eels rippled the water, catching the moonlight. She wondered if they missed the bread she'd once thrown to them.

Once in town, Theo took over. They kept to the shadows and made quick work of the empty streets.

The delicious aromas from Bakery Row reached them before the lights of the bakeries came into view, but they had nothing to worry about from those folks. All the workers cared about was getting their dough made and set to proof so that their customers could have fresh breads and pastries for breakfast.

Had Theo still been living here, she would have been one of those workers. She glanced at the shop that had employed her up until last week. Pickett's Bread Box. They were decent people. Understanding, too. They didn't deserve to live under Vesta's rule.

Robin gave her a little nudge. "You okay?"

"Lost in thought. This way."

He grabbed her hand before she could move. "Whatever you and your father need when we get back to Shadowvale, I'll take care of it."

"Thank you, but since I gave Amelia my mother's necklace to create the starstone operation, we should be fine."

"That could still take a few months. I just don't want you to worry about anything."

She nodded and gave him a little smile. "I appreciate that."

"I know you do. Now, let's get your father out of here."

She cut through the same alley she'd taken for work, stopping at the cross street to make sure it was empty. A rat scurried past, but otherwise, not a soul. Their little house was three doors down. The windows were dark. "We'll go around the back."

"Lead on."

She did, taking them behind the houses, past lines of drying laundry, and up the rickety steps to her back door. It was surreal being here with Robin. She hoped her father didn't freak out.

"Door, open," she whispered. It didn't budge, which meant it was locked. She reached under the middle step to a hidden ledge on the riser and found the spare key.

The back door let them into the small kitchen. It smelled of coffee and burnt toast. "Kitchen, night light."

The light under the stove vent came on. It seemed like a beacon in the dark, but she knew it would be barely noticeable to anyone else.

A dirty pot sat soaking in the sink, a few beans still glued to the bottom. The curtains, pulled tight over the window above, looked dingy and limp. Everything did after living in Robin's house.

And even though Theo's mother had once cooked

in this kitchen, Theo didn't need to this house to remember those old days. She put a hand on Robin's chest. "Stay here. Let me wake him and explain. If he sees you dressed in full battle gear, he might have an attack."

"Good plan. I'll be right here."

"Thank you." She tiptoed to the back bedroom and pushed the door open. Her father's snoring was deep and even. His curtains weren't as tightly closed as the ones in the kitchen, and a little light spilled through from the street.

She crept to his bed and sat on the edge. "Dad." She gave him a little shake. "Wake up. Dad, it's me, Theo."

"Hmm?" He mumbled something else, blinking and rubbing at his eyes. He smiled when he focused on her. "Theodora. Am I dreaming? What are you doing here, girl?"

"You're not dreaming, I'm really here."

He pushed up on his elbows. "What's going on? You have that same worried look your mother used to get."

"You're in danger. You have to come with me. I'm here to take you back to Shadowvale."

"What?"

"Please, just trust me. I don't have time to explain. Gather whatever you can't part with, put shoes on, and then we're leaving. We have to."

"Vesta?"

"Yes."

He got out of bed, moving with more speed than

she'd seen from him in years. He dressed, tucking his nightshirt into his trousers before donning a vest and his jacket. He put on a cap, then found a sack and started adding things to it.

"There's a man in the kitchen waiting on us. A friend of mine. You can trust him." She'd tell him later that man was Robin, but they didn't have the time right now for all the questions that revelation would bring.

"If you trust him, I do, too." Her father took a few last things from his desk drawer and stuffed them in the bag. Then he turned toward the shelving above the bed. "Oh no. I forgot about my books."

She grinned. "Where we're going, you won't lack for books."

"All right." He reached for the shelf anyway. "Just this one. Your mother gave it to me." He put it in the bag, slung the bag over his shoulder, and nodded. "Ready."

She stood. "We're probably never coming back here."

He slowly smiled. "It won't be such a hardship if I'm with my girl."

She leaned in and kissed his cheek. "Stay close now."

She led him back out to the kitchen. Robin was standing by the door. "Dad, this is my friend…Rob. Rob, this is my father, Welten."

Robin gave him a nod. "Pleasure to meet you, sir. We're going to travel fast, but if you need a break, just let us know."

"I still have some fight left in me, son." Welten tipped his head, his rheumy eyes narrowing slightly as he stared at Robin.

"Good to hear. Can I take your bag?"

Welten hesitated. "I'm all right. If it gets heavy, I'll let you know."

"Yes, sir." Robin put his hand on the door handle and looked at Theo. "We should go."

"Same way back."

"Yes."

She glanced at her father. "Ready?"

"Ready."

Robin opened the door and checked that all was clear. "Looks good."

He went out and down the steps. Theo followed, her father behind. The moon was starting to sink. Dawn wouldn't be far behind.

They went through the houses, moving only a little slower than they had on the way in. Theo hoped her father had the energy to make it. If not, maybe Robin could carry him. She couldn't leave her father behind. Not knowing what Vesta had planned for him.

The castle loomed in the not-so-far distance.

Her father picked up his step to match her pace. "What portal are we going through?"

"A private one."

"Which is where?"

She was a little afraid to tell him. "In a courtyard up ahead."

He gave her a stern look. "Fangmore's the only thing ahead of us."

She ignored the look like she'd done so often as a child. "So it is."

"Theodora."

"Dad, we'll be fine." She finally glanced at him. "How do you think we got here?"

"I shudder to think." He hitched his bag a little higher on his shoulder. "Speaking of castles, how are things working out for you in my place?"

"Just fine."

"The man treating you all right? Not making improper gestures, is he? Putting his hands where they don't belong? I know how men can be. Especially the desperate ones."

Ahead of them, Robin made a soft, choked sound. A suppressed laugh, most likely.

Theo did her best not to laugh herself. "Dad, shh. We'll talk later."

Robin's pace slowed. "You're right to be worried, Welten. A man like that, on his own for so long…" Robin grimaced and shook his head. "Probably desperate in ways men like us can't even imagine."

"See?" her father said. "Rob knows."

Theo brought them to a halt in an alley diagonally across from the bridge that led to the servants' gate to the castle. "Be quiet, both of you."

"Women," she heard her father mutter.

To which Robin's murmured reply was, "Mm-hmm."

She rolled her eyes, even though neither of them could see her do it. Then something on the other side of the bridge made her stiffen as if a cold wind had just blown down her spine. "We have a problem."

"What?" Robin asked.

She flattened against the wall but kept her eyes on the servants' gate. "The guard's awake."

CHAPTER TWENTY-NINE

Robin could see only one logical way through this. "Theo, you need to do that thing you do."

She made a face and flicked her gaze at her father before looking back at Robin and answering, "*Not* a good time."

"It's the best time." A half second later, he realized Theo's father must not know she was a changeling. Apparently, when she'd told Robin that she'd kept the ability a secret her entire life, she'd really meant it.

That didn't change the situation they were in or their need for a solution. "Theo, our time here could be running out. We need to get back through that portal as quickly as possible."

Welten cleared his throat softly. "There *are* other portals."

Theo frowned. "None that will take us close to Shadowvale. The one I used required a long bus ride as the final leg. And that won't work for Rob. His travel is kind of...restricted."

Robin's gaze was on the soldier guarding the gate. "We're definitely not getting through the gate without a plan. A really good one."

"Why?" She turned her head to see what was going on.

"Because," Robin said, "he's got help staying awake now."

The guard was leaning against the wall, digging into a pouch of crilla leaves for a bunch to stick between his cheek and gum. Crilla had been around forever. The herb was known for its invigorating properties. A lot of Overwatch used it to keep themselves alert on night shifts. Some bakers and miners who worked early mornings added crilla powder to their coffee. Robin had often done the same when he'd gone out starstone hunting.

She sighed. "He's not about to fall asleep anytime soon."

"Nope," Robin said. "If you have any other ideas on how we get through that gate, I'm listening."

She faced him again. "What about going for your mother?"

He couldn't answer for a second. "I would love to check on her. See if she'd go back with us, but I don't think I have time." He looked past Theo at the guard. "And that doesn't solve this problem."

"I would really like you to be able to check on your mother. What if you went to her now while I get my father through the portal, then I'll come back and try to catch up to you? With him safe, we'd have a little more leeway."

"But we have so little time. Dawn will be here before you know it. From here, it'll take at least twenty minutes to get to the highlands. And I have no idea what kind of reception I'll get when I arrive."

"Then wait for me to take my father through, and when I return, I'll go with you. She might open the door for me. That would at least give you a chance to speak to her." Her gaze held such sweetness and sincerity he didn't want to say no. "This could be your last opportunity."

He took a breath, hoping to clear the sudden ache in his chest. "I know."

"Then it's settled. I'll take my dad through, then come back and join you so we can see about your mom."

"You have a plan to get past the guard?"

"Sort of." She slipped by him to get to her father.

He hoped her plan, whatever it was, would work. There were a thousand ways it might go wrong. But now that Theo had brought it up, he didn't want to leave without checking on his mother. Even if just to hear straight from her that she never wanted to see or talk to him again.

Humans called it closure. He needed that. To no longer wonder what if. To give his heart a chance to heal.

Theo faced her father. "Dad, I'm about to do something that might shock you, but we're in a situation where I don't see any other way out than for me to make use of a very special gift I have."

Welten smiled. "You're going to shift into someone else?"

Theo's mouth fell open. "You know?"

"Girl, your mother and I didn't have any secrets from each other. Yes, I know. Now, go on and do what you need to do so you can get back and help the lad with his mother."

"Well, then." She snorted. "All right, just go along with whatever happens."

Welten nodded. "Will do."

Before their eyes, Theo disappeared. A faint buzzing filled the air as a swamp fly darted past them and through the servants' gate.

A second later, "Queen Vesta" approached from inside the castle. Her blue caftan billowed out around her. She stood behind the guard for a moment. Robin held his breath until she looked in their direction and gave him a wink. Then she scowled again and snapped her fingers. "Guard."

The guard startled, turning sharply and coming to attention. "Your Highness."

"There is a leak in the west dungeon wall. See to it immediately. I do *not* want that dampness seeping up to my quarters."

That was good, Robin thought. There was always a leak in the dungeon somewhere.

"Your Highness, I...I'm assigned to this gate. And I don't know the first thing about fixing leaky walls."

She looked at the entrance, lip curling. "This is the servants' gate. Why on earth does it even need guarding?" Then she leaned in with a haughtiness

303

that seemed like it had come from years of practice. "And patching a leak simply requires mortar, you fool. Now go. Before I have you thrown to the eels."

He blanched, nodded, and darted away. She turned to watch him, then after a few seconds, motioned to Welten.

Robin patted the man on the back. "Coast looks clear. I'll see you back at the house."

"Thanks for helping my girl, lad." With a nod, Welten took off. He wasn't fast, but he made it across the bridge safely.

Theo, still in Vesta's form, gave Robin a glance, then she and her father disappeared into the darkness of the castle's courtyard.

He wasn't sure how long it would take her to get the portal open, get them both through, then return. She'd have to give Amelia a little explanation. She couldn't just drop her father and go.

Minutes ticked by, and although the sky wasn't really lightening, Robin felt like he could feel the dawn coming. He scratched at his beard. It was incredibly itchy. He stayed as flat to the wall as he could and continually checked the opposite direction for traffic.

A few miners passed by on the next street over. Going to work or going home, he couldn't tell. There were mines in both directions, and it was too dark to see if they were covered in dust.

"Psst."

He turned abruptly. Theo was standing beside him. Relief filled him. "Everything go all right?"

"Yes. I'm so glad Amelia decided to stay. My father's going to sit on the bench with her until we get back. But she said we need to hurry."

"Then let's go." The highlands were going to be a trek, but once they got out of town, it would be safer. Less chance of running into someone who might care.

"Right behind you."

He pointed north. "Highlands are that way, right?"

She smiled. "You really have been gone a long time. More like..." She adjusted his finger to the east slightly. "That way."

"Maybe you should lead."

"Come on." She took off in that direction and kept a good pace.

Before long, the town was behind them, and they were climbing. The path through the forest was worn, but narrowed the farther they got. Higher still and the trees thinned, giving way to some open spaces of grass and brush.

Here and there, a few cottages and treehouses appeared. The path widened and was joined by others that branched out toward the homes. Lights burned in some windows, and the smell of beeswax and sage was strong.

They came to a crossroads with a hand-painted signpost in the center. The path here was wide enough to be called a road. Theo stopped. "Where exactly does your mother live?"

"Her address is Crane's Rest."

Theo shook her head. "Are you sure that's right?"

"Yes. I write that address on an envelope once a week."

"Something about that seems…off." She glanced up at the sign. "We're close, though." She tipped her head in the same direction that one of the signs pointed. "That way."

They walked side by side, but Theo seemed to be lost in thought. He nudged her lightly with his elbow. "What is it?"

"Something just doesn't feel right to me. Crane's Rest sounds familiar, but I can't remember why. But then, the highlands isn't an area I've ever spent any time in."

"It is kind of the artsy part of Limbo. No one ever really comes up here unless they have a good reason. Or they live here."

"Why do you think your mom moved up here?"

He shrugged. "I don't know. Bad memories in the old house? She wanted to get out of town? Away from people? Life up here is definitely simpler."

The sweet, faint tones of a flute broke the stillness.

Theo nodded. "And it's kind of live-and-let-live. I can see the appeal. Although, if that was a trumpet, I'm not sure I'd feel the same way."

He grinned. "Yeah, me either. But I guess when you live up here, you have to expect the unexpected."

"Oh no." Theo stopped. "Now I know why Crane's Rest gave me such a weird feeling."

"Why?"

She pointed up ahead.

He looked to see what she was gesturing to and found a carved but worn sign that said Crane's Rest hung between two trees, marking the entrance to a rambling patch of ground that could have passed for a garden at first.

But another moment told the truth. Crane's Rest was a cemetery.

From head to toe, he went numb. He couldn't do anything but stand there and stare and pray that this wasn't the reason his mother hadn't answered any of his letters. A knot formed in his throat.

"Robin?" Theo asked softly. "Are you okay?"

His gaze stayed on the graveyard. "I don't know what I am."

She slipped her hand in his.

He clung to it, to the warmth of it, to the connection that meant he wasn't alone. A falling star streaked across the sky. He felt empty. And angry. And unconsolably sad. He swallowed at the clog of emotion making it hard to breathe. "I should at least find her marker and say goodbye. Then we can go."

"I'll help you look."

He frowned. "Maybe we should just go. It's awfully dark. We're not going to be able to read—"

"Hang on." Theo disappeared, and a small cluster of lightning bugs took her place.

Despite his mood, he gave a short laugh. "Thanks. That will help."

Together, they entered the cemetery. Theo hovered over the headstones, the wooden placards, and the ground markers while he read the names. He looked for both Gallow and Rosebloom, his mother's maiden name. Just in case.

"Who are you looking for?"

Robin turned. A large man in rough linen overalls and a felt cap stood at the entrance. He had a stick in his hand that might have been for walking or protection. Robin had to be careful with his answer. Saying too much could reveal who he was. And that was trouble they didn't need. "I'm looking for a distant relative. A woman by the name of Pryn Gallow. Maiden name Rosebloom. Do you know where she's buried?"

"Who are you?"

That question was even trickier to answer. Robin didn't want to lie, but he certainly couldn't tell the truth. "I'm from the Gallow side of the family. I don't live around here anymore. I didn't mean to intrude. I just wanted to pay my respects. Do you know where her marker is?"

The man stared at him. Hard. After a second, he shook his head. "No, but I know someone who does."

Then he just walked off.

Robin glanced at the swarm of fireflies near his shoulder. "That was odd."

The fireflies seemed to nod as a group.

"Maybe we should go."

The fireflies flitted back to the last stone he'd inspected.

"I take that to mean you disagree." He went in

that direction. They'd checked another row of markers when the man returned.

He wasn't alone this time. A woman stood at his side, but a little behind him, her face partially hidden by the hood of her robe. Strands of long silver hair peeked out. The man did the talking. "The woman wants to know your name before she tells you where the marker is."

Robin took a few steps closer to see them both better, but it wasn't as dark as it had been. Dawn was truly on its way, and their time was slipping. There was something familiar about the woman. "It's better if I don't say."

"Then she has nothing more to share with you."

"Does she know where my…" He caught himself. He'd almost said *my mother*. "Where my relative is buried? Please. I'd just like to see her resting place."

The woman's hand came up to rest on the man's arm, and she stepped out from behind him. "Robin?"

Her voice was soft and weathered with age, but it shot through Robin like a pulse of electricity. The reason for her familiarity was plain. It couldn't be. But then, it *had* to be. He spoke without thinking or caring. "Mom?"

She pushed her hood back and smiled. "Hello, son."

Chapter Thirty

Theo flew behind a tree and shifted back into herself, then went straight to Robin's side. He wasn't in that spot long, however. He started toward his mother and she toward him, and they met halfway in an embrace that almost made Theo weep.

Robin clung to his mother with a desperate joy that Theo completely understood. She would have hugged her mother the same way if she'd been able.

After a long moment, Robin pulled back and looked at her. "You're alive. I thought—"

"It had to be that way."

"But why? And why didn't you answer my letters?"

"There isn't time to fully explain, but it wasn't safe." Pryn shook her head. "It's not safe now. You shouldn't be here. If the queen were to find out…"

"I'm here for you. Come with me." He glanced at Theo. "With us. Back to Shadowvale."

"Where you were exiled?"

He nodded. "It's safe there, and life is good. Please. You're right that there isn't time to fully explain. Just trust me. Please come."

Pryn looked at the man behind her. He nodded. "Go. It's the only way you'll ever be safe. We'll be fine."

Pryn nodded. "Thank you for your kindness and your protection, Marken. Thank your wife and boys, too. And everyone else who's helped me."

"I will. It was our pleasure to be of service." He smiled and then looked at Robin. "Maybe someday the throne will be yours again, Sire."

Robin shook his head. "I doubt that. But I am forever indebted to you for the help you've given my mother."

Theo glanced at the sky. "We should go. We have to get back to town, and darkness won't hide us much longer."

Marken stepped aside. "Be well."

Pryn touched his arm. "Be well."

The trio made the return trip in silence and with as much speed as possible, but the sky was nearly lavender by the time they reached the servants' gate. And the guard had returned from his job in the dungeon.

They huddled in the same hiding spot as they had before. Theo groaned softly. "I don't think the leaky-wall ruse will work twice."

"We have to get into the castle?" Pryn asked.

"I'm afraid so," Robin answered. "The portal is in the courtyard."

Pryn snorted. "It's one guard. I say we take him out. The odds are in our favor."

Theo's brows shot up. "I like your mother a lot.

311

And that gives me an idea. Since time is running out, we really have no other option but to just do this. Let's go."

Robin's hand on her shoulder stopped her. "What do you mean just do this? What are you going to do?"

Theo grinned. "Act like we belong inside. And if that doesn't work, tell him the truth. Either he lets us through, or you're going to toss him into the moat."

Pryn nodded. "Solid plan."

"There's nothing solid about that." Robin shook his head. "What if he sounds the alarm? Which is highly likely."

Theo understood Robin's concern. He had his mother to think about now. "Then you toss him into the moat and catch up to us, because we're already going to be at the fountain."

Robin frowned. "This is not a good plan."

Pryn gave him a stern look. "You have a better one?"

"No, but I don't want to see you in Vesta's clutches."

"I don't see what other choice we have. We need to leave." Theo checked the guard again. "There's no change. We just have to do this." She started walking toward the gate.

She heard a grunt of disapproval behind her, but it was quickly followed up with soft footsteps. Good. Robin and his mother were coming along. Theo did her best not to smile. She was supposed to be a servant arriving for work at the castle.

The guard tracked her as she approached. She yawned like arriving for work was the most boring, mundane thing. When she was halfway across the bridge, she made eye contact with him. "Two kitchen staff." She hooked her thumb over her shoulder at Robin and Pryn. "And another maintenance crew behind me."

His eyes narrowed. "You don't look familiar to me. None of you."

"New hires," Theo answered. "Part of the twenty who were brought on yesterday."

"Twenty?" He frowned. "I wasn't told about that."

She put her hands on her hips as Robin and Pryn came to a stop behind her. "Something to do with a leak in the dungeon and being short staffed and it not happening again."

He grimaced slightly. "That's been fixed."

Theo shrugged. "Whatever. But if the queen's getting fresh biscuits for breakfast, you'd better let me through."

He hesitated. "IDs, and you'd best sign in."

Robin snorted as he looked over the man's shoulder. "Sign in on what?"

The guard went over to the small alcove that housed the lever to raise the bridge. There was a clipboard there, but it was empty. He grumbled something under his breath about not being able to do his job properly.

"Listen," Theo said. "I was told she gets cranky if those biscuits aren't hot and ready. Let us in, and I promise to run back here with a basket of them for you as soon as she's served. I'll even put some nightberry jam in there for you. It's our first day. Cut us a break, will you?"

The guard stopped muttering. "Nightberry jam, eh?"

Robin cracked his knuckles while making an impressive scowl.

Pryn laughed and put her hand on his arm. "Now, now." She smiled at the guard. "Jeb has a tendency to overreact when things don't go his way. And I probably shouldn't have told him the eels will eat just about anything that falls into the moat."

The guard swallowed. "Go on. Go." He stayed by the alcove as they passed, moving only to call after Theo, "Don't forget those biscuits."

"I won't," she answered. "See?" she whispered when they were a safe distance away. "It was a good plan after all."

Pryn was still smiling. "You are an impressive liar, my dear."

"Thanks. Self-preservation is a great teacher."

"Hold up," Robin said as they rounded a bend toward the large open courtyard. "We need to make sure there's not a patrol going by. Although there should be a shift change coming up soon."

They took refuge behind an enormous potted elestia tree. They peered between the seed pods to check every direction of the courtyard.

"Looks okay." Robin pushed a branch out of the way, snapping a piece as he did so. "But with all the plants and trees, it's hard to say if there's anyone else here or not."

A soft splash echoed from near the servants' gate. The three looked at each other. Pryn shrugged one shoulder. "Probably the kitchen dumping scraps in the moat. The eels have to eat something."

She went back to surveying the courtyard. "That's all who's awake right now. Servants and Overwatch. I don't think the queen ever gets up before the sun. And thankfully, I don't see any Overwatch."

Theo looked up. "Not even on the walkways." Which seemed odd. A little warning bell went off in her head. "Something's not right. It's too quiet."

"Maybe. Maybe not." Robin scratched at his beard, and a clump of hair came off in his fingers. He made a face. "Either way, we should take advantage of it and get to that fountain now."

Theo couldn't argue with that, but the feeling of unease remained with her. Getting out seemed like the best possible solution. "All right."

"I'll lead. Mother, you stay in the middle, and Theo behind. On three."

"On three," Theo repeated.

He counted down and on one, they took off for the center of the courtyard. The fountain bubbled like an oasis in the desert, the frothy palms and blooming plants surrounding it only adding to that illusion.

A few feet to go.

Vesta stepped out of the greenery in a dress patterned with leaves and fronds and flowers.

315

Obviously, her attempt at camouflage. A successful attempt, sadly. In her hand gleamed the royal sword known as the Heartseeker. It was nearly half her length and held a ruby the size of a toddler's fist embedded in the pommel.

With a speed that surprised Theo, Vesta brought the sword to bear on Robin's chest, stopping him from doing anything with the dagger he'd pulled from his hip sheath.

"Drop that, or Heartseeker will taste blood." There was nothing pleasant about Vesta's smile.

He let the dagger fall.

Her nasty grin widened. "Did you think a ratty moustache and beard would fool me, husband dear?"

"We aren't married, Vesta. And haven't been for nearly twenty years. Now let us pass, and I'll let you live."

She laughed and leaned on the sword a little harder. It bent slightly as the tip dug deeper. Theo prayed Robin's battle leathers were doing their job. "You always were given to flights of fancy. But it's time for you to come down to earth and see that I have the upper hand. I have had it since day one. And now that you've threatened my life, I cannot allow you to go unpunished. Guards!"

A small troop of Overwatch sprang from the recesses of the courtyard, swords drawn. Theo wanted to cry and scream and launch herself at Vesta, no matter the outcome. She didn't, though. She stood there and watched the guards surround them. Four of them. And Vesta. She must have expected them to fight.

Or she was far more afraid of Robin than she let on.

Vesta was still smiling, her sword still against Robin's chest. "I will kill you myself. I think that's only fitting, don't you?"

A soft whistle rang out in the otherwise quiet courtyard. It was loud enough to be heard above the water's bubbling, but it ended as quickly as it had begun with five new sounds. *Thunk. Thunk. Thunk-thunk. Crack.*

Those were the sounds, Theo realized, of arrows finding their targets. The feathered shafts bloomed almost simultaneously from the backs, shoulders, and torsos of the men around them.

The arrow intended for Vesta sliced open her upper arm, but found its home in the palm behind her. Blood spilled from the wound, staining the sleeve of her green gown. Six inches to the right, and it would have pierced her heart. Terror filled her eyes. The sword in her hand had fallen away from Robin's chest to tremble at waist-height. "What have you done to me?"

Robin looked as shocked as she did. "This wasn't my doing, as much I wish I could lay claim to it."

Marken and two other men ran in, bows strapped across their backs and swords in their hands. Marken addressed them while his men went to work securing the fallen Overwatch. "Sire, Lady Pryn, are you all right?"

Pryn nodded. "Yes, thank you for rescuing us."

Marken grabbed the Heartseeker from Vesta's hand and held it to her chest the same way she'd just done to Robin. "I hereby arrest you for crimes against the citizens of Limbo. On your knees."

With a whimper, Vesta sank to the ground. She clutched her injury while glaring at Robin. "How dare you? You set me up. Once a traitor, always a trai—"

Marken closed Vesta's mouth with the point of Heartseeker under her chin. "You will not speak to the king that way, prisoner."

She made no further argument, other than some low, angry grunts. Another man with a bow strapped to his back joined them and began tying Vesta's hands behind her.

Marken spoke to them while watching Vesta. "This is my son. I have more men outside securing the castle. Some of the Overwatch were already with us."

Theo couldn't help but ask, "And the guard at the servants' gate?"

The corners of Marken's mouth twitched. "Gone for a swim."

Robin put his hand on the man's shoulder. "We owe you a debt."

"This kingdom owes you." Marken switched swords then, exchanging his own for Heartseeker. That blade he held out to Robin. "The throne is yours again, Your Highness."

Theo almost gasped. She never imagined this

outcome. Robin, on the throne again. She would lose him if that happened, she was sure of it. But that was selfish of her. Limbo needed a strong, kind ruler.

Despite knowing that, she felt her heart ache with the loss that seemed inevitable. That was her life, though. The good things never seemed to last.

Robin shook his head. "My life is no longer here. I am sorry. I appreciate your loyalty more than I can say. And Vesta's rule absolutely needed to come to an end, as does the magic she's bound me with. But I am not the king this kingdom needs." He smiled at Marken. "I believe I am looking at that man."

Marken's brow bent with sudden disbelief. "But I never intended—"

"Perhaps not." Pryn stepped forward. "But you will be an amazing ruler, my friend. And Limna will be the kind of queen this realm has long needed. Say yes."

"Lady Pryn, what you're asking of me…"

"I know what I ask. What a sacrifice it is," she said. "But I wouldn't ask if I didn't think you are more than capable."

His brow relaxed as the idea obviously became more palatable. "Will you stay?"

Her smile was slight but held a happiness that shone through. "I will go wherever my son goes."

"Of course." Marken took a breath, then straightened a little. A world of emotions seemed to pass through his eyes. "If my kingdom needs me, then I shall serve." He looked at Robin. "You say the traitor has bound you with magic?"

"She knows what she's done." Robin looked at his ex-wife. "Remove it, Vesta. And perhaps the new king will grant you some leniency."

Theo held her breath. Would Vesta do it?

The ousted queen glowered at him, but grudgingly mumbled a long string of fae words. "There. Your boundaries are dissolved."

Robin smiled at Marken. "I look forward to your coronation. Now let's get this woman into a cell. I have another life to return to and responsibilities there that require my attention." He looked at Theo. "Unless you think we should stay here?"

"We should go back." She shook her head, hoping the tears in her eyes weren't obvious. She loved this man for so many reasons. "But is there any reason we can't return at some point? Just to visit? With Shadowvale as our home?"

"No reason at all. If Marken will allow it."

Marken snorted like that wasn't even something that needed to be discussed. "I would be happy to entertain you anytime you wish."

"Then it's settled." Robin took her hand. "What my queen wants, my queen gets."

CHAPTER THIRTY-ONE

Nearly a half hour later, most of Robin's magical beard and moustache had fallen out or been scratched off. He imagined he looked about as awful as a person could look while feeling about as good as a person could feel.

In that half hour, he and Theo had assisted Marken's crew of highlanders in locking down the castle, securing Vesta in a cell, and seeing to the wounded Overwatch. Vesta's arrow scratch had been treated with a simple bandage.

As word spread throughout Limbo of what had occurred, the citizens arrived to cheer on the regime change and pledge their allegiance to the new sovereign. For all general purposes, Marken had become king the moment he'd taken Heartseeker out of Vesta's hand.

The coronation would come in the days ahead, but no one doubted who the kingdom's new ruler was. Robin had a good feeling about the man, and not just because Pryn liked and trusted him. Limbo had never been governed by a highlander before, and Robin thought the change in ruling style would be welcome after Vesta's dictatorship.

At last, goodbyes were said, and Robin, his mother, and Theo returned to the fountain. He knew Welten and Amelia must be desperate with worry. The concern on Theo's face made him wonder if she wasn't thinking the same thing. "We'll be back soon."

"I'm ready." She looked up at him. "But are you sure you're all right with that? You could be king again."

"I'm very much all right with it. I never intended to be king in the first place. Unless…" He tipped his head, squinting at her. "Do you…want to be queen?"

"Me?" She shrank back like the idea was unfathomable. "I would be rubbish at that. No, thank you."

"You wouldn't be rubbish. You'd be spectacular."

She frowned at him. "Did you get hit on the head?"

"I'm serious. Even if you don't see it, I do."

"I just want to go home."

Had she just called his house and Shadowvale *home*?

She shook her head. "I mean—"

"I know what you mean. I want that, too. I want to finally get to know the town I've lived in for the last twenty years. And I am very much looking forward to doing that with you at my side."

"I can't wait. I'm excited at the prospect of living somewhere besides Limbo. And not having to work every waking hour to get by. And not worrying so much about my father." She smiled. "And the thought of spending more time with you is pretty great, too."

Pryn approached them, slipping her arm around Robin's waist. "Today was a good day. One for the history books."

Robin put his arm around her as well. To have his mother back again after so long was just amazing. "I hope everyone accepts Marken as their king."

"You mean the fae?"

He nodded.

"I don't think that will be an issue," Pryn said. "Limna is fae, so they will be well represented."

"That will definitely help. Are there a lot of fae in the highlands?"

"Some," she answered. "But more with mixed blood." She smiled at him. "Interested in your heritage, are you?"

"My heritage?" He frowned. "I'm not sure I know what you mean."

"Your great-grandmother on your father's side was fae. And my mother had a little in her blood as well."

"What?" He shook his head. "This is a discussion for another time, but I want to know more. Right now, we need to get back to Shadowvale and the people waiting on us there, who have to be absolutely frantic that we've been gone so long."

Theo's brows knit with worry. "I never meant to leave my father this long."

Pryn stepped up onto the fountain's edge and held out her hands to Robin and Theo. "Then let's go. I want to see this land called Shadowvale."

Robin took one of her hands, and Theo took the other as they joined her on the edge. Robin glanced over at Theo. "Ready when you are."

She smiled at him, then spoke the words to open the portal. *"Peri peri nixie ta."* The blue glow appeared instantly. She looked back at him. "Let's go home."

When they stepped out of the fountain on the other side, Welten put a hand to his chest as he came toward them. "You're back. I was starting to think I'd never see you again."

"I'd never leave you, Dad." Theo embraced him. "And look. We brought Robin's mom with us."

Amelia, never one to appear all that worried about much, actually seemed relieved. She glanced at Pryn, then at Robin. "Is that what held you up? Or did you have trouble?"

"A little of both, but it all worked out," Robin answered. With a smile he couldn't contain, he introduced his mother. "Amelia Marchand, Welten Middlebright, this is my mother, Pryn Gallow. Mom, Amelia is the founder of Shadowvale, and Welten is Theo's father."

Welten stuck his hand out. "How about that? Nice to meet you, Pryn."

"You, too, Welten. Your daughter is a real treasure."

He beamed. "That she is."

Pryn turned to Amelia, who took Pryn's offered hand. "What a pleasure to meet you."

"Thank you. It's a pleasure to be here." She smiled at Robin. "And to be with my son again after so many years."

Amelia's gaze held a deep understanding. "I'm sure you missed him terribly."

"I did. But now that I'm here, I'm looking forward to seeing the place he's called home all these years."

"Shadowvale is a marvelous place," Amelia said. "But then, I'm rather biased." She glanced at Robin. "Will you be able to explore the town now, or..."

"Vesta was not only deposed as queen, but she was forced to remove the curse she put on me. I guess we'll soon see if that's what she actually did. Otherwise, I'll be making another trip back to Limbo."

"Deposed?" Amelia asked. She flattened her hand against her stomach as if something had just upset it. "I see. I suppose that means you'll be taking the throne back, then?"

"No. I'm staying right here. Limbo is in far more capable hands than mine." He gave Theo a smile. "But we'll be visiting now and then."

Amelia exhaled. "I am very glad to know we won't be losing you. In fact, I'm even happy that you both have family with you now. Speaking of, I'm sure you have a lot of catching up to do. I should go. I have work of my own to attend to."

"Amelia," Robin said. "About that. If I could have a word with you?"

"Of course."

Then he noticed his mother had taken a seat on the bench. "Mom, are you all right?"

She nodded. "A little tired is all."

Welten was leaning on Theo. "I suppose we all are after that adventure."

"Let's go inside, then."

Theo shook her head. "Have your chat with Amelia. I'll take them in. We'll be in the dining room, too, because I can already smell Mrs. Applestock's biscuits. Amelia, you should join us for breakfast."

"Thank you, but I don't want to intrude on time with family. We'll get together soon, I'm sure."

"All right. Thanks again for your help."

"You're welcome, Theodora. Welten, don't forget what we talked about." Amelia gave them a wave, and as Theo left, taking Pryn and Welten with her, Amelia turned to Robin. "Now, what was it you want to talk to me about?"

Theo decided on the small dining room. The one where she and Robin had had their dinner. She couldn't forget that he'd told her he'd pictured family meals in there, and breakfast with his mother and her father seemed to fit that bill.

She got Pryn and her father seated at the table, then ran to the kitchen to let Mrs. Applestock and the rest of the staff know what was going on.

To a person, they all seemed genuinely excited to have Robin's mother in the house. As expected, Mrs. Baton and Elswood were less enthused about the arrival of Theo's father. She ignored their lukewarm response and asked for coffee to be sent up with biscuits and jam as soon as possible. It had been a long night and a tiresome adventure. They were in need of sustenance.

Mrs. Applestock promised to get the coffee and biscuits out to them quickly, followed by the rest of the breakfast she was already preparing.

As Theo left, Elswood was loading a cart with the things she'd requested. She got back to the dining room and found her father and Pryn in a deep conversation about something that they immediately went silent about. Probably her and Robin, if she had to guess.

The man himself walked in a few moments later. His battle leathers had been replaced by track pants and a T-shirt.

She gave him a once-over. Whatever he had on, he was a sight to behold. "Everything all right with Amelia?"

"Very all right." He kissed her cheek. "Thank you, by the way, for everything you did in Limbo."

She grinned but shrugged. "Everything *we* did. We did all that together. And I have to say we make a pretty good team."

"You make a wonderful team," Pryn said.

Welten raised a finger. "I'll second that."

Robin and Theo took their chairs. With them now

at the table, every seat was filled. He looked out over the group and smiled. "This is really something."

Theo smiled. "A family meal in the family dining room?"

He nodded. "Exactly."

Elswood arrived with coffee, tea, cream, sugar, biscuits, two kinds of jam, pear butter, and marmalade. He filled their cups, then piled the table with the food and disappeared again with the promise to return shortly with more filling fare.

They tucked in. Robin started with coffee. "There are plenty of rooms in this house, so we'll find some that you like and get you both settled in. Then, if I may be so bold, Welten, we need to get you to a doctor and see what help is available. Theo said you've been unwell."

He nodded. "I have. And about that…" He looked at Theo. "Your friend Amelia out there. She's a witch, you know."

"I know." Theo spread nightberry jam on her freshly buttered biscuit and wondered where this was going.

"Well, she said there's the taint of fairy magic on me."

Theo stopped spreading jam to look at him. "Is that what she meant when she told you not to forget what you'd talked about?"

He nodded, looking a bit sheepish. He gave Robin a quick glance, then went back to Theo. "Seems my, uh, illness was a little bit of fairy dust your mother sprinkled on me years ago."

Theo put her knife down. "Mom *cursed* you? I don't believe that for a second."

He sighed. "Not a curse so much as... encouragement."

"In plain language, please."

He sighed harder this time. "When I gamble, I get sick."

She stared at him. Hard. "Are you serious? All this time, I thought you were dying, and you were just losing money?"

He made a frustrated face. "Well, we're all going to die sometime. I was just hoping to do it with a little bit of coin in my pocket."

A moment of silence passed. Then Pryn snorted. And Robin laughed. Soon, Theo couldn't help but join in, and Welten followed.

He wiped at his eyes. "I'm sorry for everything I've put you through. I know I haven't been the best father. And your life hasn't been easy."

She was too happy to be truly mad. "It's all right. You know, if you hadn't been sick, and I hadn't thought you were dying, I never would have ended up here." She looked at Robin. "I guess in a way, I have my mother to thank for all of this."

Out of habit, her hand went to her throat, where the necklace used to be. Her smile faded.

"Speaking of your mother..." Robin got out of his chair and walked around to her, digging in his pocket as he approached. "I have something for you."

He held out the necklace she'd given to Amelia for the starstone mine.

Her mother's necklace. Theo almost sobbed as she shook her head. "Thank you. But that was supposed to make our way. Without that...we don't have a thing to our names."

"Yes, you do. When we were in the courtyard, I took a handful of seed pods off that elestia tree. Just now, out in the garden, I explained to Amelia that starstones aren't mined. She understands completely. She's going to start a grove of elestia trees in a protected park. The Caralynne Middlebright Grove. You and your father will have plenty to take care of yourselves with."

Theo took the necklace and pressed it to her heart, doing her best not to cry. "I can't say thank you enough. You've changed my life."

He knelt at her feet. "And you've changed mine. For the better. In ways I can't even express."

He took the necklace from her and fastened it around her neck. "There is one more thing you could do for me, though."

"Anything. Just name it."

"Marry me, Theodora. Because I cannot imagine being without you. Because you said yourself we make a pretty good team. Because I am so in love with you that I will die if you say no."

She laughed, no longer able to hold back the tears of happiness spilling down her cheeks. "That's really unfair. Now I can't say no."

"Was that a possibility?"

She grinned wildly. "No, Your Highness. Not even remotely. But are you sure you really want to hitch yourself to a woman like me for the rest of your life? I have a reputation, you know."

"I like moody women. Well..." His mouth twitched into a smile. "Just the one, really."

"In that case...yes."

EPILOGUE

Robin wrapped Theo just a little tighter in his arms as they reclined on the chaise watching the stars on their balcony. On the side table were a plate of iced oatmeal cookies and two hot toddies. The night was clear and slightly cool and utterly flawless. He'd never imagined his life could be this perfect, but here he was without a want in the world and the most profound sense of contentment he'd ever experienced. He kissed her temple, just above her braid.

She tipped her head back to see him. "What was that for?"

"Just for being you."

With a smile on her face, she snuggled in closer. "The coronation ceremony was perfect, wasn't it? Simple but beautiful and regal in a way that wasn't the least bit gaudy."

"Such a contrast to everything Vesta was."

"For sure." She stretched a little. "Soon they'll all be here."

He smiled. "Yes, they will be."

"I can't believe I'm marrying the former king of Limbo and that the current king and queen will be at our wedding."

"And what a spectacular wedding it will be."

"Thanks to all the help we're getting from your mom and Gracie and Em." She shook her head. "I also can't believe you invited the entire town. This wedding is going to cost a fortune."

"What better way to get to know our neighbors? And the cost doesn't matter. There will be buckets of starstones in our future when the grove starts producing."

"I have to pay my father's debts off first. But according to Amelia, that could be as soon as a month from now. Her magic must be incredibly powerful to grow those trees so fast."

"Her magic is very powerful and nothing short of amazing." He slipped his hand under hers, and she interlaced her fingers with his.

Then she sighed a happy little noise. "Life is good."

"Yes, it is." Suddenly, movement caught his eye near the edge of the balcony. He sat up. "Pepper?"

The little black cat sauntered over and sat near the chaise, giving Robin a look that clearly said dinner had better be forthcoming.

He looked at Theo, then back at the cat, then at Theo again, frowning.

She sat up, too. "What?"

"You can't be in two places at once, right? I just want to make sure."

She coughed out a barely suppressed laugh. "You

thought I was the cat? Sneaking up here to spy on you?" She gave the cat a wink. "Nice job, Pepper."

"So you weren't? Aren't?"

"No. That would be sort of devious." Her smile was sly and mischievous. "But I love that you thought I'd do something like that. I mean, it keeps you on your toes, doesn't it?"

"Yes. Wait. Hold up. The second time I talked about having a cat visitor, you knew Pepper's name without me telling you. How do you explain that?"

"I'm sure you mentioned it."

"I didn't."

Her mouth bunched to one side, and she tipped her head coyly. "A good guess?"

He narrowed his eyes, so amused with her he could hardly stand it. "Theodora."

"*Okay!*" She bit her bottom lip. "I might have been the raven in the tree."

He snorted. "Oh, I see. Cat is devious. Raven is fine." He chuckled. "I didn't know what the rules were."

"I was just checking on you. To see if you needed company."

He pulled her close, pushing them both back against the cushion. "I always need your company."

"I don't know. You were pretty busy scratching Pepper and rubbing his belly."

"Jealous, huh?"

She giggled.

Pepper meowed, clearly less amused by their banter.

Robin sat up again. "I think someone wants some dinner. Hey." He looked over his shoulder at her. "How do you feel about adopting this stray and spoiling him silly? I'm talking about moving him into the house. Getting him his own bed. That sort of thing."

She sat up, looped her arm through his, and studied the little animal. "I think he'd be a welcome addition. Would you like that, Pepper?"

The cat jumped up onto the end of the chaise, turned around once, then lay down. He lifted his head and meowed at them.

Robin slanted his eyes at Theo. "I think that's a yes."

She shook her head. "I think that's a reminder that he still wants his dinner."

"I'll ring for Elswood."

"I'm glad Marken told us that Vesta confessed that she didn't have any spies in Shadowvale, but do you think Elswood and Mrs. Baton will ever get used to the idea of my father and me living here?"

"Yes. In fact, I think they've already softened a little since they've seen how happy you make me. Really though, they just need something new to be cranky about."

"Well, in that case, Pepper is a perfect addition."

Robin laughed. "Yeah, they aren't going to like having a cat in the house at all."

Theo leaned toward the cat and gave him a scratch on the head. "You just became my new favorite resident of Gallow House, little one."

"Thrown over for a cat. That didn't take long," he teased.

She chuckled. "Don't worry, I'm still going to marry you."

He sighed in mock relief. "I'm glad to hear that." He dug into his pocket for the ring he'd been planning to give her over dinner tomorrow. "I'd hate to have to return this."

She gasped. "Oh, Robin. Is that real? It's stunning. Huge. But stunning all the same."

He smiled. "You'd better believe it's real."

"That might be the biggest starstone I've ever seen outside of the royal jewels. And are those emeralds surrounding it?"

He nodded. "I thought that would be a nice tribute to your mother. She's the reason we're here, after all." He slipped the ring on her finger.

She held her hand out, turning it slightly to let the gems catch the light. "How thoughtful. I love that. And I love you. Thank you, Your Highness."

"You're welcome, Moody."

Pepper meowed, a much more plaintive cry this time.

Robin swung his feet to the floor and stood. "I'd better get his tuna."

Theo caught his hand. "I could go for another slice of that cake Mrs. Applestock made for last night's dinner."

He shook his head in amusement. "With ice cream?"

"Is there any other way?"

"On it." He looked down at Theo and Pepper, his new little family, and thought about his mom and Welten off in their own rooms and realized that he'd gone from feeling like the loneliest man in the world to one of the luckiest.

Gone were the thoughts of regret, revenge, and loss. His mind was filled with happy plans for the future now. His life had completely changed, and the bouts of dark rage he'd once fought against had vanished.

Moody had tamed the beast.

*

Want to be up to date on new books, new audiobooks and other fun stuff by Kristen Painter? Sign-up for my newsletter on my website, www.kristenpainter.com. No spam, just news (sales, freebies, releases, you know, all that jazz.)

*

If you loved the book and want to help the series grow, tell a friend about the book and take time to leave a review!

OTHER BOOKS BY KRISTEN PAINTER

PARANORMAL ROMANCE
Shadowvale series
The Trouble with Witches
The Vampire's Cursed Kiss
The Forgettable Miss French
Moody and the Beast

Nocturne Falls series
The Vampire's Mail Order Bride
The Werewolf Meets His Match
The Gargoyle Gets His Girl
The Professor Woos the Witch
The Witch's Halloween Hero – short story
The Werewolf's Christmas Wish – short story
The Vampire's Fake Fiancée
The Vampire's Valentine Surprise – short story
The Shifter Romances the Writer
The Vampire's True Love Trials – short story
The Dragon Finds Forever
The Vampire's Accidental Wife
The Reaper Rescues the Genie
The Detective Wins the Witch
The Vampire's Priceless Treasure
The Werewolf Dates the Deputy

For more Nocturne Falls
Try the Nocturne Falls Universe Books
New stories, new authors, same Nocturne Falls world!
kristenpainter.com/nocturne-falls-universe/

Nothing is completed without an amazing team.

Many thanks to:

Cover design: Design & derivative cover art by Janet Holmes using images under license from Shutterstock.com

Interior formatting: Author E.M.S

Editor: Joyce Lamb

Copyedits/proofs: Chris Kridler/Lisa Bateman

ABOUT THE AUTHOR

USA Today Best Selling Author Kristen Painter is a little obsessed with cats, books, chocolate, and shoes. It's a healthy mix. She loves to entertain her readers with interesting twists and unforgettable characters. In addition to Shadowvale, she currently writes the best-selling paranormal romance series, Nocturne Falls, and the cozy mystery spin off series, Jayne Frost. The former college English teacher can often be found all over social media where she loves to interact with readers.

www.kristenpainter.com

Printed in Great Britain
by Amazon